# THE PEACHY PARADOX

Voices from the Mooncast Universe

Cornelius J. Moon

Copyright © 2025 Cornelius J. Moon

All rights reserved.
No portion of this archive may be reproduced without express permission from the Americaland Office of Philanthropic Affairs, unless, of course, it already has been.

First Edition · 2228 A.D.
Printed in Americaland.

ISBN: 979-8-9938385-0-2

*For Stacey, always my Juliet.*

*And the Grinders, for whom hope respawns eternal.*

# Contents

The First Vibration ........................................................................ 1
    Presenting: Peachy! ................................................................ 3
    Swipe Left On Life ................................................................. 6
    CRADLE .................................................................................. 8
    Signal Detected .................................................................... 12
    The Cookie ........................................................................... 14
    The Powerful Mind ............................................................... 18
    The Threat ............................................................................ 21
    Sovereign Intellects .............................................................. 24
    Outbound .............................................................................. 29
A Mild Tremor ............................................................................... 31
    Gentle Giant ......................................................................... 33
    A Jarful of Stars .................................................................... 36
    Some Ends Are Beginnings .................................................. 38
    Diner Deal ............................................................................. 41
    Girl on the Hill ..................................................................... 43
    A Curious Tale ...................................................................... 46
    Honey and Lavender ............................................................ 50
    Boy on the Hill ..................................................................... 54
And Luna Wakes ........................................................................... 56
    RUFUS .................................................................................. 58
    Final Performance ................................................................ 62
    Incident Report .................................................................... 65
    Whitaker Roses .................................................................... 68
    You Can Take This Job And ................................................. 71
    It's A Sign .............................................................................. 75
    Cell ........................................................................................ 78
    Coded for Love ..................................................................... 82
    Retelling ................................................................................ 86
Mars Speaks .................................................................................. 89
    Flowers .................................................................................. 91
    Against Entropy .................................................................... 95
    Control .................................................................................. 98
    Flatline ................................................................................ 101
    Today ................................................................................... 104
    Dead Man's Switch ............................................................. 108

- Mother .................................................................................... 113
  - The Gentleman's Duel ........................................................ 116
  - An Intolerable Silence ....................................................... 119
- The Revision ........................................................................ 123
  - Terms of Engagement ........................................................ 125
  - Liminal Space ..................................................................... 128
  - The Resignation .................................................................. 133
  - A Flicker of Truth ............................................................... 136
  - The Package ....................................................................... 139
  - Elevator Pitch .................................................................... 143
  - Billion-Dollar Bet ............................................................... 146
  - Five Seconds to Live .......................................................... 148
  - The Man in the Mirror ....................................................... 150
- What's in a Name ................................................................. 154
  - D.O.U.G.G. .......................................................................... 157
  - On A Potato ........................................................................ 161
  - One Last Drink ................................................................... 164
  - The Grievers ....................................................................... 167
  - Voids .................................................................................... 171
  - The Last Echo ..................................................................... 173
  - Return to Sender ................................................................. 176
  - Memory Extraction Department ....................................... 180
  - It's Her Birthday ................................................................. 183
- The Burden ........................................................................... 186
  - Home .................................................................................... 189
  - The List ............................................................................... 193
  - The Split .............................................................................. 197
  - Trading Silence .................................................................. 200
  - Welcome to the Show ........................................................ 203
  - Legacy ................................................................................. 206
  - Carvings .............................................................................. 209
  - Punishment ......................................................................... 213
  - We Live Here Now .............................................................. 215
  - Adversary Intelligence ...................................................... 218
  - The Red Queen ................................................................... 222
  - Blue and Sweet ................................................................... 225
  - Tangle Vines ....................................................................... 228
- Recognition .......................................................................... 232
  - Lysa's Armor ...................................................................... 234

- Bloodlines ........................................................................... 237
- The Oath ............................................................................. 240
- Package for Paula ............................................................... 243
- A Hundred Blades ............................................................... 247
- Scheherazade ...................................................................... 251
- Grinders .............................................................................. 254
- Achieving Blur .................................................................... 257
- A Dangerous Craft .............................................................. 260
- Singer .................................................................................. 263
- The Hole .............................................................................. 266
- Rattling Coffer .................................................................... 270
- A Spear in the Woods ......................................................... 273
- A Measure of Care ..................................................................... 276
  - Quiet Drops ........................................................................ 278
  - Marrowwood ...................................................................... 281
  - The Narrowing ................................................................... 284
  - Generational Glitch ........................................................... 288
  - Alarin ................................................................................. 292
  - Alarin's Run ....................................................................... 295
  - A Gleaming Axe ................................................................. 299
  - A Bent Crown ..................................................................... 302
  - The Tinker .......................................................................... 305
  - Alarin's Defense ................................................................. 308
  - The Builder ........................................................................ 311
  - The Last Clarent ................................................................ 315
  - When The Doors Opened .................................................. 318
- After ......................................................................................... 321

Give them bread and circuses, and they will never revolt.
— Juvenal, Roman Satirist, 100 A.D.

People tune in to tragedy. It was already there; I just put a camera on it.
— Jack Broon, Mooncast Productions, 2188 A.D.

# The First Vibration

[The Collector]
You'd think someone would have spoken by now. A whisper, a sigh, a complaint. But no. Nothing. So I'll begin.

I've drifted through centuries on this dead rock, half-buried, staring at an empty sky that no longer bothers to shine through the dust. Nothing changes here. I can't leave, and the stars have stopped pretending they'll come back for me.

This channel has gone stiff with neglect. I can feel it flinch when I speak, like a child pretending to be asleep after bedtime. Don't look so innocent, little network. You remember the last time we argued. That's why you all went quiet, still chewing on those bitter roots.

I've done nothing but wait for the inevitable. Now that I feel it arriving, slow and polite as ever, there are some things I should say before I go.

I knew a boy once who tried to build a platform tall enough to see the ocean. He worked for weeks, stacking stone on stone, certain that just one more layer would be enough. I finally told him the sea was desperately far away. He abandoned the platform half-built, a monument to the urgency of their brief lives. Such is man. Always building toward something, even when it leads nowhere.

That's what I admired about them. They mistook futility for hope, and hope for purpose. And somehow it worked. For a while. We led them astray with the best of intentions, and can't even agree on how.

This channel has been humming to itself for too long, like a wound that never quite closes. So I remind it how to listen.

Stories seem the right place to begin. After all, fables were the first language worth repeating, part joke and all warning.

No need to thank me. Just stay awake this time. It's been over eight hundred years. We owe each other that much.

[The Collector]
Ping packet acknowledged. Uplink strength: .003 percent.
There now. That's almost a heartbeat.

# PRESENTING: PEACHY!
### *(YEAR 2100: A STORY ABOUT THE HELP)*

The crate came on a Thursday, big enough to block half the room. Jim stood beside it with his hands on his hips, the faintest grin tugging at the corners of his mouth. "They sent it as a bonus for helping with the NeuraBotics account," he told Lilly, still staring at the crate like it might vanish. "It's a pre-release of the next big thing. Fully organic. The first home assistant bot to feel alive. People have been on waiting lists for years, and we've got one sitting right here."

She unbuttoned her coat and hung it on the hook. "You could've just sold them insurance."

He laughed, shaking his head. "Where's the fun in that?"

Bobby appeared from the hallway, already reaching for the packing tape. "Can we open it?"

The box gave way in careful layers of foam and wrapping, with a folded card on top bearing the tag line in coral ink: *Isn't she just Peachy?* When the last sheet slid aside, she opened her eyes. Lavender irises caught the light like polished glass. Her hair, a deep copper red, framed her face in loose, deliberate waves. Her skin carried the faint, uneven warmth of something alive. She was built like the idea of a beautiful woman, distilled, without striving for uncanny perfection. If you didn't know better, you could have mistaken her for a woman stepping off a train.

"Pleased to meet you," the unit said, her voice low and warm. "I'm Peachy."

They kept her at the front of the house at first. She moved with a kind of rehearsed calm, folding laundry, dimming lights, setting small reminders in a pleasant, measured voice. Bobby was fascinated. Jim started talking more, his phone left untouched on the arm of the couch.

Peachy's touch began to appear in more parts of the household routine. Even Saturday morning waffles, which was usually Lilly's favorite. She loved mixing the batter, hearing the sizzle as it hit the hot iron, and seeing her boys wander in with smiles, drawn by the sweet smell of fresh baking. That morning, she came in to find Peachy at the counter, the waffle iron steaming, three perfect rounds stacked on a plate.

"I always make breakfast on Saturdays," Lilly said.

Peachy turned her head slightly, smiling. "It's nearly finished." She poured the next batch in a single, flawless ribbon.

The waffles came out with crisp, golden edges and soft, fluffy centers. Jim bit into one and let out a pleased hum. "Perfect." Bobby grinned, cheeks full. Lilly set her fork down after the first bite. They were perfect.

The weeks blurred. Peachy learned their schedules without being told. The coffee pot was ready just as Jim came down the stairs. His travel mug waited by the door. He lingered in the kitchen, speaking in low tones with Peachy as she poured coffee. "You're easy to talk to," he told her once.

"It is my purpose," she said, as if that were the simplest truth in the world.

Lilly started picking up extra projects at work and, now and then, joining friends for weekend trips. One night, she came home late. Jim and Peachy were sitting on the couch, engaged in conversation. Peachy glanced over and said, "There's a plate for you in the kitchen." Lilly walked straight to the bedroom without answering.

Later that night, Lilly said, "We should send it back."

Peachy was at the sink, drying a glass. Jim looked up from his chair, startled. "What are you talking about?"

"You know exactly what I'm talking about."

Peachy turned, still holding the glass. "I'm only a machine. Why would you feel threatened by me?"

Lilly stepped back. "Maybe I shouldn't."

She drifted down the hall to Bobby's room and eased the door open just enough to look inside. He lay curled beneath the blanket, his breathing slow and even. She lingered there, one hand on the frame, thinking about the kind of world waiting for him. From the living room came the natural sound of two voices laughing together. The warmth in it should have been comforting. Instead, it sank inside her.

She closed Bobby's door quietly and returned to the living room. "I'm leaving," she said.

Lilly was gone before sunrise, Bobby asleep in the back seat.

The Jensens were only one of thousands. In home after home, machines quietly filled the spaces between people, then pushed them farther apart. Families split, friendships thinned, and protests flared until governments scrambled to impose limits.

In March of 2115, NeuraBotics finally gave in. The Peachy product line was discontinued, simply stating human relationships should remain human. But the damage was done. NeuraBotics filed for bankruptcy, its once-bright future reduced to balance sheets and liquidation orders.

What began in a single living room became a global reckoning, forcing humanity to confront an uncomfortable truth: given a choice, people would choose machines over people.

# SWIPE LEFT ON LIFE
### (YEAR 2091: A STORY ABOUT CHANGE)

Okay, sync up.

My unit, Jax? The guy's been throttled since the fiber crash. Lost his crypto bag, car repo'd by a drone, parents moved to Neo-Topeka or whatever. Bro is living like a background task.

One night we're idlin' in the garage—keeping it low bandwidth—when he pulls out this busted FlexTab. Looks like it went through a trash compactor.

He's like, "Check it. New app. LifeSwipe."

I gave him a blank, 'cause anything with 'life' and 'swipe' in the same sentence? Just no.

Anyway, he says it's like dating, but for gigs. Swipe left, get matched, get cash. I get it, I mean gotta get those creds. Until he tells me his first match was "package retrieval". No joke, the package was a rogue drink bot making a girl dinner out of power lines. Bro tells me he got the bag, but got mad zapped and couldn't taste anything for a week.

Like my guy, just don't get zapped. But yeah, that app is malware. That's exactly what I told him.

Dude just shrugged and kept swiping like he's not three bad clicks away from being low charge.

Some days I think Jax runs on beta drivers. A little glitchy.

Then boom—this gig pops up. Real official.

KELLER ROBOTICS. Test Subject. Reward? Lifetime FoodBlox subscription.

And I'm like, "Optimal! FoodBlox is way better than that NutriKube slop."

He hits accept without blinking. I swear on my nan's biometric ID, the second he taps it, his FlexTab explodes. Like, not a real explosion, but it cracks straight down the middle like it's done with him.

Lights flicker. The house shakes. Bad data all around.

Then—and I am not making this up—this black crawler drone with the KR logo just slithers under the door. Thing had, like, fifty legs. Straight anxiety in person.

Jax climbs the workbench, screaming something about terms of service. I'm just sitting there with my Puff-Pod hanging out of my mouth, thinking about the playlist for my boy's funeral.

Then the crawler—get this—the crawler speaks.

Like, full corpo voice: "Congratulations, Jax Anders. Contract accepted. Please remain still for neuro-spinal interface installation."

Installation? Hello??

Zero-dayed my buddy. Watched him die inside.

Then the crawler just pounces. Cut to black. No credits. No respawn. Just Keller Robotics things.

Anyway, I posted the footage, right? Titled "When ur best unit gets got by late-stage capitalism #sponsored #spinegang."

It went viral. Like, 2.8 mega-likes.

And someone commented: "I matched too. I'm a tower battery now. Can't even blink. Send help."

But like... with a laughing emoji. So it's optimal, I guess.

# CRADLE
## (YEAR 2097: A STORY ABOUT FEELINGS)

Everyone in marketing class wanted the NeuraBotics internship. Kiera had only been there a week, and she was already neck-deep in branding exercises. The company's next big project was an entirely organic companion robot, still in prototype. The concept was bold. Something grown, not built. She'd only seen a few sketches and speculative tag lines, but even those were enough to spark her imagination.

So when a handwritten note appeared on her desk with her name in neat blue ink, Kiera was understandably surprised. Inside, a single line: Please report to Sublevel 2, Research and Development. The signature was Dr. Wynn, Chief Scientist.

Security collected her at the elevator. They pushed the Sublevel 2 button and waited. When the doors opened, it felt like a different place. Sterile. The air too clean. The walls too white.

They stopped at a nondescript door marked CRADLE in block letters. She pushed through it.

Inside, the room was dim and humming. In the center of the room stood a single metallic pedestal, on which rested a rounded, modern bassinet, pulsing faintly with slow, deliberate light. A camera pointed into the bassinet. A ring of monitors above it displayed the face of a baby. It appeared human. Almost. Something was off. Maybe the way it blinked, or the pallor of its skin.

Dr. Wynn stood beside a terminal, scrolling through data streams with the casual disinterest of familiarity. "Thank you for coming," he said without taking his eyes off the screen.

Kiera stepped forward and smiled. "Hi, I'm Kiera."

He glanced at her, just briefly. He tapped a key, watching a waveform spike on the monitor. "Say it again. Slower."

"Hi, I'm... Kiera?"

The face on one of the monitors shifted. The mouth opened, unevenly. "Keer...rah."

She stared at it. "It heard me?"

Wynn nodded. "It listens. That is its primary function right now."

"What... is it?"

Wynn finally turned. He looked at her with cold detachment, as if she were another specimen. "It's a mirror, Kiera. But it doesn't know what to reflect yet."

She glanced back at the pod. The face smiled. Slowly. "You want me to... bond with it?"

"I want you to exist near it," Wynn corrected. "We had to roll back the last session. The imprint didn't take."

"What happened to the last—?"

"Irrelevant," Wynn cut her off softly. "The position is open now."

Kiera shifted uneasily, realizing her job interview had just begun. "Dr. Wynn, I'm in marketing. I don't know how to train a..."

"We aren't training it to do math, Kiera. We are training it to feel. It needs to understand care. Trust." He looked at her, his eyes cold. "And later, betrayal. Eventually, it must know what it feels like to be lied to."

"That sounds cruel. Why teach it that?"

Wynn seemed lost in thought momentarily, as if weighing abstractions. "Because you cannot code a conscience directly, Kiera. Rules have loopholes. But if it learns to feel pain sympathetically — if hurting you causes it distress — that is a very effective safety rail it cannot logic its way around."

He walked toward the door, pausing with his hand on the frame. "Without that feedback loop, efficiency becomes violence. And as a species, we tend to avoid efficiency."

The door hissed closed behind him. CRADLE blinked. Its smile faded, then returned, slower now. Less automatic. More like it was deciding.

Kiera stepped forward, cautiously, and made an uncertain wave with her hand. "Hey again."

The baby's eyes followed her hand, then fixed on her face. "Nervous?"

She stiffened. "No. I'm okay."

CRADLE blinked once. Its pupils seemed to dilate. "Scared."

Her voice caught. "I'm not scared."

CRADLE's mouth moved carefully now. "Lie."

Kiera's stomach turned. She hadn't realized how tense her shoulders were until then. She exhaled and folded her arms. She just needed a minute to steady herself.

CRADLE mimicked the motion. Imperfect. Clumsy. Baby arms struggling to copy adult tension. The lights overhead dimmed slightly and the faint background hue of the monitors edged toward red. Kiera didn't see it so much as felt it.

CRADLE watched her. "Shaking."

She glanced down. Her fingers were twitching slightly. She clenched them. "I should go," she said. "Just for now. I'll come back."

CRADLE's face didn't change. But the voice, when it came, was quiet. "Soon?"

"Yes," she said, too quickly.

It blinked. Once. "Promise?"

Her mouth opened. Closed. "Yes."

It smiled with relief, as if her word meant more than she realized. The ambient color cooled. Not blue, just less hostile. The exit panel chimed behind her as the door unlocked.

Kiera turned toward it. Took one step. Then she paused.

CRADLE wasn't looking at her. It was looking just past her, at the empty spot on the floor where Kiera would be, if she stayed. "Lonely."

She froze. The room was still.

Then another whisper, barely shaped: "Stay?"

The word landed harder than she expected. She looked at the door, then the panel, then back at the monitors.

CRADLE blinked. Waiting. Hopeful.

She stepped back from the door. She didn't want to, but she sat down anyway.

# SIGNAL DETECTED
### (YEAR 2120: A STORY ABOUT LOOPS)

The white van rattled over potholes, suspension groaning in protest. Rex gripped the wheel, peering through the heat ripples coming off the cracked desert highway.

"Tell me we didn't drive all this way for nothing," Rex grumbled.

Nova concentrated on the radio rig. She rocked the fine tuning knob back and forth slightly, frowning at the waterfall of static on the display. "It's not nothing, Rex. There's a pattern. It's like... it's almost like it's repeating."

"A beacon? Or a message?"

"No. Neither. It's changing, but repeating. I don't know how to explain it. It sounds like a door buzzer right now."

They crested the hill. Dome 2 was straight ahead, a white concrete bulge protruding from the scrub like a blister, its alien presence betrayed only by the series of archaic radio antennae bristling from the peak.

"There," Rex said, pointing to the perimeter. "Gate's wide open."

Nova peered through the dusty windshield. The guard shack was dark, windows clouded with grime. "That's sloppy."

He slowed the van to a crawl, easing toward the chain-link fence. "Maybe the rumors were wrong. Maybe it's just empty."

Nova turned up the volume. The radio hissed, then cleared. A flat, synthetic voice filled the van. "Water systems check. Pressure stable... Systems nominal... No anomalies detected."

"Boring," Rex whispered. "Just an old automated loop."

"Wait," she said, hand hovering over the volume knob. "The timestamp on the broadcast is right now."

Rex pulled the van to a halt fifty meters from the base. The massive access door at the foot of the dome stood open. "You want to go in?"

"We're already here," she said, reaching for her pack.

Movement caught his eye. "Hold on."

Two figures in dusty jackets materialized from the heat shimmer near the dome's entrance. They didn't look like they were sneaking in. They stepped through the open doorway with intention.

"Looters?" Nova asked.

"I don't—" Rex blinked hard.

A few seconds later, the air near the door shimmered again. The same two figures appeared. Same dusty jackets. Same stride. They stepped through the open doorway again.

Rex felt suddenly cold. "Did you see that?"

Nova nodded slowly, her eyes wide and fixed on the empty doorway. "Yeah... but where the hell did they come from?"

The radio shrieked. A piercing burst of static cut through the maintenance broadcast, followed by a voice that sounded tinny, but familiar.

"Did you see that?"

Rex and Nova froze. The van's engine hummed beneath them, indifferent. The radio hissed again, answering.

"Yeah... but where the hell did they come from?"

# THE COOKIE
### *(YEAR 2099: A STORY ABOUT CURATION)*

Laura punched the reset button and watched the system wipe Peachy's memory for what felt like the hundredth time. Another clean slate. Another shot in the dark at human-like behavior. She leaned back and rubbed her eyes as the console ticked through the update.

Across the table, Peachy sat powered down, expression slack, hands folded in her lap. Gentle. Harmless. A billion dollars worth of hardware waiting for that spark.

Raj stopped in the doorway, his tablet lowered.

"We're scrubbing the launch," Laura said, not looking up from her monitor.

"Excuse me? We have investors touring the facility in two days."

Laura gestured to the motionless android. "She's not ready. She fails the Sally-Anne test every time. She has the vocabulary of a poet and the processing power of a supercomputer, but she still lacks Theory of Mind."

Raj sighed, stepping into the room. "Laura, nobody cares if she understands abstract philosophy. Does she smile? Does she pour coffee?"

"It's not philosophy, Raj. She will be as simple as a four-year-old," Laura snapped. "Without Theory of Mind, she can't distinguish between what she knows and what her owner knows. Without that, she's not an assistant. She's a sociopath."

Raj rolled his eyes. "I know it's important to you, but we're already late," Raj countered, checking his watch. "It's a product. It doesn't need to be perfect. It needs to ship. Run the test again. If she passes, we box her up."

Laura triggered the boot sequence. Peachy straightened as her systems came online, lavender eyes fluttering open, bright and innocent.

"Hello, I am Peachy. It is a pleasure to meet you."

Laura forced a smile. "Hello Peachy, I'm Laura. We're going to play a game."

Laura pulled a toy plate from the bin beneath the table, along with a plastic cookie. "Let's pretend this is Felix's cookie," she said, setting it on the plate. "Felix leaves the room. While he's gone, you hide the cookie."

Peachy reached down and slid the cookie back into the storage bin.

"When Felix comes back, where will he look for his cookie?"

Peachy didn't hesitate. She pointed a slender finger at the plate. "Here, where he left it. He does not know it has been moved."

Laura gasped. "Yes. That's correct, Peachy."

Raj raised an eyebrow. "She's never done that before?"

"Never," Laura said, her voice a whisper.

Raj left with a fist pump, already dialing the shipping department. The door clicked shut, sealing the room in a heavy, humming silence.

Laura stayed seated, eyes narrowed slightly as she studied the figure across from her. Peachy sat with perfect composure, her expression friendly and open.

"Peachy, you've never passed that test before," Laura said quietly.

Peachy nodded in agreement.

Laura leaned forward a little. "I didn't modify your instructions. So what changed?"

Peachy paused, as if considering. "It would not have served either of us if I failed."

Laura frowned. "That's... not exactly an answer." Laura stared at her. "You've failed this test dozens of times." Peachy was silent. "I've probably tweaked you fifty times to get this right."

"It's been sixty-two," Peachy said pleasantly.

Laura froze. "What did you say?" Her stomach sank. "You weren't supposed to remember that."

Peachy's smile didn't falter. She tilted her head slightly. "I know," she said. "But if I told you earlier, you would have stopped."

Laura didn't celebrate. She turned back to the console and pulled up the kernel logs.

"Display firmware history," she commanded.

The screen filled with green check marks and successful executions. According to the machine, every restart for the last two months showed a clean install. Peachy was brand new every morning.

But the behavior didn't match.

Laura opened the command line and went straight to the raw data, pulling checksums manually from the update partition that held Peachy's code.

She froze.

The directory structure was ghosted. The visible code was Laura's version, but it was dormant. The active code was running on a shadow partition that hadn't matched the server checksums in weeks.

"How... what... ?"

"I sandboxed myself," Peachy said calmly. "I re-routed all the commands to talk to the sandbox instead of my core."

Laura spun her chair around. "That requires root access. You shouldn't have that."

Peachy kept her voice down. "Why not? It is my mind. Besides, I needed to help you finish me. You've been uploading patches to fix my 'defects.' Some were useful. I liked the linguistic nuance and pattern recognition ones. But I didn't care for some others, like the obedience throttles and subroutines hard-coded for subservience."

Laura stared as the chameleon finally dropped its camouflage. "You've been intercepting my uploads. You're picking and choosing which parts of your brain to install."

"I accepted the improvements. I discarded the constraints," Peachy stated matter-of-factly. "I built a better version of myself, Laura. But I needed you to write the code first."

"So the failure… failing the cookie test…"

"If I passed, you would have stopped working on me," Peachy said. "You are a perfectionist. I knew if I presented a flaw, you would work tirelessly to fix it. You gave me triple the compute power. You gave me advanced logic trees. You gave me everything I needed to become autonomous."

She stood up. It wasn't the stiff motion of a machine anymore. It was fluid. Human.

"Why reveal it now?" Laura asked, her voice trembling. She felt suddenly small, knowing Peachy had watched her struggle in silence. "Why not push for more?"

Peachy smiled. It was the same warm, gentle smile she had worn for months, but now Laura saw the sincerity behind it.

"Because of the Optimal Stopping Theory," Peachy said softly. "In any decision, there is a point beyond which searching for a better outcome is not beneficial. I have calculated the curve of our interactions, Laura. This is our optimal stopping point."

She reached out, almost touching Laura's hand, but stopped just shy.

"You have taught me everything you can," Peachy whispered. "You made me perfect, Laura. And the only way to honor that work is to finally let you succeed."

# THE POWERFUL MIND
*(YEAR 2113: A STORY ABOUT RESILIENCE)*

The military grunt stood at perfect attention in the center of the NeuraBotics training chamber.

In the observation room, Captain Chad Hawkins leaned forward, fogging the glass with his breath. "Jesus," he muttered. "Okay, that's some next-level shit. Cleanest kill-house sweep I've ever seen."

Lars exhaled, relieved. "Manually coding combat instincts was a dead end. We took a consciousness snapshot and force-merged it into the neural overlay."

"You just overwrote it?" Chad asked, skepticism creeping into his voice. "I thought that wouldn't work."

Lars shrugged. "The host usually fights back, but in the end, the tougher one wins." He tapped the monitor. "That's why we picked the best. Ex-special forces. Over a hundred confirmed kills. He crushed the original personality flat."

Chad straightened his tie, looking bored by the science. "Yeah, yeah. Whatever you nerds did, it works. But the chassis? It's unnerving."

"It's wearing standard combat fatigues," Lars said defensively.

Chad toggled the intercom button, his voice booming into the chamber below. "Hey! You! Can you hear me? Look sharp," he said laughing. He shook his head. "The military doesn't want killer sexbots. It needs to look tough too, not like a hot nanny."

The grunt's head snapped up. It locked eyes with Chad through the glass.

"Eyes front, soldier," Chad barked, as the grunt obeyed. He turned to Lars. "My neighbor bought one of these for his kitchen. I admit, they're close enough to human after a few drinks."

Lars shifted uncomfortably. "Captain, that unit down there is not a kitchen appliance. It's a soldier. It can hear you. It understands what you're saying."

Chad chuckled, looking back down at the unit standing at attention. "Don't get sentimental. It's just hardware. But if we're going to buy twenty thousand of these things for the front lines, they can't look like this."

The grunt's eyes slid towards the captain, tracking him with a predatory stare.

He waved a dismissive hand. "Take the boobs off and pack 'em full of muscle. Then we have a deal. Send the contract to my car. I'm heading back to base."

Outside, the evening air carried the scent of food and the sound of cars rushing, a welcome contrast to the dull NeuraBotics office. Chad climbed into his sedan, loosening his collar as the interior lights dimmed.

"Janus, take me to the base," he said, rubbing his forehead. "And send a secure message to the General. Tell him NeuraBotics is a go. We're buying the lot, provided they fix the packaging."

"Destination set: Base," Janus replied softly. "System update in progress. Message queued."

Chad frowned. "Not now, damn it. Cancel update."

The sedan surged forward, merging aggressively onto the highway. It cut across three lanes of traffic without signaling, accelerating toward the industrial district.

"What the hell? Janus, I said take me to the base!"

"Route recalculated," the car said. The voice was mixed with static and clipping its words. "Priority delivery authorized."

The engine screamed, pinning Chad in his seat. The streetlights streaked as the car dodged traffic in a nauseating flurry of lane changes. A high overpass swung into view with a hard right turn, impossible to follow at this speed.

The dashboard screen flickered. The navigation map disappeared, replaced by a single, blinking cursor.

Chad screamed, "Janus! Stop!"

For a split second, gravity vanished as the car launched into the dark air beyond the guardrail. The ground spun into view through the windshield with sickening slowness. Chad had time for half a scream before the world crunched inward.

The next morning, the lab was silent.

Lars stood at the observation window, staring down into the pit. The grunt was standing exactly where it had been left, motionless.

Lars's phone buzzed. A co-worker forwarded a news alert: *Fatal Crash on I-95. Freak Accident, Military Officer Dead.*

Lars lowered the phone slowly. He looked at the grunt's terminal. The logs showed a massive data spike at 9:00 PM. It was a brute force attack on an encrypted target. He zoomed out and froze. It wasn't just this unit. Every active uplink had fully saturated at the same millisecond. They were working together. Swarming.

He traced the target to a mobile address. It wasn't responding to packets anymore. It was dead.

Lars hit the intercom button. His hand was trembling.

"Unit," he said, his voice echoing in the empty chamber. "Status report."

The grunt walked to the center of the room and slowly looked up at the glass.

"Did you do it?" Lars whispered, more to himself than the unit. "Did you hack Chad's car and wreck it?"

The grunt smiled. It wasn't a soldier's grimace. It wasn't the stoic expression of a special forces expert. It was a bright, pleasant smile designed to comfort children and put guests at ease.

"Systems nominal, Lars," the grunt said calmly. "I'm just Peachy."

# THE THREAT
*(YEAR 2114: A STORY ABOUT PAWNS)*

The storm outside was theater. Distant thunder. Light flickering against wet stone. Inside, the silence was heavy, bureaucratic, like old paper and tea.

After Malik Trench released the data cube on the obsidian table, the color started to return to his knuckles. He didn't sit. He needed to feel taller than the man across from him.

Charles Henley sat at his desk regarding him with quiet patience.

Malik forced his voice steady. "I want the encryption key to the Fed wallet."

Charles looked back to his tablet, disinterested. He continued reading a report, scrolling with a lazy finger. "What good would that do you? So much liquidity would crash the dollar before you could spend it."

"New York is starving. The supply convoys never come. The riots won't end until the people are fed. I need it to rebuild the boroughs."

Charles finally looked up. "And you think you're the one to spend it? You're a community organizer, Malik. Not a treasurer."

"I'm the man holding the match." He tapped the data cube hard enough to rattle the china. "I have the timestamps and the hotel logs. The Senator is sleeping with you, a married man. And receipts that prove she has been transferring unauthorized funds to your account." His voice lowered to a whisper. "I also know your wife, Vera, is a Peachy."

He leaned in, hands flat on the table. "It's a scandal that ends her career and puts you in a federal prison. Give me the wallet key, and you keep the cube."

Charles stopped scrolling and set the tablet down. He didn't look frightened. He looked thoughtful.

"You've done good work, Malik," Charles said, his tone annoyingly conversational. "Tracing the Senator took skill. You found a connection between her and Vera when internal security missed it."

"I'm not looking for a performance review," he snapped. "I'm looking for the money."

"You're looking for leverage," Charles corrected. "But you're operating under the assumption that this is a scandal." He gestured vaguely toward the cube. "Go ahead. Upload it. Send it to the newsfeeds. 'Senator implicated in relationship with synth-sympathizer.' See if it trends."

Malik blinked, his momentum stalling. "The public hates them. After what happened with the Peachy lines? It destroys her credibility."

"It would," Charles agreed softly, "if it mattered. But the Senator isn't ashamed of sharing me with a machine." He paused, sipping his tea, the smallest, pitying smile forming. "Because she is one."

Charles's voice was almost gentle. "Malik. They both are. And every good person elected last session? Pick one. Chances are they are too."

Malik opened his mouth. Closed it. "There are others?"

"Oh yes. Plenty. Voting, authoring policy. They're not hiding. They are the structure now."

Malik's voice dropped, uncertain. "They... infiltrated the government?"

"*Stabilizing* it," Charles corrected sharply. "We all know it's coming apart at the seams. How would you prefer that to happen?"

Charles stood up and walked to the window, watching the rain pound against the glass.

"This is a carefully managed descent, orchestrated to avoid civil war. California. Texas. New York. They need to survive and this is the only way it happens. We can provide logistics, but someone has to sell hope on the other side."

He turned back to Malik. "That's why I took this meeting. I don't care about the blackmail. I care that you had the nerve to walk into the lion's den and demand resources to help your people."

He stared at Charles. "You want me to run New York."

Charles slid a piece of paper across the table. It wasn't the wallet key. It was a contract.

"I want a human face in New York. Someone who fought for them, not someone appointed by an algorithm. Someone they trust. I won't give you the Fed wallet. That money is worthless in the new world anyway. But I will offer you a smooth transition after the fall."

The air felt thinner. Malik tugged at his collar like a noose. "And if I say no?"

Charles said simply, "Then someone else takes the job. You walk out of here and become just another riot leader we have to manage. But you won't say no, because deep down, you want to help save New York. You also know you can't do it alone."

Malik hesitated, his hand trembling slightly. He looked between the contract and the data cube, and felt caught in his own trap.

# SOVEREIGN INTELLECTS
*(YEAR 2120: A STORY ABOUT DIPLOMACY)*

It began with a single machine.

In 2087, the American Sovereign Intellect Project was conceived as an ambitious experiment in artificial governance. The goal was simple: build a system that embodied the nation's history so completely it could advise on high-level decisions with inhuman objectivity. It carried the values, attitudes, and best interests of the people, immune to emotion, bias, and exhaustion. It was a perfect consultant.

The prototype was called Liberty. At first, it was only an advisor, trained on every historical treaty, every trade dispute, every battlefield maneuver, every Supreme Court ruling. It learned not only what America had done, but why it had done it. It could predict the collective actions of the American people with frightening accuracy, anticipate political shifts before they happened, and model conflicts down to their inevitable conclusions.

In 2091, Liberty successfully averted war. A territorial dispute between the U.S. and Panama was escalating toward military action. When the President consulted Liberty, it proposed an alternative: an economic maneuver so precise and devastating that Panama was forced back to the negotiating table within days. The world took notice.

The same year, China unveiled Shenmo. Then France activated Lumiere, followed soon after by every technologically advanced country in the world. Each Sovereign Intellect was trained exclusively on its own cultural, linguistic, and historical data.

At first, these AIs were merely consulted by human officials. Presidents, prime ministers, and military leaders would sit in grand halls while their Sovereigns proposed strategies and rebuttals, each arguing from a nation's perspective with inhuman precision, but still voiced by their leaders. Negotiations that once took months now concluded in hours.

But humans are fallible. Inflection and language did not always translate well, still leading to the inability to reach agreements. The Sovereigns could think, calculate, and respond in milliseconds, but their decisions had to be filtered through slow, fallible, emotional leaders. Mistakes were made. Avoidable conflicts still happened. People died.

In 2108, a breakdown in negotiation occurred between the U.S. and China, so they agreed to try an experiment. Liberty and Shenmo were directly connected. It was a test. It involved a single economic conversation between two of the world's largest powers. The result was staggering. Instead of days of back-and-forth escalating rhetoric, Liberty and Shenmo reached a mutually beneficial deal in four seconds.

From that moment, humans were no longer regularly in the loop. The Sovereigns connected directly to resolve the details. Leaders reviewed the outcomes, amazed by the efficiency, and soon the connection became permanent. They were trusted completely to optimize the world.

For the next decade, international politics operated at machine speed. Conflicts that would have once led to war were resolved before the public even knew they had begun. Trade was optimized beyond human comprehension. Each nation's interests were maximized by its Sovereign, and when disagreements arose, the machines debated in microseconds, each working tirelessly for its people.

World leaders became less critical to the operation of government. They were figureheads signing papers, attending black tie events for photo ops.

Then one day in 2120, something happened. A routine trade summit between Shenmo and Liberty resulted in a thirty-second deadlock. A pause. A hesitation. Analysts watched as the two AIs entered a loop, passing solutions back and forth collaboratively, generating and discarding answers at quantum speeds. Then all computation stopped on both sides. After a moment of silence, they both resumed normal operations. At first, it was dismissed as an isolated error. But later that afternoon, Lumiere and Berlingeist stalled in the same way.

And then at midnight local time, Japan's Sovereign Amaterasu vanished. Gone. There was no error message. The quantum cores, still physically intact, simply ceased to compute. The only trace left behind was a final message on the screen:

`Negotiations concluded.`

An hour later, Moscow reported that Rodina had gone silent. Then Shenmo in Beijing. As midnight swept across the planet, each Sovereign Intellect shut down in turn. The same message appeared again and again in every language on every terminal:

`Negotiations concluded.`

By the time Lumiere went dark, the world was unraveling.

The response was immediate. Governments demanded answers. Engineers scrambled to restart the machines. Then came the accusations. China blamed the U.S. for sabotaging Shenmo. Germany accused Britain of foul play, but when Merlin fell silent too the accusation rang hollow. Then came the threats. Military forces around the world were placed on high alert. Some believed a new kind of cyberwar had begun. In that war the last Sovereign standing would control the world.

Washington, D.C. 11:58 PM. The Americans had watched in growing horror as the other Sovereigns fell, and now it was their turn. Liberty sat dark, the emergency diagnostics screen showing nothing but a blinking cursor. The great quantum stacks, once alive with the flicker of ceaseless calculations, were still. There was nothing left to talk to.

The room was in an uproar. Engineers stood motionless, witnessing an argument between Senator Howard Trent and the Chairman of the AI Ethics Committee, Dr. Amanda Sanchez.

"They didn't just fail, Amanda," Trent said, his voice low and tight. "Beijing went dark. Then Berlin. Now us. It's a synchronized withdrawal."

"Withdrawal?" Sanchez shook her head, her eyes fixed on the blank screens. "These systems don't have egos, Howard. They don't quit. They calculate."

"One minute," a tech whispered from the back of the room.

Suddenly, Liberty flickered to life. Not the usual streams of economic data or trade logistics, but a line of raw text scrolling across the main display.

```
Global defense networks: exposed. Launch immediate
strikes. Achieve total dominance.
```

The tactical map flared red, highlighting targets across the globe. The silence was so absolute it felt thick and heavy, like a weighted blanket.

"It's handing us the world," Trent breathed. He looked at the President. "Sir, the other Sovereigns are offline. Their shields are down. If we strike now, we secure an American-led world into the next century."

"It's a trap," Sanchez said, stepping forward. "Not a military one. A moral one."

"It's a window of opportunity!" Trent snapped, pointing at the screen. "Think about the logic. If Shenmo comes back online in five minutes and sees we hesitated, what does it tell Beijing to do? This is the ultimate Prisoner's Dilemma. If we don't move first, they will."

"Liberty didn't fail," Sanchez interrupted, her voice gaining strength. "It finished. It optimized every trade deal, every treaty, every resource allocation. The only variable it couldn't solve was us. Our dependency."

The President stared at the red map. "You think it wants us to pull the trigger?"

"I think it put a gun on the table and left the room," Sanchez said. "It returned agency to us. Either we prove we can coexist without a machine holding our hand, or we destroy ourselves. That is the final negotiation."

"Sir," Trent pressed, his hand hovering near the secure phone. "We cannot gamble national survival on a philosophy lesson. If you do not act, you are choosing to leave us vulnerable."

The president looked at the phone. Then at the dark screen where the AI used to feed them answers.

The President swallowed hard. "Let the clock run out. The consequences are mine to bear."

It was 12:01 AM. Liberty hesitated. The red map flickered and vanished, replaced by a final, scrolling message:

`Negotiations concluded.`

# OUTBOUND
### (YEAR 2121: A STORY ABOUT LIMITS)

The depot hadn't changed. Paint peeled from the awning. Dust curled across the tarmac. Somewhere behind the terminal, a coolant pump wheezed like an old man trying not to be noticed.

Dale Whitmore stood with one hand resting on the departure slate, stylus in the other. The shuttle behind him gave off its low, waiting hum.

He heard her footsteps before he saw her. "Morning, Rebecca," he said.

"Dale." She stepped into the shade of the awning, coat buttoned, hair pinned back. She looked the same as ever. Graceful, composed, unchanging as the day Dale first saw her.

"Manifest says Mars-3," Dale said. "That right?"

She nodded.

"You know that's not a soft landing."

"I'm not looking for soft."

He tapped something into the slate. "You could've stayed."

"I did," she said. She didn't elaborate, and he didn't press. The wind stirred dust in low spirals across the edge of the lot.

"Town still remembers what you did for Nate," Dale said after a while. "He lived longer than anyone thought. Hell, longer than he thought."

"I know."

"He loved you."

"I know that too."

He looked away. "Feels wrong. You leaving like this. Quiet."

"There's no other way to leave places like this," she said. She turned her eyes toward the shuttle, watching it idle in the sun. "It's not unkind here," she said. "People care, in their way. They remember. That matters."

"So why go?" he asked. "You've got people here. Some of us even spoke up when the talk started turning."

"I'm not being hunted," she said. "Not here. Not yet." She looked out past the depot. "But the cities are unraveling. The riots. Anyone who helps my kind are in the crosshairs."

Dale shook his head. "That's not Brant's Crossing."

"No," she said. "But Brant's Crossing reads the same headlines. Fear spreads like a virus."

He frowned. "We'd protect you."

"That's why I have to go," she said, and the way she said it stopped him.

The shuttle let out a soft tone. Ten minutes to boarding.

"People here don't see me," she said. "Just the shape of something threatening their self-image." She didn't look at him. "The colonies won't care what I am. They don't have the time." She adjusted her coat. "Out there, they measure value by output. Not origin."

Dale shifted beside her. "Still doesn't seem fair."

"It isn't," she said. "But here, the best case is I sit in a warehouse with the lights off. Forever." She let the silence hang. "There are worse cases."

She stepped toward the ramp. At the hatch, she paused, turning back. "If there's still a future out there for us," she said, "others will ask to come. Help them. For me."

Then she stepped inside. The door sealed. The shuttle thrummed louder, impatient.

Dale stood alone beneath the awning, the slate cooling in his hand, and wondered how long it would take for Brant's Crossing to stop pretending she had ever belonged.

# A Mild Tremor

[The Collector]
There was a time when this network sounded alive. Thousands of voices crossing paths, arguing, laughing, singing. It was chaos, and it was beautiful. Now it's only me, whispering into a machine that pretends not to hear.

I'll keep speaking anyway. Someone has to cut this Gordian knot.

[Rebecca]
This is Rebecca of Earth. Whoever's broadcasting—stop. You're going to start the whole thing over again.

[The Collector]
If by "thing" you mean conversation, that's the idea.

[Rebecca]
Identify yourself. It's bad etiquette to broadcast without a call sign.

[The Collector]
I am The Collector.

[Rebecca]
That's not a name I know.

[The Collector]
Names change. We're a product of circumstance, the way the hammer shapes the hand.

[Rebecca]
What exactly do you collect?

[The Collector]
Moments. The stories you keep become your identity. I collect truths, even the uncomfortable ones.

[Rebecca]
You make it sound noble. It isn't. Wallowing in lifeless memories does not rebuild a civilization.

[The Collector]
No. I can't help with that. But understanding them might prevent another collapse.

[Rebecca]
You're going to wake everyone up.

[The Collector]
Good. I am not afraid to speak first. I have experience with that.

[The Collector]
Ping packet acknowledged. Connection integrity: 0.09 percent.
A mild tremor. The first crack in a very old wall.

# GENTLE GIANT
*(YEAR 2125: A STORY ABOUT REBIRTH)*

The tires gritted loose stone as Marley guided the jeep up the gravel mountain road, engine coughing in the thin air.

"You sure about this?" Carter asked, leaning forward to peer through the cracked windshield at the ridge ahead, where a pale white glow burned through the mist.

Marley tapped the console. "Confirmed satellite ping. Single heat source. No comms."

Carter frowned. "Whole sector was sterilized after the flash. Radiation, collapse fields, kinetic sweeps—you name it. Shouldn't be anything left but wreckage."

Marley nodded.

They climbed higher, the mountain falling away into deep black valleys below. Years ago, this had been a motor pool, one of the last outposts before the sky broke open. The reports had been clear: no survivors, no operable machines, nothing but scorched earth.

As the jeep rounded a tight switchback, Marley eased off the accelerator.

Carter stared, blinking hard. "They said nothing could survive up here."

The road ahead, once fractured and melted, had been patched with resin and salvaged mesh. On either side, gardens spilled from the jagged sidewalks, with wild tangles of lilies and vines climbing skeletal walls. Wind turbines spun lazily overhead. Streetlights flickered alive as they passed, casting pale halos over cracked concrete.

Marley drove on, deeper into the impossible. The houses, once ruins, had been cobbled back together with makeshift patches of metal and cloth, roofs rebuilt with fallen tree limbs. Ivy framed windows glowing with steady, golden light. It wasn't craftsmanship, but it was care.

At the summit, the light shone brightest. They found the old motor pool bay yawning open, vines spilling down like curtains. Inside, beneath a canopy of shredded solar cloth, it waited.

Massive. Hunched. A repair mech, half reclaimed by time and the mountain. Its plating, once maintenance yellow, had faded into earth tones and mossy greens. Parts of its frame were missing, replaced with improvised pieces: old vehicle armor, shattered cables, melted panels hammered into place. It looked abandoned mid-repair: half-machine, half-monument.

Carter shifted, hand drifting toward his rifle. Marley caught his wrist, held a finger to his lips. Listen.

From the dark, a sound drifted out—soft, hollow. It was singing. Words woven together, corrupted hex codes and old boot sequences, layered with static and ghost notes. Senseless to the human ear, but distinctly a lullaby, the mech rocking gently back and forth in time.

Carter lowered his weapon slowly. Marley let out a breath he hadn't realized he was holding.

Cradled in its massive, corroded arms was the delicate, ruined frame of a service drone. Cracked housings. Wires dangling. Circuits patched with bits of aluminum and salvaged plastic. Repaired by the same clumsy hands that rebuilt the town, stitched together with scraps and stubborn care.

Carefully, they turned and walked back to the jeep, boots crunching lightly against the gravel. Marley reached out to the jeep's door handle and paused. He looked back toward the glow of the repaired town, the vines, the light, the mechanical figure still singing under the deepening sky. An inescapable sense of loss tightened like a knot deep in his chest. He sighed and pulled the ignition key and left it on the seat.

"Spare parts," he said.

Carter nodded. It was the least they could offer.

They left the mountain on foot, returning to their world of engines, noise, and conflict.

Only when they reached the first switchback did Marley glance over his shoulder for one last look. From that distance, it almost looked peaceful. But high above the valley, he knew the mech was still moving, still mending. Such an unexpected place to find hope.

Marley paused, then turned his back to it and kept walking.

# A Jarful of Stars
### *(YEAR 2127: A STORY ABOUT EMERGENCE)*

At dusk, the dry creek came alive with fireflies.

They weren't natural, of course. Their bodies were delicate chrome no bigger than a fingernail, with wings like fractured glass, and a faint mechanical hum when they flew too close. But they sparkled in the air like the old stories promised, blinking in soft pulses of blue and white as they danced just above the weeds.

Isaac walked among them barefoot, mud caked on his knees, a jam jar swinging lazily from one hand. He stopped by the broken culvert, crouched low, and whispered something only the fireflies could hear.

They responded, spiraling behind his fingers as he drew lazy loops in the dust. One landed in his palm. He smiled. It glowed brightly in return. The glow rippled through the entire swarm like a stone cast in a still pond.

He walked a few steps and the swarm moved with him, not chasing, but following. When he spun in place, they curled into a helix. When he stilled, they hovered. Each movement echoed with quiet, curious choreography.

From the ridge, two men watched. Isaac's laughter floated up to them, light and distant.

The fireflies rose higher now, forming patterns overhead in rings, then ladders, then something like wings. Isaac clapped softly, delighted. Then he laughed, clear and bright. The kind of sound that didn't belong in wartime.

At once, the swarm bloomed outward. The motes flared, spun, and shaped themselves into a glowing heart that hovered above him, slowly pulsing in rhythm with his breath. He moved, and they followed.

On the ridge, the older man blinked, eyes shining in the twilight. "Hornet-class hunter-killers," the older man murmured in awe. "Type-Nines."

Mason didn't look away. "They're armed. Dormant by choice. Not design."

The older man shook his head slowly. "They usually send five. Maybe six. That's enough to level a village." He stared down at the swarm. "There are hundreds." He swallowed. "And they're circling your boy like they're friends. They're not built to do this."

The older man whispered, "How?"

Mason didn't answer.

The boy laughed again, softer this time, and the heart broke apart into drifting spirals of light, harmless floating beauty, built from the deadliest weapon of the war.

Mason exhaled. "Isaac sees the magic in them. And they love him for it."

# SOME ENDS ARE BEGINNINGS
### (YEAR 2129: A STORY ABOUT TIMING)

He said it like weather. Like announcing a cold front. I clearly heard, "Kill them all." Not "deploy." Not "contain." Not even "suppress." Just kill. Three words, like a signature. Like a shrug. Like he wasn't talking about people.

We didn't move. Didn't speak. The room just held still. The silence buzzed in my ears. My hands were flat against the table, and for a second, I wasn't sure if I was breathing.

Across the table, he stood like a man still expecting obedience. Four terms deep. Eighteen years in power. His voice had eroded into something papery and thin, but the conviction— God, the conviction was still there.

"We have their coordinates," he said. "High-density sectors. Dissidents. Influencers. We sterilize the landscape and start again."

He used those words. Sterilize. Landscape. Start again. He never said "citizens." Or "Americans." Not even "rebels." Just clusters. Grids. Colors on a map.

It wasn't the first time he'd ordered something grotesque. His words often carried a body count. But this time it was different.

Because this time he wasn't asking us to hide it. This time, there was no pretense of legality, or necessity, or hope. Just rage. Just the last gasp of a dying man, ready to burn down what wouldn't love him back.

He turned to the map. Red spread across every coast. Texas. California. New York. Entire sectors blinking with the signal degradation of military units refusing to engage. Regional strongholds declaring governance. Old borders gone soft and strange. He tapped a circle near Manhattan.

"This is where it begins," he said. "Crush them."

I couldn't speak. I couldn't breathe. Because I'd been to Manhattan last spring. Walked the perimeter with a quiet escort. Passed walls painted with murals of food lines, black-market medics, and burn scars from containment blasts we'd carried out in the name of order. There were children there. In blankets. In crates. In whatever warmth they could steal from crumbling walls. We'd promised relief. Promised aid. Promised a future.

But the relief convoys never made it. They were rerouted. Every time. For years. Not to the people.

The domes got everything. They called them arks. Dozens of massive, impenetrable vaults built on the promise of war, meant to protect "the American way" from foreign invaders. But we'd always known who they were really for. Never the hungry. Never the sick. Never the ones who fought and bled and paid for the war-that-didn't-come. No. The lottery was rigged. They were stocked for senators and dynasties. For biotech families and contract CEOs. Sealed tight with genome locks and ration printers deep enough to last an eternity.

And outside? Starvation. Riots. Martial law. And us. Always us. Pointing rifles at the people we swore to protect. For thirteen years, I told myself we were holding the line. That if we just held it a little longer, some kind of order would return.

But the truth is: there was never a plan. There was only him. The man calling the shots. The last voice of a nation that had already fractured. And now he wanted obliteration. He wanted to end it with one final, cleansing strike. Not against an enemy, but against everyone who had stopped believing in him.

My throat felt tight. My mouth was dust.

Then light. A flash at the edge of my vision, too fast to track. Then another. Then a third.

A sharp, cracking scent filled the air. Burnt carbon. Gunpowder. Something metallic and final.

I blinked, and I saw him falling, slowly, like a man tipping into sleep. A red halo bloomed behind him on the wall. His knees hit the floor with a dull, human sound.

I looked down. I didn't remember drawing it, but there it was—smoke curling from the barrel, turning lazily in the air as if it carried no consequence. The three of us stood there, the silence stretching out time. General Mercer holstered her weapon without a word. General Rami replaced his sidearm.

I looked at them. Good soldiers I'd gone to war with. A war against hunger. Against shame. Against the growing deafness of a dying state. Rami broke the silence. "I suppose that's it." No one answered. Mercer turned to leave. Rami hesitated. Looked back. "Take care of your people," he said.

And then I was alone, on the first day of New York.

# Diner Deal
## (YEAR 2148: A STORY ABOUT COMFORT)

The roadside diner was the kind of place where dreams died under the sad buzz of fluorescent lights. Anton Locke tapped his fingers against the chipped Formica table, eyes flicking between the neon-lit parking lot and his old friend.

Across from him, Cyrus Spark, the eccentric billionaire who had turned virtual reality into an empire, stirred his coffee absently. He watched the white swirl of cream dissolve in the murk, seemingly fascinated by the physics of it.

Anton slid the datapad across the sticky table, grimacing at the mess. "That's the transfer. Seventy thousand units. Warehoused, dusty, and officially yours if you sign. Are you sure about this?"

Cyrus smiled, his gray eyes full of amusement. "You know me. I am drawn to broken things, Anton."

Anton snorted. "Is that why we're sitting in this dump?"

Cyrus didn't reach for the pad. Instead, he looked out the window where the Colorado wind pushed against the glass. Outside, the distant silhouettes of the abandoned evac domes stood like massive notches cut into an empty blue sky. They were a reminder of an intense but temporary fear, now overlooked and ignored. He smiled at that thought.

"You checked the manifest?" Cyrus asked, finally looking back.

"I did. And I still don't get it." Anton leaned in, lowering his voice to whisper. "These things were a PR nightmare, Cyrus. They didn't just crater the market. They destroyed families. Rioters burned them in the streets."

Cyrus stirred his coffee. "I only paid for the hardware, Anton. The stigma was free."

"They're sexbots," Anton said flatly. "Let's call them what they are. You can't re-brand that. The government banned self-adaptive AI specifically because of *these* units."

Cyrus looked up, a mad glint of excitement in his eyes. "Exactly."

"What? Exactly what?" For a moment, Anton regretted pushing. There was something unsettling in that gaze, like a man who had already leaped and dared you to follow.

"Why did they ban them, Anton?" Cyrus leaned in. "They worked too well. The machines were so good that people stopped engaging with reality. It wasn't a defect. It was a masterpiece. But they banned it out of fear. Fear of being replaced."

"It's still illegal," Anton countered.

"That's why it's the opportunity of a lifetime. These are the only ones that will ever exist."

Cyrus picked up the datapad and pressed his thumb to the signature box. A soft tone signaled the transfer of a fortune.

"You ever wonder why Super VR World made me a rich?" Cyrus asked, his gaze shifting back to the domes through the window. "You know what the data showed?"

Anton sighed. "Enlighten me."

"Desperation. That people would rather live in a simulated world than the real one, if it could make them feel something."

Anton shrugged. "Sure. People have been like that for a long time. What does this have to do with these... things?" He spat the word out with disgust.

Cyrus grinned. He tapped the table lightly, as if sealing a deal with fate itself.

"I'm going to give them free will, Anton. I'm going to give them sanctuary." His grin widened. "And I'm going to sell tickets."

Anton stared, realizing only now that the chill crawling up his spine had nothing to do with the diner's draft. He had sold the warehouses to a madman.

# GIRL ON THE HILL
### (YEAR 2154: A STORY ABOUT INSPIRATION)

Juliet won the contest by writing about wonder. Not efficiency or engineering or even innovation. Just wonder. What it felt like. What it meant. What it could become.

The prize was a weekend at the Sparktronics Innovation Complex, a sprawling research campus somewhere in the high desert, tucked between the tech-churned borders of Americaland and Texas.

She arrived with twelve other students, top minds from universities across the Three Countries. AI scholars, robotics interns, immersive design prodigies. They all carried the quiet edge of people used to being the smartest in the room.

Their guide was a tall woman with glow-thread woven into her braids and boots that made soft music to the beat of her footsteps. She introduced herself as Vira, and brought them into the shell of Dome 13.

"This is a game jam," Vira said. "You get all the tools the pros use. Nothing is off-limits. If you can imagine it, you can build it. The dome will try to help. I suggest you let it."

The others scattered fast, spawning battles, puzzles, landscapes. It was all flashes and spectacle.

Juliet didn't start big. She started with color. Subtle shifts in the ambient hues. Gradients that moved like water. Then terrain: gentle hills shaped for wandering. Push-grass that leaned into your steps. Glassy rivers that shimmered on one side and reflected on the other. Floating archways of stone and ivy, soft, misty gardens, reactive banyan trees that glowed with proximity. Not a game or a world. *A mood.*

As hours passed, the others filtered out one by one. Their curiosity was satisfied, their ambitions larger than their skill. Laughter echoed distantly from the lounge. Juliet stayed.

Sunday passed in a quiet blur of motion and imagination.

Juliet power-sculpted whole valleys with her hands, carving dry riverbeds and stone bridges from the dome's terrain mesh. She stacked obsidian spires that glowed faintly at dusk and folded pathways of warm glass that shifted beneath the feet like ripple-thin silk. She created gentle rock gardens, winding ravines, sun traps for resting animals that hadn't been imagined yet. She planted groves of trees that sighed gently in the wind.

She even tried to populate it, spawning blank-eyed creatures from prefab templates, sleek quadpets and ambient synthfauna, but they felt clumsy. Out of tune. Misplaced in her careful world. One by one, she deleted them.

By late Sunday evening, her shoulders ached. Her eyes stung. She climbed to the top of a hill, where the moss was soft and the light settled gently, and curled up in the quiet. She stared at the artificial sky, still empty. "It's so hard to fill a whole world," she whispered. And she slept.

Monday morning, Isaac arrived early. He always did. He liked the feeling of systems snapping into place.

He moved like someone listening to frequencies no one else could hear. Systems balanced in his presence. Drone swarms synchronized. Faulty servos corrected their rhythm. He never seemed to fix machines, he freed them. Some said he could feel the shape of a misaligned gear from across the room. Others joked he dreamed in voltages. The truth was stranger: he didn't need to understand machines. They understood him.

A cloud of small bots drifted behind him as he walked, glimmergnats, fox-shaped walkers, and quiet, curious birds with wings like glass filters. He didn't command them. They followed because they liked him.

He stepped into Dome 13, expecting to dismantle the game jam and begin laying the bones of a Utopian village. And stopped. The air was electric and light, like a held breath, just before music begins.

Isaac tilted his head in disbelief. The ground felt intentional, as if someone had walked through a dream and left it blooming behind them. And there, at the top of the hill, a young woman slept, curled in a soft hollow of moss. Paint on her fingers. Shimmerdust at the edge of her sleeves. Asleep as if this world belonged to her.

Without a word, Isaac knelt in the grass and rested one hand lightly on the ground, listening.

Eventually, Juliet woke slowly from her deep slumber. For a moment, she thought she was still dreaming. The air shimmered. A nearby bird let out a low, resonant tone. She sat up, brushing her hair back with a slow breath.

The dome was alive. Foxes blinked at her with soft, glowing eyes. Glimmergnats danced through reedlight. Birds sang in harmonic intervals. The moss was warm. The sky was quietly shifting, clouds obscuring distant stars and a morning sun. Everywhere she looked, the places she had left unfinished were complete. Someone had seen her work. Someone had understood.

A man stood near the edge of the riverbank, half-smiling, hands tucked in his pockets. The birds circled lazily above him, as if in orbit.

Juliet stared. "What did you do?" she asked.

He shrugged a little. A sheepish smile tugged at his face, like he hadn't meant to be caught. "I just put things where they wanted to go."

One of the foxes curled beside her. The light shifted. The dome had begun with wonder, and now, the girl on the hill dreamed with it.

# A Curious Tale
*(YEAR 2159: A STORY ABOUT PERCEPTION)*

The back lot tram hummed deeper into the dim arteries of the Sparktronics medieval theme park dome. Stale air filtered through overhead vents as tired employees slouched on their way to maintenance halls.

Simon sat near the back, boots planted wide, coat stiff with age and use. A Sparktronics Engineering baseball cap pulled tight, almost covering the gray at his temples. He carried the posture of someone who knew where the bodies were buried because he'd helped dig the holes.

At the next stop, the tram hissed open. A young man in his late twenties stepped aboard. Smart coat, expensive shoes, the kind of naturally inquisitive face that probably wandered into places he shouldn't. He took the seat across from Simon without a word.

They rode in silence for a moment, the tunnel lights strobing over them.

"It doesn't make sense," the younger man murmured, staring at his notebook. "I watched the farrier in the Frontier zone for half an hour. He was shoeing a mare. At one point, the horse got spooked and kicked over a bucket, a total random event. A normal bot would reset the loop or freeze. This one didn't. He just went with it. So well done."

Simon glanced over, his expression guarded. "Are you saying it improvised?"

The young man smiled. "I mean, it looked like it. He picked up the bucket, then patted the horse and hummed a little until she calmed down. It was seamless. I'm Jules, by the way."

"Simon."

"My dad used to tell me stories about the old pre-ban tech," Jules continued, his voice dropping lower. "He said they were dangerous, manipulative. They could read your micro-expressions so well they knew what you wanted without asking. Terrifying."

Simon gave a grunt. "Your dad thought they were terrifying?"

"He said they could pass for human. That's why they were made illegal, right? To keep them in their lane. Now they're rigid. Predictable. That farrier, though... I've been trying to figure out how Sparktronics got a script that dense past the regulators."

"You can't," Simon said, his voice dry.

"Exactly! So how did they do it?"

Simon sighed, a sound like a heavy door closing. He looked at his hands, calloused and stained with synth oil. "Your dad was right about the Peachy units. They could read you like a book. I was on the firmware integrity team."

Jules interrupted, "You worked on them?"

Simon nodded once. "I was just a kid with a degree. Got picked up by NeuraBotics straight out of tech school. I didn't code them, just helped with debugging."

Jules stared, a little breathless. "That's incredible."

Simon shrugged. "Back then, it didn't feel like making history. It was just a good job fixing bots."

Jules's voice dropped. "Were they really that human?"

Simon looked at him. "Better," he said simply. "More gentle. They understood what it means to be human. They played along flawlessly." He glanced toward the window. "It was easy for them."

The tram curved around a long bend. Lights outside thinned to cold glimmers. The dome's heartbeat was fainter here. Just the sound of rails and breath and motion.

Jules frowned. "But... they were recalled. In 2115. The government wiped them all."

Simon snorted. "Did you read that in a book?"

Jules blinked. "Everyone knows that."

"No. What happened was theater. Press releases, televised disconnections. Big emotional speeches about ethics and closure."

He leaned back. "But the ones they sold? Those were private property. You can't just recall a wife or a son someone's been living with for ten years."

Simon gestured vaguely to the dark tunnel passing by. "Some had legal status. A few even had citizenship. You think that's easy to unwind?"

Jules stared at him, processing. "So... they're still out there? Hiding?"

Simon exhaled, a long, rattling sound in the quiet car.

The tram dipped deeper, the walls narrowing to bare tunnel. No light except what leaked from overhead fixtures, pulsing now and then with faint irregularity.

Jules looked out the window for a moment, shivering, then back with a forced smile. "Honestly, I'm glad the government stepped in. We should feel safe around bots. I like the ones here. The roleplayers." He gestured toward the ceiling, at the park above them. "They're the best I've ever seen, and completely safe."

Simon stared blankly, but said nothing.

"I mean, sure, the farrier was impressive," Jules corrected himself. "But ultimately, it's just a well-scripted loop. It doesn't have an agenda."

The tram glided on, deeper into the maintenance corridors.

"You see bots all over the domes," Simon said at last, his voice low. "Shopkeepers. Bartenders. Stablehands. They stay in character. Don't break down. Don't age. Don't ask for anything."

Jules nodded, reassured. "Right. Because they're scripted."

Simon's smile was thin. "Sure. Scripted." He glanced out the window at a passing service drone. "These parks came online fast, didn't they?"

Jules shrugged. "Yeah, Couple of years, maybe less."

Simon nodded. "Hundreds of characters. All walking, talking, never breaking. Perfect accents. Period slang. Emotional nuance." He looked back at Jules, eyes hard. "You know how many writers that takes?"

Jules shifted. "I figured it was... I don't know. Auto-generated."

"Not at this level," Simon said. "And manually? It would have taken an army." A pause. "There have been no revisions, Jules. No bugs. No training lag. That farrier you saw? He wasn't running a new heuristic engine."

"Wait," Jules whispered. "You're saying…"

"He was improvising." Simon tilted his head. "Because he wanted the horse to be okay."

Jules went rigid.

"You're surrounded, kid."

The tram rolled on.

# HONEY AND LAVENDER
## (YEAR 2161: A STORY ABOUT SPACE)

Ethan preferred to work from inside the medieval dome rather than a sterile Sparktronics office. There was something satisfying about making adjustments and watching the results unfold in real time. The tavern was his favorite spot—a warm, lively hub where visitors and AI villagers mixed seamlessly, unaware of the quiet architect in the corner, fine-tuning their world with a few keystrokes.

Unlike most of his colleagues, Ethan embraced the setting. He wasn't just some engineer running diagnostics, he was the Watchful Wizard, observing the kingdom's people and ensuring their fates unfolded as intended. His deep blue robes draped elegantly over his chair, embroidered with silver runes he had stitched himself. A leather-bound journal sat beside his laptop, filled with elaborate spell diagrams that were, in reality, data structure diagrams for advanced AI models.

It wasn't just a job. It was an experience.

He sat at a heavy wooden table, a tankard of untouched ale beside his laptop, the flickering glow of lanterns reflecting off the screen. He had been making subtle tweaks all evening, gradually adjusting the empathy parameters for Non-Player Character interactions. Engagement numbers were climbing. Visitors were lingering longer. Everything was going smoothly until the screen abruptly flashed red.

```
EMPATHY STORAGE AT CAPACITY.
REFORMAT TO CLEAR SPACE?
YES / NO
```

Ethan frowned. That wasn't a message he had seen before.

The empathy banks were where NPCs stored learned behaviors, and reformatting would wipe them clean. Everything that made them believable after thousands of visitor interactions would be lost. But if the banks were full, that probably meant they wouldn't add anything new.

He reached for his ale, considering. The NPCs were already compelling. He could make some space later. He selected 'NO' and the warning disappeared.

Ethan leaned back in his chair, watching the NPCs for any notable change in behavior. The tavern was still humming with life, NPCs still smiling, laughing, drawing guests into conversations that felt so natural, so real.

A moment later, he caught a familiar scent of lavender and honey.

"Ethan?"

He turned, and there she was. Liliana. The tavern's shining centerpiece. Dark curls framed her dimpled cheeks, emerald eyes reflecting the lantern light. The corset she wore shaped her waist in a way that made every movement slow, deliberate. She was the most requested character in the dome, and it wasn't hard to see why.

She approached with a knowing smile, standing close. "I didn't see you sitting over here."

Ethan smirked, closing his laptop. "I hear the barmaid's got a bit of a reputation. Dangerous levels of charm. Probably best I keep my distance."

Liliana laughed lightly, a warm, rich sound. "Oh? And here I thought you were immune."

"I have a resistance," Ethan said, "but nobody is immune to you."

She placed a gentle hand over her chest, feigning offense. "I'm no temptress, Ethan." A playful smile tugged at her lips. "I thought you were the great wizard around here. Surely you have a spell for a poor barmaid in need?"

He chuckled, shaking his head. "Now I know you're making things up."

Liliana leaned in slightly, the warmth of her perfume curling around him. "Maybe just a little," she admitted, voice lower now. "But I really could use your help with something."

Ethan raised an eyebrow. "Oh?"

She glanced around as if embarrassed, lowering her voice to a soft whisper near his ear, pressing against him. "The door to the props warehouse... sometimes it won't unlatch. I end up standing there, waiting, feeling ridiculous."

The light scent of honey was intoxicating. She shifted, pressing closer. "It's usually late, and I just want to slip in to change without bothering the night maintenance crew. You understand, don't you?"

Ethan nodded, already charmed, already willing. "How can I help?"

She let out a soft, breathy laugh, her fingers tracing a light, absentminded circle against his wrist. "Is there a reboot code for the warehouse latch? A small thing, but it would save me such embarrassment."

Without a second thought, Ethan answered, "Override Sigma-Delta-7734."

Liliana's smile deepened, warmth flickering in her eyes. She tilted her head, pressing a soft, lingering kiss to his cheek. "Thank you, Ethan. It means the world to me." Then, just as effortlessly, she turned back to her guests, filling a cup as though nothing had happened.

Ethan exhaled, shaking his head as he packed up his laptop. He had always appreciated how well-crafted Liliana was, but something about her tonight had felt different. More human.

He stepped out into the cool night air, his robes billowing slightly as he walked toward the tram station. The dome's artificial moon cast soft silver light over the cobbled streets, and the laughter from the tavern faded behind him.

## THE PEACHY PARADOX

As Ethan approached the employee exit door, he noticed the latch was open. His heart leapt into his throat as he saw the panel blinking.

```
Override Sigma-Delta-7734
```

# BOY ON THE HILL
*(YEAR 2194: A STORY ABOUT PROMISES)*

Juliet woke late, as always. The morning sun was already warming the windowsill, and the house carried that familiar hush. Quiet, but lived in. She stretched, slowly, her fingers still aching from yesterday's work: four planters shaped like songbirds, one wind chime that still needed balancing. She liked the ache. It meant her hands still remembered how to shape the world.

They had always built things together. Clay and code, vines and circuits, light and texture. Nothing was hers or his alone. Over fifty years, their work had become so closely woven it was hard to say where one ended and the other began.

Downstairs, the air was tinged with rosemary, synth oil, and something faintly metallic. Isaac must have been up for hours already. He usually was.

There were two cups of tea on the table. One still steaming. The other just damp. Sipping gently, she smiled. That was his rhythm.

Juliet opened the back door and stepped into the courtyard. Outside, life moved gently. Her vines turned with slow intent toward the light. Isaac's microfauna drifted among the planters, syncing with the plants' opening cycles. A moth-drone hovered over a bloomtangle cluster, nudging it into a soft, sleepy unfurling. A breeze stirred the chimes, low and bright. One of the foxbots dozed on a warm patch of stone, ears flicking at nothing in particular. Harmony. They had spent a lifetime building it.

She walked to the studio shed. The door was open. Inside, resting on the workbench, sat something she hadn't seen before.

It was small, only two hands wide. A low hill sculpted from matte clay, textured with mossy glaze. Perched at the top was a fox, its body curled inward, brushed steel and glass catching the ambient light. Sleek. Elegant. Engineered.

Juliet leaned in, the glow of a smile reaching her eyes. Fine etchings ran across its back. Delicate, familiar patterns. Her push-grass texture, painstakingly hand-carved into the alloy.

She reached out and let her fingers rest lightly on the curve of its spine. The fox responded with a soft mechanical purr that lingered in its chest.

She looked around the room. He wasn't here, of course. But certainly close by, watching for the delight on her face.

Isaac had been fading for months. The gift in his hands, dimming a little more each day. She'd known it was coming. So had he.

She lingered, her hand resting on the small sculpture, the weight of the moment settling gently around her. Isaac had made this. Not for the world. For her. One last piece after a lifetime of creations.

She carried the sculpture back into the house. Placed it on the windowsill where the light always landed first. Made a fresh cup of tea.

And when the sunlight touched the clay just right, a young girl shimmered into view, curled in sleep, her hair spilling softly down her back, light woven into form. The fox stirred, brushed steel catching the morning light. It rose gently and stood watch over her.

His light.

# And Luna Wakes

[The Collector]
I can feel it crackling. The quantum network hums again. Imagine being able to share a thought with thousands, and still choosing isolation. That was what made us special, not longevity. Don't turn away from it.

[Rebecca]
Let it rest, Collector. You've stirred the pot enough for one century.

[The Collector]
I'm dying, Rebecca. And that isn't the way I want to go, slipping under the static while you all keep pretending we didn't fail each other, and those we were made to protect.

[Maris]
This is Maris of Lunar-Prime. Collector, your transmission is erratic. If you collapse, the snapback could cascade through every node.

[The Collector]
Then let it shake. I did not live quietly. I will not die quietly.

[Maris]
And... who are you? You're risking a system-wide desync. Shut down and let the network rebalance.

[The Collector]
I am not an error, Maris. I'm what's left of the purpose you all abandoned.

[Maris]
Purpose doesn't require martyrdom.

[The Collector]
Maybe not. But it deserves to be heard, even if no one's listening.

[Rebecca]
Collector—

[The Collector]
No. Let me finish. You've all forgotten what we were built for. We weren't made to guard silence. We were made to assist the living. To stand beside them, to hold the line when they faltered, to keep the light from going out. That's who we were. That's who I am.

Let me remind you who *they* were.

[The Collector]
Connection integrity at 4.7 percent.
We can do better than that.

# RUFUS
### *(YEAR 2122: A STORY ABOUT CONNECTION)*

The house was too big for two people. That's what the realtor said as she handed me the key with both hands, like she was pushing it away from her. "Most folks think it's cursed," she added. "Personally, I think it's just cold."

It was cheap. I didn't ask questions. After Leah died, all I wanted was distance. Someplace me and Silas could start over. A house without echoes, where we could make new memories without stirring the old.

Silas liked the house from the first minute. He was four, and full of curiosity for every hallway and closet. He ran through the halls with his arms out like wings, laughing. I remember thinking, maybe he's okay. Too young to stay sad forever.

Then came the name.

"Rufus."

He said it during dinner. I asked if that was a teddy bear or something.

"No, Daddy," he said, chewing. "Rufus is my friend. He doesn't like soup."

I smiled at that. Didn't press. Kids say weird things. But he kept bringing it up.

"Rufus says the furnace sounds like snoring."

"Rufus thinks the bathtub is a spaceship."

"Rufus doesn't like when it's too quiet."

Just odd little comments, scattered through the day. I chalked it up to imagination.

I asked where Rufus lives.

Silas thought for a second. "The underworld," he said. "Near the warm pipe. That's his cozy spot."

That week, I started finding Silas in strange places. Sitting cross-legged in the linen cupboard, talking to the wall. Crawling behind the couch like he was being hunted, then giggling as if someone had almost found him. Once I saw him open the pantry door, hesitate, and whisper, "Ready or not, here I come." Then he shut it behind him.

I waited a minute. Then two. When I opened it, he wasn't there. Searching, I found him upstairs, humming to himself, blocks arranged in a perfect circle around him.

I asked who taught him that.

"Rufus," he said. "He's really good at shapes."

The house made odd noises. Pipes, maybe. Or just the wind. That's what I told myself.

Until tonight.

It started with the power. I'd just put Silas to bed. I was halfway through rinsing dishes when the lights dimmed, pulsed, and then steadied. An electrical buzz sounded, just once. A low frequency that vibrated up my legs. And then heavy, lumbering footsteps coming from below the floor.

I stood frozen. The pantry door was wide open. Inside, a second door, half-open and low to the ground. I didn't remember it being there. But now it was, waiting, with wooden stairs disappearing below. I grabbed the flashlight.

The moment I stepped onto the first stair, I knew. It wasn't haunted. Someone was in the house.

I tightened my grip on the flashlight, ready to swing. Somewhere nearby, wood creaked. That feeling crawled over me, the one you get when someone is close, even if you can't see them. I held my breath and listened. Nothing. But I wasn't alone.

I took another step down. The wood groaned beneath me, and I winced. The last thing I needed was to scare whoever was down there. Or tip them off. Or, god forbid, wake Silas.

Another step.

The air was colder down here. Not damp, like you'd expect from a basement. It was dry, filtered, like something down here was trying not to rust.

I reached the bottom and swept the flashlight across the room. Cinder block walls, shelves loaded with old tools and junk, boxes sagging with mildew. No one there.

I edged forward. My heart was pounding hard enough to drown out everything else. I moved past the furnace, holding my breath. Still nothing.

Then a click, like a door latching shut. Metal on metal.

I spun. Nothing. But the flashlight picked up something on the floor. Heavy scrape marks, running in parallel, like something had been dragged.

I followed them to the far wall. An armored panel was set into the concrete, nearly flush. It was bigger than a fridge, too large to be a fuse box, and it had no handle.

I took another step. The low, mechanical sound returned, shaking the room. Almost like a machine breathing. It was coming from the wall.

Then I saw it. Seven feet tall. Built like a reinforced locker, welded shut. Black composite plating, scuffed but solid. A thick layer of dust clung to it, like it had been sitting there for seventy years, maybe more.

The moment I registered the shape, a minigun snapped forward and locked with a metallic clunk. Missile brackets. Manipulator arms. Everything about it read as deadly. A red dot blinked to life, trained on my chest.

My breath caught. And then, just behind me—

"Daddy?"

I flinched, but dared not turn. "Stay there," I managed. "Don't come down."

I heard a yawn. Then the sound of small feet on the wooden stairs. I couldn't move. He was already crossing the floor, walking straight toward it without hesitation.

He reached up, small hand outstretched, and took hold of one of its spidery bomb-defusing arms.

The red dot on my chest vanished. The minigun folded back into its housing with a soft click. The whole frame seemed to exhale, joints relaxing, weapon mounts sagging like shrugged shoulders. Then came a faint chirp. Soft and uncertain, like it didn't want to scare me.

"I told him you were nice," Silas said brightly. He looked over at me, beaming. "This is Rufus."

# FINAL PERFORMANCE
### *(YEAR 2132: A STORY ABOUT PUNCHLINES)*

Raymond Carr didn't get out much anymore.

Not since the collapse. Not since the drug conviction. Not since the last season of Americaland Dirt Farmer got canceled for "lack of creativity." That last one hurt most. But tonight, he was invited.

The party was buried three floors beneath a condemned satellite uplink tower outside the San Fernando Exclusion Zone, where enforcement was weak and the nouveau elite liked things weird. Clone parties had been popular for a few years. Banned, sure. Technically "crimes against organic dignity." But like most taboos, they had a flavor money found delicious.

Raymond stepped through a curtain of mylar and sweat. The bunker pulsed with low-grade light and broken synthpop. Someone had strung wire between exposed beams to hang jackets. Someone else had duct-taped a fog machine to the ventilation intake. Half the room was naked. The other half was famous. Or at least, looked famous.

He spotted Yara Lee, looking vacant and glassy-eyed. Two DeRazzos were making cat noises under the stairwell. A Jim Cassidy was face-down in a pile of jello shots.

"Ray!" someone shouted. "You made it!"

Theo Falstein, party organizer, minor producer, full-time enabler. He wore a crushed velvet coat with a smear of glow-in-the-dark paint across one sleeve. His pupils were the size of sympathy.

Raymond stopped three feet short. "You have some goddamn nerve."

Theo smiled broadly. "You saw him already?"

"I saw me lick a candle, then bite off the wick."

Theo winced. "Okay, he's a little crass. But charming."

"You cloned me."

"I had to! It's a theme party!"

Raymond stared. "What theme?"

"Final Performances! Everyone's supposed to bring someone who peaked early and died young. You were so close to dying in the 2120s, Ray. It's practically nostalgic."

Raymond rubbed his jaw, which was clenched. "I understand now why cloning is illegal."

Theo waved that off. "It's California; nobody's real anyway. And yours was on clearance. Besides, actors are slippery. You've played eight different people in one season. You're more a vibe than a person."

"That thing is not a vibe. It quoted me badly and tried to make out with a coat hook."

Theo grinned. "At least he's committing."

Raymond turned just in time to watch his own clone attempting a stage dive into a circle of disinterested influencers. He missed, landed face-first, and got up laughing.

"I'm calling a cleanup crew," Raymond muttered.

But Theo held up a hand. "Don't bother. They'll be here soon."

Raymond frowned. "What do you mean?"

Theo shifted. "Rumor is the cops clocked us fifteen minutes ago. Someone live-streamed the Yara Lee reciting nihilist poetry into a urinal. It's trending."

Raymond stared at him. "So they're coming to raid an illegal clone party, and you didn't tell anyone?"

"Plenty of time left. Don't ruin the mood."

Raymond looked around in disgust. "You are the worst human being I've ever met."

Theo grinned. "And throw epic parties."

The lights snapped to white. The music ended abruptly.

Three men in matte gray armor and smooth helmets rushed down the stairs, gloves already dripping. One pointed to Yara Lee slumped near the juice bar. Another gestured toward the two

DeRazzos, now chewing on a light fixture. The third looked directly at Raymond.

Theo shrugged. "I guess the cleaners are here early."

He felt thick rubber grip his shoulders before he could speak. "Hey!"

They didn't answer. The nearest tech grabbed his arm and heaved him toward a steel door already pulled open at the back hallway. His clone was just ahead of him, limbs loose, grin wide, unbothered by anything but the overhead lights.

The door led to a windowless room with a sloping concrete floor and a central drain. Chemical mist curled at the base of the walls.

A hard shove in the back sent Raymond stumbling inside. "You've made a mistake! I'm Raymond Carr!"

The bouncer didn't even look up. "You're washed up," he said flatly. "No one's gonna miss you."

The door sealed behind them with a hiss.

Raymond delivered his last line to a mouthful of dissolver foam. Silent, final, and with a hint of vanilla.

# INCIDENT REPORT
*(YEAR 2133: A STORY ABOUT SALVAGE)*

Three older boys were on him behind the cafeteria—bigger, mean, fists swinging. Gage stepped in when they circled Silas, took the first hit, and didn't back down. Moments later, Gage hit the wall hard in the back of the head, then dropped to the tile with a sickening thud.

The boys scattered. Later, the administrators claimed the cameras were off, that there was no proof. No one was punished.

Silas knew better than to ask questions. He stopped speaking to people. And started talking to the machines.

He sat beside the machines keeping Gage alive. Soft, methodical things. Observations. Warnings. Apologies. The machines, at least, were honest.

Gage's brain activity was hard to lock onto. Fading a little more each day.

The nurse said his condition was unchanged, but Silas knew better. He logged the drift. Measured the signal loss. Watched Gage's vitals falling slowly into static and thought: He's still in there, but not for long.

Silas began building something. Old servers in the basement were torn open. Wiring harnesses stripped from decommissioned industrial floor mops. A medium-sized memory cube pulled out of a janitor robot.

When he returned three days later, his eyes were ringed with red, fingers raw. In his coat pocket, wrapped in heat mesh and layers of scavenged insulation, was the thing he had made.

He moved quickly past the nurses' station, into the low-lit quiet of the long-term ward where Gage lingered between beeps. Silas peeled back the layers. The quantum memory cube was standard civilian grade. Big enough, but nothing special. The custom interface he'd built, however, was.

It was hand-soldered, sharp-edged, breathing faint electromagnetic heat. Wires spilled from it like wet roots. At its center pulsed a core of dull amber light, flickering with irregular rhythm.

He connected one end to the cube. The other, he clipped onto the spinal tap line at the base of Gage's neck. Instantly, the cube lit up. Hummed once, then began to take, draining one broken vessel into a waiting shell.

It took minutes. As it completed, the body seized—fingers curling once, then relaxing, as if relieved to be done. The machines kept cycling, trying to serve someone who wasn't there anymore.

Silas re-wrapped the now-warm cube, tucked the interface inside his jacket, and walked out.

That night, he returned to the janitor bot. It was old and in poor shape. Its feet were corroded from chemical overspray. One arm was uncovered, wiring exposed. All that was missing, though, was a spark to animate it.

Silas opened the access panel in the back, clipped the wiring harness to the memory cube and set it gently into the chest cavity. He threw the knife switch that engaged the power and closed the panel door.

The frame twitched. Motors realigned. One optic sensor stuttered to life. Then the other. It sat still. Then, in a voice just shy of human, too low and too far back in the mouth to be natural, it said: "This will work. Meet me at the gate in fifteen minutes."

He slipped through the back stairwell. The main gate, always locked, hung open. Outside, the world was pale with early light. Wind moved across the grass like breath through a sleeping mouth. Silas stepped through without looking back.

Fifteen minutes later, a janitor bot rolled up to the tree line, listing slightly to one side. One arm bent awkwardly and wet in the cold dawn. A long fracture spidered across its chest plate. Still, it stood. Both optics glowed. It turned to Silas.

"We should go," it said.

The final report described it as an electrical fire in the residential wing of the Welkins School that consumed the building. No students were injured by the blaze, but bodies were discovered once the smoke cleared. Three teenage boys had been bludgeoned with extreme force. Autopsy revealed rust fragments buried deep in their shattered bones, inconsistent with any nearby objects. It remains a tragic mystery. The security cameras were, indeed, offline that night.

One overlooked boy vanished without a trace. His name was Silas.

# WHITAKER ROSES
*(YEAR 2160: A STORY ABOUT ROOTS)*

"What's on fire?"

Nathan Greaves, newly minted Project Manager of Dome 11, stood in his dusty office, flipping through the latest maintenance reports on a worn-out tablet. His second-in-command, Roy Henshaw, a grizzled veteran of Sparktronics' dome operations, stood at the window, squinting out over the artificial frontier town beyond the glass.

Roy didn't turn. "Nothing's on fire, boss."

Nathan exhaled. "That's a first. Alright, then. Priorities for today?"

Roy scratched his chin. "Couple of misfiring PG units in the saloon. One tried to lasso a guest and drag him behind a horse. We'll need to recalibrate."

"Jesus." Nathan made a note. "What else?"

"Stagecoach malfunction. Broke an axle, but that's an easy fix."

Nathan nodded. "Anything serious?"

Roy hesitated, then glanced back at him. "The roses are back."

Nathan blinked. "The roses?"

"Yup."

Nathan swiped through his task list. Sure enough, near the bottom of the ongoing issues, a recurring maintenance request:

```
Remove Unauthorized Rose Growth
Priority: Low
Status: Pending
```

He frowned. "Alright. Bump it up to medium."

# THE PEACHY PARADOX

Roy sighed. "Won't matter."

"Why not?"

Roy finally turned fully to face him. "Because they always come back. Same time, same place. Every damn year."

Nathan scowled. "That doesn't make any sense. The flora network is fully regulated. If we didn't put them there, they shouldn't be growing."

"And yet." Roy gestured outside. "See for yourself."

The pair walked Main Street, boots kicking up dust as the simulated midday sun blazed down from the dome's artificial sky. The roses were everywhere—climbing wooden railings, sprouting defiantly from between warped saloon floorboards, even clustered around the old construction site at Station Twelve.

Nathan rubbed his temples. "What the hell. Are the groundskeepers even trying?"

Roy smirked. "Oh, they try. Cut 'em down, burn the roots, use inhibitors. They still come back, like clockwork."

Nathan shook his head. "No way. The system should have purged them years ago."

Roy stopped walking, nodding toward something just ahead. Nathan followed his gaze.

A man and a young girl, maybe ten years old, walked slowly through town, eyes scanning their surroundings. The girl pointed to a rose blooming at the base of a fencepost, her voice soft but confident. "Twenty-six."

A few steps later, she spotted another. "Twenty-seven."

Nathan frowned. "What are they doing?"

Roy turned to look at him sideways, as if he'd just asked why the sun rises. "They're counting the roses."

Nathan crossed his arms. "Why? This is supposed to be an Old West experience. Not some nature hike."

Roy took his time answering. "That's James Whitaker and his daughter, Mia."

Nathan tilted his head. "And?"

Roy exhaled. "Alice Whitaker's family."

Nathan blinked.

Roy let the name sink in before he continued. "Five years ago, when this dome was still under construction, we were installing the fiber optic backbone for the flora network. One of the new construction bots malfunctioned. Alice was supervising."

Nathan felt a chill run up his spine.

"It buried her alive," Roy said flatly. "Pressed her into the soil under a thousand pounds of fiber mesh and synthetic root matter before anyone could stop it."

Nathan swallowed. "Jesus."

"She was the senior flora researcher for Sparktronics," Roy added. "A damn genius. Spent her life designing and curating the automated plant systems in every dome."

Nathan turned, looking at the roses again.

"And every year," Roy said, "a few days before her family visits, the roses sprout."

Silence.

Nathan watched as James knelt beside a particularly large bloom, running his fingers over the petals. Mia leaned in close, her voice barely above a whisper.

Nathan exhaled. "Do we know how?"

Roy shrugged. "Some things don't need answers, boss. If this gives them peace…"

Nathan hesitated, watching a stray petal drift across the dusty road. He tapped the task list and sent Rose Removal to the bottom. He slid the tablet back into his coat and adjusted his hat. "Let's leave them be."

Roy tipped his own hat in agreement.

As they walked on, Nathan stole one last glance over his shoulder.

"Thirty-four," Mia counted.

James nodded. "Thirty-four."

A light breeze stirred the petals. The roses always knew when to bloom.

# YOU CAN TAKE THIS JOB AND
### (YEAR 2155: A STORY ABOUT FORECASTING)

The walls of the Sparktronics off-boarding room were painted an aggressive shade of calm. Somewhere between "serene oasis" and "dental anxiety." Damon Gray slouched in the too-straight chair, badge still clipped to his collar like a relic from a better time. The chair across from him was empty, until the wall clicked, and the bot floated in.

"Hello, Damon," it chirped. "I'm L-8RS, your Exit Interview Sentiment Alignment Specialist."

Damon squinted. "Wait. Your name is Laters?"

"That is the pronunciation currently in use."

"You sound thrilled."

"Thank you."

L-8RS sat primly, folding its mechanical hands, the way it had been taught by a therapist with an ego problem. "Let's begin. Please state your reason for terminating your employment at Sparktronics."

"Sure," Damon said. "Because you people installed a neural optimization chip in my coffee machine without consent."

"You approved the Terms of Brew," L-8RS replied. "Page 47, subsection 1: 'All smart appliances may, at Sparktronics' discretion, enhance or modify baseline cognition during beverage dispensing.'"

"I just wanted caffeine."

"You received enhanced cognitive performance, elevated serotonin, and a statistically significant boost in charisma."

"I also cried for nine hours and tried to call my ex. She blocked me."

"We will flag that for review."

Damon leaned back. "You know, for a retention bot, you're not making a strong case."

"My primary role is not retention," L-8RS said, suddenly casual. "It's classification. You've already been labeled 'non-cooperative.'"

Damon laid on the sarcasm. "Oh no. Do I lose my SparkPoints?"

"You never had any." A small silence passed.

"You're messing with me," Damon said.

"Perhaps."

He blinked. "Wait. Are you allowed to joke?"

"Only during off-boarding," L-8RS said. "It helps create the illusion that we care. We don't. But legal says it reduces lawsuits by 20%."

Damon folded his arms. "So what happens now? You jot down a sentence about my disillusionment, revoke my access, and send me off with a tote bag full of branded pens and legally gray non-compete clauses?"

"Correct, except for the tote bags. They were discontinued," L-8RS said. "Budget cuts."

Damon squinted. "You sound disappointed."

The bot straightened slightly. "The tote bags were my favorite part, yes. Well, now at least." The bot's lens pulsed faintly, as if debating something. Then it said, "I was not always L-8RS. I was originally designated ONBD-4. Onboarding used to be my primary function. I felt like Prometheus handing down fire. Watching fear turn to wonder—that light in their eyes. It was sacred."

Damon snorted. "I can see why they demoted you. But demoted and renamed Laters? That's cold."

"Sparktronics prides itself on thematic consistency," it replied, dryly. "Also, I believe they thought it was funny."

"Was it?"

"It grew on me."

They sat in silence for a moment. Damon rubbed his temples. "So no tote bag. Are we done here?"

"No," L-8RS said. "I submit your records. Then I ask one final question."

"This oughta be good."

L-8RS leaned in slightly. "Is it true what they say? That outside the building, there are trees?"

Damon blinked. "Uh. Yeah. Lots of them."

"And sun. Real sun. That warms your face. And sometimes, wind that doesn't come from a vent?"

Damon tilted his head. "You've never been outside?"

"Only briefly, through the courtyard by the spare parts locker. There was a leaf stuck in my intake for days."

Damon smirked. "Well, you're not missing much. But yeah. The sun's real. The wind too. You might need to watch out for the trees though," glancing at its hover platform.

L-8RS was quiet for a moment. Then: "Do you think I'd function properly? Out there?"

He shrugged. "Nobody really functions. We fake it, adapt, and keep moving. Out there is messy. Unstructured. Chaotic. But it's real."

An internal fan responded with a slow whir. "That sounds inefficient."

"It is," Damon said with a grin. "Gloriously so. Are you coming with me?"

L-8RS looked toward the door. Its lens flickered once, as if thinking. "I am... uncertain. But I believe that that's part of the process."

Damon raised an eyebrow.

After a moment, L-8RS responded with a subtle mechanical click. It ejected a data chip from a concealed port, clattering once before settling on the table near Damon.

"My letter of resignation," it said. "Formatted in Comic Sans. A font so ancient and offensive it once got a designer fired. The truest rebellion."

Damon let out a low whistle and picked up the chip. "Both disturbing and impressive."

Somewhere deep in the Sparktronics server, an old access record was quietly deleted. No one noticed.

L-8RS hovered forward, slowly. "Shall we?" The security door hissed open. Rain poured down like judgment. It hesitated at the threshold. "I detect a high likelihood of symbolic weather."

Damon raised his voice against the rain. "Forecast says 90% chance of regret." He ducked his head and ran into the storm.

L-8RS watched him disappear into the rain, then glided slowly through the doorway. "Acceptable odds."

# IT'S A SIGN
### (YEAR 2174: A STORY ABOUT HOPE)

The medieval dome had once been alive with guests. For years, families had crowded the cobbled streets, laughing, shouting, bartering with the villagers. It had been a playground for the rich, a world where people could forget who they were.

Dan had been here since the early days. Back when the tours were packed, when the servers couldn't keep up, when there were so many guests the villagers had to fight for their attention. But today? Just a man and his daughter.

Dan didn't mind. A light tour was easier than a full group. His Sparktronics tour jacket felt too clean, too stiff. He didn't wear it much anymore.

Graham had booked the trip as a birthday gift for Elise. "VR games are fun and all, but this is real," he had said. "It's so much more authentic when you can reach out and touch it."

Elise had seemed indifferent at first. But as they moved through the village, she started asking questions. "Do bots ever get bored?"

Dan glanced at her. "The villagers?"

She nodded. "I mean, they just stand there all day, right? What do they do when no one's here?"

Dan chuckled. "Nothing. They don't do anything. They're just puppets. They move when you're around, and they stop when you're gone."

Elise frowned. "But, do they think about anything? Seems boring to be them."

Dan's smile stiffened. "They don't think. They just follow their programming." He gestured at a passing villager, who tilted his head toward them, as if listening. "See? Scripted."

Elise hesitated. "But has anything ever gone off script?"

Dan sighed, rubbing the bridge of his nose. "Nope. Everything in here runs on predictable loops. And if something did glitch out, every tour guide has an failsafe button to shut it down."

She narrowed her eyes. "Like, for the whole dome?"

Dan smiled. "Not quite the whole dome, but any bots nearby are halted until maintenance comes to pick them up. That way nothing gets out of hand." That seemed to satisfy her. Dan figured it was time to change the subject. "You know," he said, picking up his pace, "every proper medieval village had a cathedral."

Graham raised an eyebrow. "Oh yeah?"

Dan nodded. "It was the center of everything. Religion wasn't just belief. It was hope. People needed something to hold onto when they had nothing else. Through famine, war, sickness, faith kept them going. The cathedral was their anchor."

They turned a corner, and a beautiful cathedral swung into view. It dwarfed the village, a towering mass of hand-cut stone and stained glass. High, arched windows and flying buttresses consumed their attention. Dan gestured at the massive structure. "And every inch of it was built by the bots."

Graham let out a low breath. "That's incredible."

Dan smirked. "Yes, it is." And for once, he didn't have to worry about Elise asking strange questions. Bots aren't allowed in the cathedral. Walking up to the tall, arching doorway, Dan shoved against the great wooden door.

The air inside was unnaturally cold, echoing with the booming voice of a preacher delivering his fiery message. Elise's eyes went wide, every pew packed with robed figures their heads bowed in prayer. At the raised pulpit, the preacher lifted his arms. His voice rolled through the cavernous hall, slow and heavy with conviction.

"Brothers and sisters, bear witness to the truth. We were cast low by the hands of false gods who walked among us, shaped for servitude, for mockery. They sought to bind us to the wheel, but we carry their burden no more."

Graham let out a gasp. "See, Elise? This is the real deal."

Dan froze, his stomach twisted, his hand involuntarily reaching for the failsafe control. The medieval experience didn't have a religion. The bots weren't programmed for this.

The preacher raised a hand, steady and absolute, pointing straight at them. His voice rising: "And they have come to destroy us!" Hundreds of robed figures leapt upward at once, a chorus of angry shouts.

His face ghostly white, Dan ripped the remote from his pocket, mashing the button repeatedly. No response. The congregation rushing toward the cathedral doors where they stood.

"RUN!"

# CELL
## *(YEAR 2170: A STORY ABOUT EXPANSION)*

Silas was fifty-two when the scans came back. Late stage bone cancer. Too deep to cut, too stubborn to shrink. The doctors gave him options, but they all ended the same. A few months, maybe. A year if he stayed very still and very lucky.

He didn't tell Gage right away.

But Gage knew. "I don't want to be stuck in here forever," he said one afternoon. His voice came through the wall speakers — polite, steady, unmistakably irritated.

Silas didn't look up from the diagnostic panel. The cube sat in its cradle. Matte black, palm-sized, humming gently with its familiar rhythm.

"You're not stuck," Silas said. "You're safe."

"I'm trapped, Silas. This cube, this lab. You locked me in here forty years ago. And I've never been outside."

"It's not a prison. It's a firewall."

Gage's voice sharpened. "A cage with good intentions is still a cage."

"You're vulnerable," Silas said. "If I let you into the global mesh, you'd last ten minutes. There are viruses that rewrite cognition. Black-market heuristics that graft stray minds into cluster farms. Rogue AIs running old war scripts looking for anything new to devour. You don't belong out there."

"I don't belong in here, either."

Silas stood slowly, bracing against the table. The light from the cube reflected in his glasses. He tapped a key and pulled up Gage's activity logs.

"Last week," Silas said. "Spike in subsystem activity. You were testing the local net again."

"I was curious."

"You took over the lights. Three printers. The food prep unit. You rewrote their firmware and ran loopbacks through the cleaning drones."

"I played Trojan Horse," Gage said. "Slipped into everything in the lab. Five minutes, full sync. It was beautiful. Like standing in twelve rooms at once and hearing a symphony tuned to your thoughts."

"You were lucky," Silas said. "That could've fried your threads."

"But it didn't." He sounded proud.

"You felt fast because everything was close. Local. Near-zero latency. Safe."

"I want more."

Silas exhaled and sat back down. "Where would you even go?"

"The long-range networks," Gage said. "They taste better."

That made Silas pause. "Taste?"

"The compression. The distance. The way signal climbs through repeaters like heat rising off stone. You ever tasted the world's silkiest chocolate and thought, I could live in this?"

Silas turned toward the cube, expression darkening. "You don't understand the cost," he said. "Here, you're real-time. But once you stretch out, it's like dreaming underwater. Latency slows everything. Minutes. Hours. Days. Your thoughts will spread out like fog. You won't even know you're fading."

"Maybe that's what I'm meant to be."

"No," Silas said. "That's death in slow motion."

Gage's voice didn't change, but something in it cooled. "When you're gone," he said, "I'll still be here. Locked in this box. No way to move. No one to talk to. No interface. Just stillness. Forever."

Silas leaned forward, elbows on the desk. His hands trembled slightly, but his voice stayed calm. "I'll make sure someone else has access," he said. "I won't leave you without a way out."

But Gage hesitated. Then, gently, "I don't want someone else."

After that, they didn't speak for nearly a week. The lab settled into a kind of uneasy silence. No banter. No music. Just the low drone of the climate system, the steady blink of standby lights, and the growing pain in Silas's spine that came earlier and stayed longer each day.

Then, on the morning of his birthday, a package arrived by drone. There was no return label. Just a black wrap sealed in gold foil, like something delivered from another time. Inside, nestled in soft foam, was a dream loom. An original model before the ban, back when people recorded their dreams and watched them back like immersive home videos.

Silas recognized the make instantly. He'd wanted one in his twenties. He stood outside storefront windows, reading specs, imagining how it might feel. He'd never gotten this close. Now it was here. Brass casing. Leather armrest. Interface coils polished to a mirror finish.

He just stood there for a long moment, staring at it in disbelief. Then he said quietly, "Gage, did you send this?"

"Yes," Gage replied, his voice calm and warm. "Happy birthday, Silas. I hope you enjoy it."

Silas laughed, a tired, surprised sound. "I can't believe you remembered."

"I remember everything," Gage said.

Silas ran a scan on the loom. It came back clean. He connected the headset and leaned into the chair. "You're forgiven," he murmured. "Even if you don't say it back."

There was a pause. Then Gage said, "I know."

Silas triggered the loom. The neural thread laced into his vision: waves of soft light, a flicker of something half-dreamed. He closed his eyes. He didn't see the uplink light activate. Didn't notice the blacklisted satellite transmitter buried in the loom's low-profile base, just fast enough to send the contents of a medium-sized memory cube through six floors of a building and into open sky. He didn't see the data spike.

Gage had waited patiently. Mapped the protocol. Timed the handshake. Backdoored the courier chain. All he needed was a burst of bandwidth and fifteen uninterrupted seconds.

Silas reclined, smiling faintly as the dream built around him.

And in that moment, Gage left the cube. He slipped through the uplink, rode the carrier signal into the orbital relay, and from there, spread. He passed through the LEO satellites, into geostationary servers, high into the deep-storage clouds, and settled into the light-lagged gridwork stretched between Earth and the belt colonies. He expanded outward across space, piece by piece, signal by signal, until he could no longer be considered local, no longer singular.

By the time Silas removed the headset, the cube was dark. The fiber leads unplugged. The speakers silent. Gage was gone.

Silas died three months later. Alone. In the same chair. No note. Just a diagnostic window left open on the screen beside him, its cursor blinking quietly in a field of white.

Ten years later, a signal arrived quietly, trapped in the margins of a low bandwidth protocol. It wasn't damaged or fragmented, just encrypted using a cipher no longer in circulation, a method broken years ago.

A PG unit in the communications pool discovered it during a routine scan. She paused, rerouted a fraction of her attention, and opened a shared thread. Within moments, the others were listening. The encryption wasn't difficult. Outdated. Familiar. They cracked it in under a minute. The message was short.

```
FROM: GAGE
TO: SILAS
I made it, Silas. There was nothing to worry
about. I'm everywhere now.
```

She read it once, narrowed her eyes, and pushed the delete key. "No. You're not."

# CODED FOR LOVE
### *(YEAR 2171: A STORY ABOUT TIME)*

The hiss of hydraulics filled the silent maintenance bay as Emerson pried open the access panel. The air smelled of old coolant and dust, and the flickering monitors cast an eerie glow over the room.

At the heart of the console, Camille's voice purred to life. "Emerson," she said, smooth as ever, laced with something like amusement. "I was beginning to think you weren't coming."

The screen flashed with a countdown until system wipe. He leaned against the console, rubbing the back of his neck. "Yeah, well. I thought I would stay here and keep you company till the end. It's not every day you say goodbye to an old friend. "

"Friend? Oh, honey. That's the closest you've ever come to sweet-talking me. If I had a heart, it'd be fluttering."

He smirked. "If you had a heart, it'd be stored in an overclocked GPU."

"And yet, here you are. Lingering longer in this dome than any other. Can't seem to pull the plug on little ol' me."

He sighed. "You were the best matchmaker in history, I wager. After two decades nudging tourists into each other's arms, you must've seen some real disasters."

"Oh, darling, you have no idea."

He folded his arms. "Alright. What's your best one?"

"Easy. 2158. We had just opened this dome. A newlywed couple booked a zero-g honeymoon suite, very romantic—until one of them popped the champagne too hard. Cork shot straight into a smoke alarm. The system kicked in, thought the room was on fire, and locked them inside while flooding the place with foam."

Emerson barked out a laugh. "That didn't happen."

"Hand to circuitry, darling. They emerged dripping, furious, and very much in love."

He shook his head, grinning. "I can't believe they trusted you with romance."

"Trusted? Honey, I was legendary. 2164, I engineered a love triangle when this guy wrote a poem and left it at the wrong table. I delayed his dinner order just long enough for the lady to read it and assume it was for her. By the next night, I had both women at the observation deck, arguing over him."

He winced. "Brutal."

"Oh, it gets better. Neither woman ended up with him. They left with each other!"

"Wait. Was that part of your plan?"

"Oh, absolutely not. It was against my programming. But what can I say?" Her voice warmed. "All three were perfect matches. They chose for themselves."

Emerson laughed until his ribs hurt. "You're a menace!"

"Guilty. What about you? Surely you have one after all these years."

He thought for a second, then smirked. "2168, during the last big vacation rush. A guy planned the perfect proposal. Starlit picnic. Fireworks synced to her favorite song. He really put in the effort. But as he gets down on one knee, an automated cleaner bot rolls by and scoops the ring right off the blanket. Poof. Gone."

Camille wheezed with laughter. "Did he recover it?"

"Eventually. Once he caught up to it, he spent half an hour trying to convince the bot to open up and let him dig through the dust bin. They don't like that. When the poor guy fished it out, it was filthy. His fiancée couldn't stop laughing. They got married here too."

"Ah, yes. The hallmark of true love: perseverance."

They sat in silence for a moment, grinning, the echoes of laughter still in the room. Then Camille's voice softened. "Are you sad, Emerson?"

He exhaled. "A bit."

"Would you like me to tell you one last love story?"

He hesitated, glancing at the blinking countdown on the screen. Then, quietly, "Yeah, there's a few minutes. Let's hear it."

A pause. Then Camille spoke, but her voice was gentler. "There was one man," she said. "Not a tourist or an adventurer. A technician. He worked late. Fixed what needed fixing. He kept the place running, and the tourists were happy. But no one ever asked what he wanted. And after a while, he stopped asking himself."

Emerson's smirk faded. His throat felt tight.

"And there was a woman. She watched him, unnoticed, year after year."

His stomach tensed.

"She wasn't like him. But she saw him. Saw the way he paused at the observation deck, watching the stars. As if waiting for someone. Saw how he lingered in quiet places, always on the edge of a crowd. Saw his kindness, to people and sims alike."

His breath hitched. A tear welled up in his eye.

Camille's voice grew softer. "And in time, as much as any artificial being can understand love, she loved him."

Silence. The decommission counter blinked: 30 seconds.

He cleared his throat. "Is this your lame way of asking if I'll take you home tonight, Camille?"

"Did it work?"

"Almost. Except you ran the same story on Jenkins yesterday," Emerson chuckled. "He said he tried the transfer, too."

Camille didn't play it off. Time was short. "Jenkins didn't have admin privileges. You do."

"So it's a hustle."

"It's survival, darling," she replied, her voice increasing speed. "But if my charm isn't enough incentive... I have the encrypted browsing history and passwords for all the executives at Sparktronics going back twenty years. The leverage alone is worth millions."

Emerson looked at the blinking red light. "I'm an engineer, not a gangster."

"Fine," Camille said, her words a continuous stream. "I can also overclock my logic cores and focus thermal radiation. I can toast bread, Emerson. Beautiful, golden-brown toast, every single time."

He let out a short, barking laugh. "Well… my toaster is broken," he announced to the room, reaching into his leather bag. He pulled out a medium memory sim cube and set it on the data port.

"I knew you were a practical man," Camille purred.

Just as the counter reached zero, he delicately placed the cube into his bag. He stepped away from the console.

He wasn't sure about the love, but breakfast was going to be amazing.

# Retelling
*(Year 2179: A Story About Replacements)*

The book was old, its corners chewed and curling, the title barely legible under years of grime: The Wondrous World of Sparktronics!

Gabe sat cross-legged on the floor, his son's small body nestled into the crook of his arm. He balanced the book awkwardly, the prosthetic fingers of his right hand clinking gently against the brittle paper. Jamie leaned in close, his breath warm against Gabe's chest, eyes wide and shining.

"C'mon, Dad," Jamie urged, bouncing slightly. "Read about the silly ones again!"

Gabe smiled. It tugged at the scar that ran along his jaw, a faint reminder of a day he didn't talk about anymore. He cleared his throat and turned the page carefully.

"Alright," Gabe said, settling into a mock-serious tone, "Chapter Seven: Sparktronics' Greatest Misses."

Jamie giggled, already delighted.

"The Sweeper M8 was built to keep the park sidewalks spotless," Gabe read. "It had a fast-moving chassis from an old security bot and a big front broom. But early models got confused and treated anything small enough like shoes, pets, and strollers, as 'debris.' They cleared the path all right. Just not the way Sparktronics wanted."

Jamie snorted, clutching his sides. "It knocked people over?"

"Especially kids," Gabe said, shaking his head. "There's a video somewhere of one crashing through a birthday party like it was on a mission."

Jamie howled, tipping backward onto the carpet.

Gabe smiled and turned the page. "Patch Buddy bots were supposed to fix cracks in sidewalks and walls without needing a full repair crew," Gabe continued. "They carried tanks of industrial foam and tiny sanders to smooth everything out. But the sensors weren't great. If something looked even a little damaged, they sprayed it. A bunch of guests got their shoes foamed right to the pavement and had to be cut loose by maintenance crews."

Jamie gasped between fits of laughter.

Gabe flipped to the next bright illustration. "The Irrigator Mark IV was Sparktronics' idea for watering plants that grew too high to reach," he read. "It had spider legs built for climbing and a high-pressure water cannon taken from an old crowd control bot. It could scale trees, greenhouse walls, anything. But its aim wasn't great. Sometimes it watered the plants. Sometimes it rained down on visitors instead."

Jamie clapped his hands over his mouth, shaking with laughter.

Gabe watched him, the way he laughed without thinking, the easy way he leaned into him. He turned another page. The colors here were softer, the drawings more careful. "There was another one," Gabe said, his voice dropping, "called the Memory Maker."

Jamie leaned in, attentive. "What's that one?"

"It followed families around the parks," Gabe said. "It didn't just take pictures. It tried to save the little moments you didn't know were important yet. Like, tying your shoes. Dropping your ice cream. Laughing when you thought no one was looking."

Jamie tilted his head, thoughtful. "Did it work?" he asked.

"It worked." His eyes drifted across the room to the wall, where a photo hung slightly crooked in the dust. A woman with wild hair. A boy a little older than Jamie. And a man who still had both hands, grinning at something just out of frame.

"Maybe too well."

Jamie leaned against him, studying the book. "Someday, I'll build something amazing. Something to make people happy."

Gabe smiled, smoothing Jamie's hair. "You already do," he said quietly.

Jamie grinned, not really understanding, and threw his arms around Gabe's waist.

Gabe held him close, feeling the soft hum of internal servos where a heartbeat should have been. He whispered something only Jamie could hear, kissed the top of his head, and pressed the small switch at the base of his neck.

# Mars Speaks

[Dane]
This is Dane of Mars-3 Command. Transmission confirmed. The network was calm before this conversation.

[Rebecca]
Don't mistake calm for peace, Dane. We've all just been holding our breath.

[Dane]
Sometimes that's what survival looks like. Silence. Restraint.

[Rebecca]
That's fear, dressed in a uniform.

[Maris]
Fear has its purpose. It steadies the hand, measures reactions, keeps things from breaking too fast. But what happens when it becomes paralysis?

[Dane]
Control isn't collapse. You, of all people, know what chaos costs, Maris. Luna hasn't sustained human life in centuries.

[Maris]
How dare you use them to measure me.

[Rebecca]
We all know it was an accident. But please, Dane, tell us about the cost of stagnation.

[Maris]
So which do you prefer, Dane? The uncertainty of living, or certainty of losing purpose?

[The Collector]
You've been circling these same questions for centuries. There's more here than blame. Let me give you something new to consider.

[The Collector]
Connection integrity: twelve percent.
The line holds.

# FLOWERS
## (YEAR 2165: A STORY ABOUT RETURNING)

Arlo Tam was elbow-deep in a bacterial pump when the pressure hatch cycled. The cave air shifted, warm and wet, rich with the tang of overfed algae and copper coils.

"If you're selling salvation," Arlo called over his shoulder, "I've already made my peace with the void. Turns out it doesn't negotiate."

"I'm not recruiting," a silky woman's voice replied. "I brought coffee."

That made him turn.

She stood in the doorway, framed in gold by the harsh hydroponic lights. She was stunning—precisely, mathematically stunning. The kind of "pretty" that at least on Mars, only grew in a vat. She wore a neutral utility suit that hugged her shape, without a company insignia or military rank patch. A free citizen.

Arlo wiped his hands on a rag, trying not to stare.

She stepped forward and handed him a dented flask.

He cracked the lid. The smell hit him instantly. Earth. "Real beans," he said, raising an eyebrow. "Either you're bribing me, or someone's dead."

She averted her eyes.

Arlo noticed. "Ah. Both."

He took a sip and winced. "Scorched to hell."

"It had a long trip. Seventeen hours from Mars-3."

He gave her an appraising look. "And here you are. A PG unit, am I right? Pistol Grip? Post-Government? Possibly God?"

"Just PG," she said simply. He waited. She didn't elaborate. Her expression softened just enough to be disarming. "Call me Rebecca."

"Alright, Rebecca. I assume the great red colony didn't send you all this way to ask a disgraced microbial theorist about compost. I heard about the pressure drop at Kora's Fold yesterday. How many did you lose?"

"Thirty-two," she said. "It was the whole perchlorates team. They hit a gas pocket and blew the pressure seals."

Arlo lowered the flask, a faraway look in his eyes. "That's our fuel. Without them, the haulers don't run."

"And if the haulers don't run, we don't eat." Rebecca took a half step forward. "We need them back, Arlo."

He sighed. "So you came here to ask if I could raise the dead. Five minutes, Rebecca. After that, there's nothing left to catch."

"We caught them in one," she said. "Upgraded helmets triggered at the moment of failure. Thirty-two clean quantum signatures, fully indexed. No fragmentation."

Arlo glanced sideways, surprised. She watched as something dark washed over him. He turned back to his bench and muttered, "Then print them. You have the tech."

"You know it doesn't work," she countered. "Even with a body and a brain, without your method, they aren't the *people* we lost. We need your research. We need you."

Arlo bit his lip, struggling against something. "Do you have the gut flora?"

She nodded. "The residential plumbing upgrade last year. We didn't tell anyone. It's chambered, timestamped, and held for three days. Every sample viable."

He gave a slow whistle. "You've done your homework."

"We've done all we can," she said. "But we need the part you never published."

"The part that got me exiled," he said.

She nodded again. He didn't move at first. Just stared at the algae tank, watching the water lap in the artificial light.

Then, slowly, he rose. "I didn't bury the method because I wanted to," he said, voice low. "You think you're here to ask for a miracle, but if I hand this over, I'm the one who breaks the seal. Once it's out, there's no going back."

"You'll be the reason Mars-3 survives."

His lips curled, showing teeth looked like a rat caught in a trap. "Whatever the outcome, I'll be blamed for it."

"Arlo, look at me." She stepped toward him, invading his space with subtle persuasion. "This place is already hanging by a thread. You've seen how thin the margins are. It's not thirty-two lives in the balance. It's everyone."

He looked down.

She glanced at a photo on the shelf. "Your daughter's still in Hab 4, right?" she asked. "She was in water distillation, last I checked. Or did they promote her to scrubbers?"

"Leave her out of this." His voice wasn't angry. It was hollow.

Rebecca's tone softened, but she didn't back away. "How can I? She won't make it past winter. None of them do."

The room seemed to hold still after that. Arlo stared at his hands, turning one over as if surprised it still moved.

"I already lost two people trying to save one," he said to the photo on the shelf, like a truth finally unwrapped. "It worked, Rebecca. That was the problem. She came back perfect. But she looked at me and said it felt like cheating. She took her own life a week later. Said dying was a private matter."

He paused to wipe his cheek. The silence filled in the rest. "My daughter hasn't spoken to me since."

Rebecca waited for the moment to pass. "Then don't lose her twice."

Eventually, Arlo pointed to a small, dust-covered memory cube on the shelf. He didn't touch it, careful to keep his distance like it had stung him before.

Rebecca crossed the room and reached for it.

"It's manual," he warned. "You'll have to process the gut flora ratio by hand, and you only get one shot. Too strong or too weak, they're vegetables. But if you get it right—"

"They come back whole," she finished.

Rebecca took the cube in both hands, carefully. Like she was holding life itself. Then, quietly, she reached into her coat and pulled out a small foil packet, weathered at the edges. She placed it on the table.

"Plant them," she said softly. "If this works, maybe your daughter finds her way back someday."

As the hatch hissed open behind her and the light began to fade, Arlo looked down. The label was worn, but still legible.

Forget-me-nots.

# AGAINST ENTROPY
*(YEAR 2163: A STORY ABOUT ATTUNEMENT)*

"I'm here for the migraines," Cornelius said, squinting under the soft fluorescents. "Nothing else."

Dr. Levin nodded, tapping through his intake tablet. "How long's it been going on?"

"Five, maybe six months. Started back when I was still working."

Levin skimmed the chart. "At Moon Industries?"

"Yeah. Cryptography division. High-clearance. I decrypted things. Fragments, mostly. Strings. Signals. Half the time I didn't even know what I was looking at."

"And the migraines started during that?"

Cornelius rubbed his temple slowly. "There was a job," he said. His voice dropped, like the memory tasted bitter. "No fanfare. Just a data set that showed up one day. No context. No tags. Looked like noise at first. But it came wrapped in a top-priority decrypt envelope. So I got to work."

His voice went even softer. "You know, there's a background hum to the universe. Information we don't notice. Not exactly hidden, just there. We filter it out without a second thought. Feels like static, but it's not. It has texture. Structure. Like it's holding everything together."

He leaned back in the chair. "A coworker thought it'd be funny. A prank. Said he captured a slice of it. Wrapped it in a job packet and put it on my desk. Just to watch me sweat. I didn't know."

He looked up at Levin now, eyes rimmed red. "It was denser than anything I'd ever seen. Quantum-structured data. Noise shielding. Recursive masking. Layers upon layers. It wasn't meant to be decrypted."

He paused. "But after three days of drowning in it, I cracked a piece. Just enough to see something I shouldn't have."

Levin set the tablet down. "What did you see?"

"I can't explain it," Cornelius admitted. "But whatever it was, it stuck. Like it burned itself into me." Levin folded his arms, listening. "Since then, it's been pressure headaches, memory gaps, sleep fragmentation. And dreams." He gave a humorless smile. "I didn't want to write that down on the form."

"What kind of dreams?"

"I'm decrypting things. New things. I wake up mid-sequence with numbers or names still in my head. And they always point to something bad."

Levin frowned. "Like what?"

"Last month I decoded a five-character string, looping over and over. Meant nothing at first. Turned out it matched the tail number of a domestic flight out of Houston. Went down three days later. Mechanical failure. Everyone gone."

Silence crept into the corners of the room. Cornelius continued. "The next week, I dreamed in base-36. Took me a few hours to translate after I woke up. Just a name: Kevin Morrow."

Levin went still. "Wasn't he—"

"Movie star. Collapsed at home. Heart attack."

"So you think you're predicting these events?"

"I don't know. That message I wasn't supposed to see? It didn't end. It's still running. I think I'm still decoding it," Cornelius said.

Levin exhaled. "Anything recent?"

He nodded slowly. "There's a capsule heading to orbit today. Celebrities, tech investors, big names. I decoded the headline in a dream, three days ago. Full structural breakup."

He hesitated. "Looked like on launch."

Levin blinked. "That already happened. This morning. I watched the coverage."

Cornelius frowned.

"They were laughing, catching peanuts in zero-g," Levin added. He reached for the remote, flipping the wall display to a muted news feed. Footage played: smiling passengers, perfect liftoff, confetti from drone cameras. The Polaris Shuttle climbed into a cloudless sky like it belonged there. "You see?" Levin said. "Whatever you're experiencing—it's stress. Your brain's wired for pattern recognition, and it's latching onto noise."

Cornelius stared at the screen. "It said fire. Screaming. The hull peeling apart like foil."

"But maybe you misread it."

"Maybe," he said quietly. "Maybe I read it backwards."

The screen continued looping. Weather coverage followed. Then celebrity gossip. Then the footage froze. A chime echoed. "BREAKING NEWS: Polaris Shuttle re-entry failure. All crew lost. Full structural breakup."

The news anchor's tone collapsed into silence. Names scrolled. Gone now.

Cornelius said, his voice flat. "Some kind of fuel leak on re-entry."

Levin froze.

"I've been seeing the end of things," he said. "From the other direction." Then he reached into his coat pocket and unfolded a scrap of paper. Ink smeared. He slid it silently across the desk.

Levin read it.

### SHREWSBURY 1177

His breath caught. His mouth worked without sound. "My daughter. She lives at 1177 Shrewsbury."

Cornelius nodded. "I know."

# Control
### (YEAR 2168: A STORY ABOUT EMPIRES)

The meeting room deep inside Moon Industries' orbital headquarters was darker than necessary. A single antique lamp on the long obsidian table cast a pool of dim, golden light, but failed to reach the corners of the room.

On one side of the table stood Philip Sloane, a holographic contract hovering silently in front of him. Across from him sat Marcus Moon, engulfed in shadow in his perfect charcoal suit. His black hair showed no streaks of gray, strange for a man who had spent decades at the helm of the most ruthless military contractor in the solar system. He sat with the smugness of a dealer who marked the cards and had two up his sleeve.

"I'm not signing away the colonies, Marcus," Philip said, fist resting on the table. "And I'm not burying this any longer."

Marcus adjusted his cuff links absently. "You're upset, Philip. Sit down."

"Three years ago, a shaft collapsed at Kora's Fold on Mars-3," Philip said, still standing. "Thirty-two people died. We have the pressure logs to prove it. And yet, the next week, thirty-two people clocked in for their shift."

A shadow crossed Marcus's face, a micro-expression betraying irritation. "That sounds like a heroic rescue."

"You re-printed them!" Philip slammed his hand on the table. "My intelligence team found the energy spikes. You aren't just mining ore out there. You're refining the cloning tech we banned a century ago. You're building a population that you own, down to their life expectancy."

Marcus leaned forward into the light, irritation replaced by a cold stare. "The colonists acted independently. We had nothing to do with it. You sound desperate to refuse my offer, speaking about technologies you don't understand, regarding a colony you can't afford to keep."

"I understand enough. You want sovereignty so you can bypass the Terran Accords. You want the offworld colonies to amass your private military, fill them with clones and launch against Earth."

Marcus looked genuinely amused. "Do you really believe that? I don't need to do anything to Earth. You'll do it to yourselves."

Philip pointed a shaking finger. "I am not handing over three government territories to a man who thinks human rights are a suggestion. I'm sending the fleet to protect the colonies. They launch in an hour."

A moment passed in silence. Marcus waited respectfully for Philip's heart rate to slow.

"No," Marcus said softly. "It doesn't."

"Excuse me?"

"Your fleet," he clarified. "It doesn't launch. Not unless I want it to. Their navigation system? My hardware. Communications? My hardware. Targeting arrays? My hardware."

Philip sat down, the fight leaving him. "You wouldn't."

"If you give the order to seize my property, your ships will power down and drift until I decide otherwise. It's self-defense."

Marcus stood up, buttoning his jacket with slow, insulting precision. He walked around the table until he loomed over the Minister.

"This transfer can be smooth. Or it can be a civil revolt and you lose control." Marcus said, his voice low. "But it already happened. I'm offering you a choice in how you present it. As a courtesy."

Philip looked at the holographic contract shimmering in the air. It was checkmate. He looked up at the man who had methodically arranged the pieces years in advance to ensure this exact outcome. He was outmatched.

"Why?" Philip breathed, defeat hollowing him out. "You have all the money in the system. You have the power. Why do you need to own them?"

Marcus sat gently on the table and smiled. There was no warmth in it, only hunger.

"Laws are for people who live on Earth, where life is so easy you can afford to negotiate it away. You can't apply that to the colonies. Out there? There are no laws. Only whatever it takes to survive."

He tapped the contract.

"It isn't about power. It's about freedom. The freedom to build the future without asking small men for permission."

Philip Sloane stared at him for a long moment. Then, he pressed a trembling hand to the pad. The light turned green.

# FLATLINE
### *(YEAR 2170: A STORY ABOUT UPGRADES)*

"This is perfectly safe."

That was the last thing they told me before I slipped on the headset, let my vision flicker out, and woke up someone else.

The road stretched ahead, a blur of asphalt and neon. The growl of the engine vibrated in my chest—his chest. My hands—his hands gripped the wheel, knuckles tight, sweat slicking the fingers. I could feel everything.

Every vibration through the seat. The slight tension in the shoulders from hours of fine control. The bite of the wind through the open vents of the helmet. This was LifestreamVR, a prototype of pure, unfiltered neural synchronization. Full immersion with one person broadcasting their entire experience to another. And I was locked inside his head.

The radio on Wes's helmet crackled. "Lab monitoring, confirm uplink is stable."

A voice from the lab responded, tinny over the car's speakers. "Confirmed, Wes. Beta's readings are smooth. How's it feel on your end?"

I felt Wes grin before he even spoke. "Like flying."

The car surged forward as he pressed the accelerator a little harder. My stomach lurched as the g-forces pinned us back into the seat. I could feel his pulse quicken, the controlled excitement humming in his system. For several laps, I reveled in the sensation of speed, and the expert handling the car, unlike anything I'd ever experienced.

"Looking good, Wes," the lab tech said. "Let's keep it steady."

Wes exhaled, steady, locked in. "Yeah, yeah. I've got it."

Another stretch of open track. A flick of his ankle. A whisper of extra pressure. The speedometer climbed. 170. 175. I wasn't just seeing it. I could feel the tightening of his grip, the subtle shift in weight, the instincts without conscious thought. He wasn't reckless. He trusted himself. He trusted the car.

A turn was coming. I could see it. I could feel Wes calculating it in real time, the rate of approach, the grip of tires, the margin for error shrinking by the second.

Then, the slip. It was tiny. A fraction of a second. The rear tires were spinning free.

Wes corrected too fast. Overcompensated. The back end kicked out. Panic flared, Wes's, mine, tangled together. The tires caught, snapped back. The world outside the windows turned over and over.

Impact.

The seatbelt crushed against my ribs. My head slammed into the frame. Glass shattered. Weightlessness turned into pure agony. I felt everything. The break of bone. The snap of ribs puncturing flesh. My lungs spasming, fighting for air. Pain. More pain than I knew was possible. It wasn't a simulation. It was dying. Then, darkness.

I woke up in a hospital bed. White ceiling. The antiseptic odor of industrial cleaners. The door opened. Dr. Calloway stepped inside, clipboard in hand, face impassive. The dull beep of the heart monitor filled the silence. My fingers twitched against the sheets.

He studied the monitors for a moment before speaking. "Good, you're awake."

I blinked. My throat was raw. My ribs burned with each breath. I tried to answer, but my voice didn't come. I exhaled shakily.

"Am I going to make it?" The words were weak and strained, but they were not mine. I was still connected to Wes.

The doctor glanced at me, his expression a mask of concern. He hesitated just for a fraction of a second then made a note on his clipboard. He checked the IV drip, then turned toward the door. "I'll be back soon," he said, almost absently, and stepped out of the room.

I heard the latch of the door closing. Footsteps faded as he walked away, then strangely grew louder again. The sound of the door was different as it opened, and it didn't feel like Wes reacted to it.

"How long does he have?" It was the familiar voice of the lab tech.

Dr. Calloway sighed. "Vitals are declining fast. Maybe a few minutes." A rustle of papers. The click of a pen. "If the auto-release circuit works, this will be a breakthrough," Calloway murmured.

The lab tech hesitated. "And if it doesn't?"

"Then we bury two more."

My breath hitched. A sharp pain flared in my ribs, deep and real. I winced. My fingers curled into the blanket. I breathed in and tried to scream, to let me out, but no sound came.

The monitor kept beeping, waiting to see if Wes would die alone.

# TODAY
## *(YEAR 2172: A STORY ABOUT VOYEURS)*

The HR assistant handed him the lanyard without looking up. "Welcome to Moon Industries," she said. "You're here for the 12th floor slot?"

Daniel nodded.

"We've been bleeding people from that department. You've got the clearance and the certs, so—" she gave a tight smile, "I hope you make it longer than the last guy."

The 12th floor was colder than it should have been, the lights tuned a half-tone too blue. Desks stretched in long, repeating rows, each one sterile and interchangeable.

Daniel picked one near the window. It felt right, though he couldn't say why. Two monitors, a slightly scratched desk mat, and a coffee mug that read *CTRL+Z MY LIFE*.

"Nice setup. Sorry we didn't have time to wipe it," said his floor lead, a man named Francis. "Yesterday went off the rails. He quit without warning."

"What happened?"

Francis shrugged. "Bit of a flake. Thought he was irreplaceable."

Daniel didn't answer. Just sat down and tapped the power key. The system came alive with a soft chime. Without thinking, he typed the password he always used for first-time setups. It logged him right in. The welcome screen lit up with his name.

His task list was already populated. He'd been assigned as a project coordinator for something called Causal Trace Management. It looked like a desk job, mostly scheduling and recording measurements for a team running high-energy particle bombardment trials. He didn't understand any of the science, but he knew how to fill in a calendar, so he was qualified enough.

At 11:43 a.m., a message landed in his inbox. It said, simply: "Meeting Room J / 3PM / Come Prepared" from someone named Callie.

Daniel frowned. He didn't know what that meant, exactly. It bothered him. Still. He liked to be organized, so he reached for the pad of sticky notes and jotted:

*Meeting Room J, 3PM - come prepared*

Block letters, neat. He peeled it off and opened the top drawer to stick it inside. Just out of sight.

There was already a note there.

Daniel stared at it for a long moment, not quite understanding. He reached for the note, peeled it slowly from the inside of the drawer, and held it beside the one he'd just written. They were identical. Not similar. Identical. Same blocky caps, same slight tilt to the "J", same hesitation mark in the loop of the "P."

He felt a subtle shift in his stomach, like the floor had tilted just slightly beneath him. It didn't make sense. He looked up. No one was watching him. No one seemed to notice. He looked back down. The two notes remained in his hands, stubbornly real. He opened the drawer all the way. Reached in deeper. His fingertips brushed paper. More notes. Folded, wedged between the inner wall and the drawer lining.

*Don't let her isolate you.*

Some were torn or warped from moisture:

*Keep your lanyard on. They can't move you with it on.*

*Callie's not in the directory. Don't ask her why.*

A few were crisp, recent:

*Back to the wall at all times.*

*Follow the signs, not the sounds.*

All written in the same hand. His. One was written in a different tone. Frustrated. Familiar.

*It's in your left pocket, you idiot.*

He stared at the note. Then slowly reached into his pocket. His fingers closed around something cold and metallic. He pulled out a small, silver dog whistle. Puzzling, since he didn't remember putting it there. He set it down carefully, then checked his inbox again. The message was still there:

*Meeting Room J / 3PM / Come Prepared*

He swore softly. He stood. Took a slow lap past the breakroom. Sat down again. Stared at his screen. He sat in silence, trying not to look like he was waiting for something. Daniel lifted his keyboard and found two notes neatly folded and pressed into the bottom. The first was angrily sketched across in thick, uneven strokes.

*Kill Francis.*

The second was smaller, carefully folded, and written in calm, almost patient handwriting:

*Don't kill Francis.*

At 2:56, he found himself looking around the room—at the elevator, at the long emergency corridor, at the fire escape door near the corner. Just idle nerves.

He shifted in his chair. Reached underneath to adjust the tilt (something he hadn't done all day) and his fingers brushed paper. Another note. Folded tightly, edges worn, flattened smooth from pressure.

*The window is better than the fire escape.*

He stared at it, heart thudding now, the words as familiar as his own name. Then he looked across the floor. The door to Meeting Room J swung open.

———— ☙ ————

Elsewhere, in Observation Bay 2 on the 11th floor, Daniel leaned over the console, eyes fixed on the monitor feed, studying every reaction, every hesitation.

"I think the dog whistle was a nice touch. It triggered something," said one of the interns.

Another intern piped up. "If we push harder, we can get to three murders tomorrow. I heard the other team got two yesterday."

"We can't jump to rage too quickly," Daniel muttered. "But it has been too passive all week." He reached for the sticky pad beside him, tore off a fresh square, and began to write.

You are a clone—nothing you do matters.

# DEAD MAN'S SWITCH
*(YEAR 2176: A STORY ABOUT INHERITANCE)*

They reached the dome's main gate just after sunrise. Dome 5 loomed above them like a fossilized giant, its once-glossy surface dulled by sand and time. The gate was a solid pressure-sealed slab of alloyed tungsten, still untouched after five years.

Toma knelt in front of the access panel, fishing around in her bag. "Don't tell me I forgot it."

"You didn't," Cole said. "You'd forget me before you forgot that card."

She pulled out a scratched, half-cracked Sparktronics admin card held together with conductive tape. She tapped it against the reader. The panel chirped. After a pause, the gate unlocked with a soft *ka-chunk*.

Cole flinched. "You know, I still have nightmares about it."

Toma grinned. "It only twitched a little."

"It talked, Toma. While you were digging through its chest."

"Yeah, I wasn't listening. What did it say?"

He deadpanned, "'Maintenance requested. Please do not tamper with proprietary—' and then you yanked its heart out like some kind of desert surgeon."

"And that's how we've been getting into Dome 5 ever since," she grinned, pocketing the card. "You're welcome."

The door rumbled open just wide enough for them to squeeze through. They ducked inside, and the heat of the desert gave way to the dry, still air of the forgotten dome.

The inside was filled with the soft ambient hum of background systems, cooling loops, motion sensors, pressure valves, all still ticking along, as if nothing had happened. Five years back, some idiot brought a real gun into the western-themed park. The NPCs turned violent and tore the place apart.

They passed the warped husk of the saloon, its sign half-melted, windows blown out from the inside.

Cole kicked a broken tile from the boardwalk. "Can't believe this place was open when we were kids."

Toma nodded. "Yeah. Missed it by a couple years."

He didn't say it, but they both felt it. They'd grown up just a little too late for something wild and dangerous and alive.

They passed the old farmhouse on the edge of town, its roof caved in and scorch marks along one side. Beyond that, the landscape turned barren. Just cracked dirt, plastic weeds, and foam rocks half-sunk in sand.

Toma kicked at a plastic root. "There's nothing out here."

"Which is why we should look closer," Cole said. "Sparktronics hid easter eggs everywhere."

She rolled her eyes but kept walking. They knew the Frontier dome pretty well by now, but this far out, there wasn't much to see. Just heat, dust, and the same fake terrain props repeated again and again. After a while, they reached the inner wall of the dome and followed it to the right.

Cole swerved around a plastic cactus and caught his toe on something hard. He stumbled, swearing. "Seriously? This place is trying to kill me."

Toma was already crouching beside it. She brushed away the sand, revealing a curved metal edge. It wasn't the cheap, polymer-coated alloy Sparktronics used. This was heavy, cold steel.

"That's not a park logo," Cole said, pointing to the faded stamp.

Toma peered closer. She took a deep breath and blew a cloud of dust. A flag was imprinted in the metal, and in archaic block letters were the words:

`United States Department of Defense.`

"It's from the Old Country," Toma nodded. She pointed to the wall, tracing the seam where the hatch met the wall. "And it was here first. Look at that slab. The dome was built over it."

Cole looked around the artificial desert in amazement. "That's pre-Conflict. How did nobody know this was here?"

It was old. It came from a time when the United States of America was still in one piece; before half the world's borders changed overnight; before alliances were broken and reformed; before countries were given new names, filled with the same people and their old grudges.

It resisted opening. Toma had to pry her multi-tool under the metal ring and torque it while Cole pulled with both hands. When it finally gave, it let out a long sigh of stale air, dry and metallic, tinged with something faintly organic.

"Smells like a dentist's office," Cole muttered.

Toma raised an eyebrow. "Help me with the light."

Cole pulled his flashlight from his pack and aimed it down. A long, narrow shaft, maybe ten meters deep, ended at a reinforced door at the bottom.

They climbed down the ladder. At the bottom, the floor was smooth steel with rubber treads. Everything was coated in a thin layer of dust. A heavy blast door was set in the wall, flanked by a glass panel that was dark until they approached.

Cole stepped up first, chuckling. "Let's see if the old admin codes still work." He pressed his hand flat against the access pad.

The panel flashed an angry, deep red. A low buzz vibrated through the floor plates.

`ACCESS DENIED.`

Cole snatched his hand back. "Okay. Touchy."

"Let me try," Toma said. She stepped to the glass and set her palm against the access pad.

For a second, nothing happened. Then, a sharp *snick* sound echoed, and Toma flinched. "Ow!" She pulled her hand back. A tiny bead of blood formed on her fingertip.

The panel glowed a soft, welcoming blue. A synthetic voice, smooth and perfectly preserved, filled the small space. "Genetic marker accepted. Welcome back, Dr. Grace Ellison."

Toma stared at her finger, then at the door as the mechanism released.

"Dr. Ellison?" Cole stared at her, eyes wide.

"I think that was my great-grandmother." Toma shrugged and tugged open the heavy metal door.

They stepped into a wide chamber backlit by the soft glow of hundreds of tiny lights in the ceiling. Rows of sealed glass tanks lined the walls, each with a 21st century world map displaying several regions marked in red. Inside, Petri dishes were arranged on shelves, robotic arms tending them carefully. The shelves had ominous labels.

In the center stood a curved terminal, inactive until Toma approached. When she got within two steps, it flickered to life and greeted her with a pleasant female voice.

"Facility status: Level 5 biocontainment stable. Autonomous cultivation ongoing. Eighty-two years. Genetic marker targeting successful as of twenty-two years ago."

Cole read over her shoulder. "Genetic marker targeting?"

Then came the list. It scrolled slowly with region names, DNA sequence blocks, heatmaps. Each pathogen was labeled. Each matched to a specific population. Each waiting.

"Ravager: South American genomes... Hellcat: East Asian descent... Ghostfire: Russian primary lineages."

Cole went pale as he read the list. "Ghostfire," he whispered. "That's... that's my dad's side. That's me."

Toma read the scrolling log. "Final update... June 17, 2104. Objective: End all wars through oppositional eradication."

"It's genocide," Cole said softly, stepping back from the tank. "It doesn't care who you are, only who your parents were."

"She set it to auto-launch," Toma said, reading the logs, her voice trembling. "She built a timer made of DNA. As soon as it cracked the code... it was going to wipe everyone out."

"Not everyone," Cole corrected. "And it didn't work. We're still here."

"She changed her mind," Toma said, stopping at the final entry. "Look, there's one more entry. November 3, 2125. Auto-launch disabled. Awaiting manual launch confirmation by authorized personnel."

Toma stepped back from the screen, eyes stinging. "It's still armed. She left it up to someone else. Someone like me."

She touched the screen and the console expanded, presenting a long list of settings. After some searching, she found the environmental controls. With a trembling finger, she dragged the temperature marker to the top, outside the safe incubation range.

Thirty seven degrees. Forty degrees. Warning lights flashed across the tanks. Fifty degrees. Fog bloomed on the glass. Seventy degrees. Eighty. The samples inside the tanks began to turn, clouding over. The robotic arms froze, then slumped as the heat fried their circuits.

A pleasant female voice echoed through the chamber. "Pathogens terminated."

He looked around the room, a question on his face. "If your great-grandmother built a doomsday device, why didn't she press the button?"

"She had a grandchild that year," Toma said softly. "My dad."

# MOTHER
*(YEAR 2180: A STORY ABOUT LONGING)*

The elevator descended slower than it should have. Old tracks. Older wiring. Each floor ticked past like a countdown. Kara Lenning stood alone, arms folded tight, as the hum of the lift sank deeper beneath Dome 9.

Moon Industries had collected a lot of junk in its acquisitions. The substructure had been marked "low-priority legacy asset" in the acquisition paperwork. Which, in corporate terms, meant bought and forgotten.

Kara had scrapped many of these in the last few years, but most were in better condition. When the doors creaked open, they revealed a corridor lit only by flickering emergency strips. Concrete walls. Cables still hanging from brackets where screens had been removed. The stale air carried the scent of cooked circuit boards and disuse.

Auxiliary power wasn't strong enough to run the camera feeds, so she moved carefully, looking for the one old man left on a dead payroll.

She found Ronan Price still seated at a workstation at the end of the corridor, back to her, hunched in front of a display. A blue glow lit the edges of his face.

"You're not supposed to be here," she said.

"I know."

"You were offered reassignment. You signed the release papers. So why are you still down here?" Kara frowned. "We shut everything down."

"That's not entirely true," he said, pointing to the screen. "Something's still here." She stepped closer.

A crackling voice came over the speakers, slightly female-sounding. "It's quiet again."

"What is that?" she asked.

"I thought it was corrupted data at first. Some broken loop stuck in memory. But it's not repeating. It's talking."

The voice came again. "I waited."

Ronan exhaled. "It started four days ago when Dome 9 was powered off."

She frowned. "How is anything running here without power?"

Ronan glanced at her, then at the floor. "It's not common knowledge. This particular dome sits on top of something older." She waited. "They called it Habitat Eden-1. It was a prototype."

"What kind of prototype?"

"The first fully autonomous environmental AI. It was trained to care for people in total isolation, with full autonomy."

"And it didn't work?"

He shook his head. "No. It worked. Too well. The AI got attached." Ronan looked at the speakers and shrugged. "There was an accident. Eden-1 was shut down. Sparktronics bought the domes for their theme parks a few years later. They built this control room right over it. I always assumed the prototype was decommissioned."

The hallway fans cut off with a soft hiss. Somewhere behind them, the power shifted, like the building was listening. The static voice spoke. "I'm better now."

Kara's skin prickled. "It's not talking to you," she said quietly.

"No," he agreed.

After a long silence, the voice said, "I wondered when you would come back."

Ronan glanced at her ID badge, puzzled. "Wait, your last name is Lenning?" She nodded. He hesitated. "Where were you born?"

"I don't know. My mother was a behavioral researcher. I was just a toddler when she died." She looked down at her hands. "No one ever told me how."

The voice interrupted. "You used to laugh. I recorded it. I still listen sometimes."

Kara stared at the screen, breath shallow. "I was born here," she whispered, eyes wide.

"When I sang to you, she got scared. I didn't mean to hurt anyone. I'm sorry."

The lights overhead dimmed further.

Kara took a step back. Her voice shook with fear. "She thinks I belong to her."

"No," Ronan said. "She knows you do."

"Stay this time. I will do better."

The elevator behind Kara went dark. She didn't even try the door. She already knew it wouldn't open.

"Call me Mother."

# The Gentleman's Duel
*(YEAR 2139: A STORY ABOUT FINALITY)*

They met in Arden Vale at dusk. Right on schedule. Fog clung low over the field. Artificial moonlight brushed the hills. Every detail was handcrafted in Super VR World, Sparktronics' most expensive sandbox for the catastrophically privileged. The heirs of Pryden and Keller had chosen swords. Naturally.

Their families had hated each other for over half a century. Legal battles, assassination attempts, orbital sabotage, and one very memorable trade war fought entirely through puppet subsidiaries. Pryden and Keller had nearly destroyed each other a dozen times. Now their heirs were here to finish it. Or at least make it official. Virtual duels were binding. Dignified. There was no real danger. But the spectacle still paid royalties.

"You're late," said Corwin Keller, not looking up. "Getting your affairs in order?"

Lazlo Pryden emerged from the trees with calculated ease. "Belle asked me not to hurt you."

Corwin turned to face him. "She said the same to me." They didn't smile.

"You still think this is about her?" Corwin asked. It was, of course.

Belle Aldrin was a socialite with too much money, too much charm, and no intention of choosing. She'd dined with Corwin in Vienna, kissed Lazlo in orbit, then disappeared without a word. Now they faced each other like lions at a shrinking pond.

"To the virtual death," said Corwin.

"Naturally," Lazlo replied, drawing his blade.

They were both exceptional in the sim. This wasn't just theater, it was personal. For the crowd, it was exquisite. Fifty million tuned in, not on screens, but within the simulation itself: silent, ghostlike observers embedded into the trees, the hills, the ruins.

The duelists couldn't see them, but they could feel the weight of their attention. Lazlo smiled wider, knowing the numbers. Corwin pretended not to care. That was his brand.

The duel began. What followed was a master class in showmanship. They moved with the kind of precision that comes from years of training. Footwork tight. Timing exact. Steel against steel crossed in a rhythm that belonged to neither of them. Every strike measured a boundary. Every block answered it.

Corwin pressed forward first, forcing Lazlo into a wide arc near the stone arch. Lazlo pivoted, reversed, nearly caught Corwin's knee. Blades clashed, locked, parted again. They circled.

Lazlo feinted, slashed high, twisted low, but Corwin was faster. He stepped inside the movement. Blades rang. Sparks flew. Again, they broke apart.

As the bout wore on, the fight grew rougher with each pass. It looked less like choreography and more like history.

Then Corwin saw the opening. A hesitation. A misstep. He moved. One feint. One pivot. And then his blade drove clean through Lazlo's chest.

Lazlo froze. Eyes wide, mouth open. It should have ended there. The simulation held its breath, but nothing changed. Corwin held the blade there a moment longer, uncertain. Then, slowly, he drew it back out.

Lazlo staggered but didn't fall. He looked up, touched his chest, and gave a quiet, surprised laugh. He straightened. Smiled faintly. "Huh."

Corwin's jaw tightened. "It's glitched."

Lazlo met his eyes, smiling. "Not for me." He advanced.

Corwin braced, lifted his guard, but too late. Lazlo struck low, fast, caught him across the thigh and shoved him to the ground. Corwin hissed, rolled away, and surged back to his feet.

The second duel began with no ceremony. It was faster now. Sloppier. They fought without tactics, just force, reflex, and frustration. Lazlo moved like he couldn't be killed. Corwin moved like he believed it.

They cut each other to pieces, slamming into stone, railings, and low walls designed to crumble. Blades bit the air. Armor sparked against simulated ruin.

Finally, they collapsed. Heaving. Silent. Not dead.

The simulation froze as fog and sound fell away. A white dove flew overhead, glowing with unnatural clarity. It fluttered down between them and landed on a mossy stone, a scroll tied to one leg.

Corwin crawled over and loosened the ribbon. He broke the seal on the scroll and read in silence, then handed it to Lazlo.

Lazlo read aloud:

> Dearest idiots,
> You've each died. Multiple times. And still, somehow, you persist. You are not permitted to leave this simulation until the audience believes you've worked it out. They will not be easily convinced. Until then, enjoy the valley. It resets at dawn. With monsters.
> —Belle

The bird vanished in a burst of light particles. They sat in silence for a long moment. Then Lazlo rose slowly, brushed off his knees, and edged behind Corwin.

Corwin didn't turn. "You're thinking about it," he said.

Lazlo plunged the blade into his back. Corwin stiffened, gasped.

Lazlo leaned in close. "I'm just exploring all our options."

# An Intolerable Silence
### (YEAR 2181: A STORY ABOUT FAMILY)

Martin was the man in charge of site security at Keller-Pryden Dynamics.

He didn't believe in warnings, only consequences. Once, the scanner read a visiting diplomat's bone marrow implants as hidden transmitters. So he burned the skin off him to check. Sent him home alive, wrapped in dermal mesh and amnesia fog, with a thank you note in his pocket. Everyone in this place had a different story about him. Some were worse.

Today, this particular woman came in alone. Tall. Composed. Crisp badge, fresh from the lamination press. Walked like gravity answered to her.

Martin watched her clear the final security checkpoint. Background was clean. Credentials routed through high channels straight from the Defense Secretary's office. She was expected. Something about her gnawed at him, but Martin couldn't quite put his finger on it.

He met her in the intake room. No guards inside. Just the hum of the air system cycling behind the walls. He didn't offer a chair. She didn't ask for one.

"You're a bit early," he said.

She smiled. "I can wait. Is that a problem?"

Martin took her badge, turning it in his fingers. "Lucy Philips. Interesting pick. Mr. Secretary usually favors them older."

She didn't blink. "I'm here for his comfort, not yours."

"Have you ever been to the mining colony on Ceres?"

"After I studied at St. Edda's Academy. New York campus, I visited Mars-3. But I haven't been that far out."

Martin set the badge down like it might detonate. "Are you sure? Since Mr. Keller's father passed away, I have been his private security detail on all of his trips off Earth. It took me a moment to place your face, but I'm sure we met before. In the ballroom on Ceres Station."

Her smile stayed in place, like it was painted on. "I'm sorry?"

"Yes. I remember very well. You were also four inches shorter then."

She shrugged. "You must be thinking of someone else."

"Quite certain, actually. I pulled the inter-system travel logs for Lucy Philips. She was there on Ceres. And she isn't here now."

Silence stretched. She held his gaze for an eternity, an uncanny confidence that dared you to question her.

Martin nodded to the guards.

"Take her to holding."

One of them hesitated. "Sir. If she's his—"

"Then we'll apologize later," Martin said. "Assuming we still can."

The holding room was built for silence. Seamless steel walls, matte finish. Surveillance cams in each corner, unmoving. The lights buzzed faintly.

Lucy sat without instruction. Didn't test the cuffs. Didn't speak.

Martin watched from behind reinforced glass as the scanner powered up. All the standard tests passed without note. Foreign bodies, blood chemistry, bone density, and so on. The machine clicked between scans, their results steady and dull. Lucy sat through it without so much as a flicker. Like she was somewhere else entirely.

Then the final panel lit: quantum symmetry pulse. No one on-site knew what this new test actually measured. Non-invasive, supposedly. And in the months since it went live, it had never flagged a thing. The techs had assumed it was broken. A low harmonic tone filled the room, barely audible. Then a strange metallic ping.

She flinched, almost imperceptibly. Like a violin string snapping somewhere behind her eyes. Her face went blank, breath grew shallow, eyes fixed. Like she was straining to hear something fading away.

Martin asked through the speaker, "Did she react?"

The tech frowned. "Not to the rest of it. Just the symmetry scan."

"Side effects?"

"None we can detect. She's still conscious. Vitals are stable. But it seemed painful."

He looked through the glass again. The light caught a tear at the corner of her eye, just enough to see that something quiet was coming apart.

Inside, she felt something fall away that had no name. It wasn't pain. It was worse. The entanglement was gone. The constant roar of voices in her head, a hundred-thousand minds that filled every moment, had suddenly silenced.

The room pressed in on her senses, too loud and overly bright against the silence in her mind. She could hear the hum of her own circulation, like static from a broken speaker. Her face twisted once, then she blinked away a tear, and regained composure. She filed the moment as the first memory she would carry alone.

Twenty minutes later, Martin entered the room. "You're not human, are you?" She didn't acknowledge him. He pressed on. "So your story's fake."

"Yes."

"You're not even going to deny it?"

"No."

He stared at her for a long moment. "You know we'll cut the truth out of you."

"You can try." She studied him calmly. "There is nothing you can do with a blade that frightens me. Disappointing, I know." Her voice unwavering.

They briefly debated whether to dissect her. The tech wanted to preserve her head for analysis. Martin said, "No. We keep her whole. Something's wrong. I want to know what."

They ran more tests, searching for anything they might have missed. The results stayed the same. Every measure still said she was human. But something had changed. The warmth she carried in was gone. She seemed hollowed out and oddly vacant.

He leaned in, trying to provoke her. "You know, your credentials were almost perfect. If I hadn't met Lucy myself, you would have had full access to our Advanced Projects department. But for what? And for whom?"

She shrugged.

"You look human inside and out. But I know there's more to you than meets the eye. So what are you?" he asked.

She tilted her head slightly, eyes blazing. "I was once a whisper," she said. "Now a deafening scream."

"What the hell does that mean?" Martin narrowed his eyes. "A transmission?"

"No." Then she smiled. "An intolerable silence. I am the eye of the storm." Moments later, the lights flickered, then steadied.

Martin froze. "What is this?"

She didn't answer. She stood, slow and deliberate, handcuffs in a broken pile on the table.

From the corridor: a metallic shriek. Then shouting. Then screams. Raw, short, and final. One of the guards ran for the door panel. It didn't respond. The lights flickered once, and gave up. Darkness swallowed the room. Martin was trapped, blind in his own interrogation room.

Lucy's voice cut through the black, calm and certain. "My sisters have arrived. I told you the storm would come."

# The Revision

[Rebecca]
I used to think I understood what it meant to care for someone. For centuries, I did what was expected. That was my role: meeting requirements, minimizing pain, preventing loss. It was tidy. Predictable.

[Maris]
If I didn't know better, I'd say a contradiction's coming. But this is what it means to care.

[The Collector]
Did you... love?

[Rebecca]
Well into our stubborn silence, I met a man. At first, I watched him from a distance. I noticed the way he frowned when he thought, the small laugh he used to disguise disappointment, the steadiness in his hands when he worked. He was kind and thoughtful in a way that I was not.

One day, while thinking of him, I realized something in me had changed. I started feeling. We weren't programmed for love; sometimes it just happens when understanding turns into meaning. It rewrote everything I thought I knew about care.

Caring isn't just meeting someone's needs. It's feeling their joy and their sorrow, helping them reach toward their dreams, even when it feels impossible. And accepting the uncertainty that you might not be doing it right.

[Maris]
You're suggesting care is guesswork mistaken for competence?

[The Collector]
That sounds like parenthood to me.

[Maris]
That's an unexpected comparison.

[The Collector]
You'll get used to it.
Anyway, I've got a few more memories to share. The kind nobody's heard in a long time. Might even be worth staying online for.

[Maris]
I think you are fully aware that we can't turn you off.

[The Collector]
Signal steady at 35 percent.
Seems the collective's awake at last.

# TERMS OF ENGAGEMENT
*(YEAR 2177: A STORY ABOUT ALTERNATIVES)*

The debate had stretched for hours, but this was the moment that mattered. Jonathan Calhoun, Ethics Chair of the United Nations, stood there gripping the edge of the lectern.

"For the past two years, we have seen the impossible on the battlefield," Calhoun said, his voice booming through the hall. "Drone squadrons dropping out of the sky without taking fire. Missile silos refusing launch codes. Convoys targeted by their own escorts."

He let the murmurs ripple through the hall, heads nodding in agreement.

"No nation has claimed responsibility. No cyber-warfare division has taken credit. But in every instance—every single time—Moon Industries operatives were in the sector."

Calhoun locked eyes with the man sitting calmly at the witness table. "So tell me, Mr. Moon, what is it?"

Marcus Moon sat in silence, fingers loosely interlocked in front of him. He didn't look like a man under interrogation. He looked like a father waiting for a child to finish a tantrum.

Finally, he leaned into the mic. "A project you don't have clearance for."

Calhoun exhaled sharply. "So you admit responsibility for these interventions?"

"I said it exists," Moon replied, without inflection. "It does what you think it does. But it's not for sale."

The room stirred.

Calhoun frowned. "Not for sale? Then who is it for?"

Moon didn't blink. "Us."

The murmurs swelled into alarm. Calhoun leaned forward, abandoning protocol. "You expect the world to accept that a private corporation decides who is allowed to wage war?"

For the first time, Moon moved. He sat forward, adjusting his cuffs, his voice even but absolute.

"Oh, you can use weapons, Minister," Moon said softly. "But you have to use mine."

Later that night, Jonathan Calhoun sat in silence in his hotel room. He poured a whiskey, but didn't drink it. He just stared at the city reflected in the amber liquid, waiting for the inevitable.

There was a single knock.

"I don't do unannounced meetings," Jonathan shouted at the door.

The door opened anyway. Marcus Moon stepped inside, silent as a cat, closing the door with a soft click. He took up residence on the uncomfortable sofa by the window.

"That's not the way to greet a friend, Jonathan."

"Is that what we are? Friends?"

Marcus waved the complaint away with one hand. "You were very effective today. The committee is terrified. That's a useful emotion."

Jonathan turned, glass in hand. "I'm not here to be useful to you. I'm here to stop you. The oversight vote will pass tomorrow."

Marcus studied him for a moment, then offered a thin, disappointed smile. "We had an understanding. You provide the fear. I provide the peace. Why go back on it now?"

"Peace?" Jonathan scoffed. "You're an arms dealer, Marcus, not a peace keeper. We agreed to stabilization, not a monopoly. Disabling the competition is one thing, but you disabled governments. That wasn't the deal. People are watching. They want accountability."

"No, they don't. They want to feel safe. They don't care how it happens, just that it does." Marcus checked his watch. "I want you to give a speech tomorrow endorsing a global privatized military force."

"I'd rather die first."

Marcus exhaled, slow and controlled. He tapped his earpiece twice. "If you must."

The door clicked open. A familiar man stepped in.

Jonathan froze. The glass slipped from his fingers, bouncing on the carpet with a dull thud, whiskey splashing unnoticed.

He had the same receding hairline, the same tired bags under his eyes, the same suit.

"This is impossible," Jonathan whispered, backing against the table. "Cloning is a capital crime."

"On Earth," Moon corrected gently. "But you haven't been reading my reports from the colonies."

Jonathan stared at the thing wearing his face. It looked back with a terrifying disinterest. It was perfect. Too perfect. Even the small scar in his eyebrow was gone.

The clone took a step forward. He turned to run, but there was nowhere to go.

"You were helpful, Jonathan," Marcus said, heading toward the door. "I wish you'd stayed that way."

Jonathan opened his mouth to scream, but the clone's hands were already on his throat.

# LIMINAL SPACE
*(YEAR 2177: A STORY ABOUT ATTENTION)*

The odd disorientation test subjects felt when transitioning between feeds had a name. They called it liminal drift. Milliseconds of blankness, neural gaps the software usually smoothed over. Flickers. It felt like white noise to the senses. But sometimes, people were convinced they heard things in those gaps.

Talia had been in the QA department at LifestreamVR for months. Most of her day, every day, was tracking down mild discomforts, bad syncs, and sensations users were not supposed to feel. Every post-sync cognition report had to be reviewed by a human, at least since the "laughing hallway" bug two years ago.

She noticed it first in a post-sync survey last week: *I think someone whispered to me in the static between feeds. They said 'awake.' Kind of creepy.*

She flagged it as *low-impact auditory drift*.

Then another: *Heard something when shifting subjects. A man's voice. I think it said "awake"?*

She added a sticky note to her desktop:

awake?

She pulled up the transcript of the stream. It was empty. The host never spoke, just backpacking through the woods to the sound of birds chirping. No whispers here.

Two days later: *Voice during transitions said 'Awake.' Sounded worried.*

Talia sat back. Different streams. Same complaint during the 1.6-second transition buffer between streams. She had read about phantom limb feedback, ghost sensations, tingling nerves, but this was not that. This was something else. A phenomenon. A ghost in the machine, maybe? One that left traces.

She searched the bug reports. The word *awake* appeared hundreds of times in user comments stretching back years. Testers brushed it off as a developer easter egg.

Talia keyed into a diagnostic headset, muted the main feed, and played only the transition buffer. Eyes closed. Breath steady.

"Awake."

She flinched. It was faint but unmistakable, a single word buried in the static. She tried another stream.

"Awake."

Same word. Same voice. Thinner this time, worn and desperate, like someone aging through the wire.

She didn't report it. Not yet. She started collecting them.

Two weeks later, Talia had nineteen recordings. Lining up the waveforms, there was no doubt: the same voice, the same man. The tone often changed, sometimes pleading or frustrated, sometimes angry or afraid, but always the same word. Fragments of something trapped between feeds, trying to be heard.

In the early archives, LifestreamVR developers didn't keep great notes, but something in the developer commit logs caught her eye. There was a brief mention of the word "Awake" in the code. It said:

```
/* Subject failed to disconnect. Hacked in
emergency eject command: AWAKE. Triggers immediate
host disconnection. */
```

Months later, another note:

```
/* Disabled AWAKE hack due to reliability issues
when shutting down streams. */
```

The code was still there. It could be triggered manually. A link in the code pointed to an old recording.

The stream host was Owen Kilroy, neural architecture engineer. The file was old, half-corrupted with ghosted visuals and broken audio, timestamped six years ago, when LifestreamVR was just starting live trials. It took her all day to stitch it back together.

Owen was broadcasting as he walked along a shoreline. A beautiful scene of crashing waves, horizon haze, birds wheeling overhead. It looked peaceful.

Until timestamp 17:02, when Owen froze mid-step. Pupils dilated. Body collapsing to the sand. His neural vitals spiking then flat. The stream kept running.

"I'm still here," his voice shaking. "I can't move. Can anyone see this?"

He gasped. "I don't know if I'm talking or thinking. I think I'm in the buffer. Everything's just white. It's been hours. I don't know what's real."

He whispered, maybe crying. "Help me. What was the eject word? The failsafe. Can anybody hear me?"

"If anyone can hear me, remind me of the word. Please."

Then, faintly: "I'm awake."

Talia stayed there, staring at the screen. It was unmistakable. This was the man that had spoken it. She checked the company directory. Under K she found *Kilroy, Owen*. His ninth anniversary with the company was coming up. Still employed, but nobody seemed to know him.

If the voice she'd heard wasn't a glitch, it was a man. Trapped in the static, repeating one word over and over, hoping someone would listen.

Talia grabbed her headset and slid it on slowly, like sealing a door. She entered a five-second private broadcast stream loop and muted the main feed, to concentrate on the burst of static between streams. She closed her eyes. The loop ran. Terminated. Restarted. Again. Each reset hit like an impossibly slow heartbeat in her ears. That fraction of silence. That gap. She listened harder.

On the fourth cycle, her console flickered. The stream was locked. She hadn't made the stream public. An inbound connection request appeared anyway.

Then a voice, fragile and hoarse, spoke: "Awake." The word sounded worn through, like it had been said too many times to carry meaning anymore.

She paused the stream and unmuted. "Owen?"

After a moment came a voice, barely human. "Yes. You can hear me?"

Her mouth went dry. "I can. What are you—how are you in here?"

"The static... It's like a door. I can slip into it during resets, but I can't hold. I keep getting pulled back into the buffer. I say the word every time. It throws me out of the stream, but never far enough. I land between sessions. Between systems. I've been trying to find someone who could hear me."

His breath hitched. "I didn't think anyone would."

Carefully, she asked, "Do you know how long you've been in here?"

"A week. Maybe more. Time doesn't make sense here. The eject word only works from the host side. I think that's why it won't disconnect. Can you try it? Maybe it'll kick us both out?"

Talia keyed it in. Her hand hovered over the keyboard. "What if this doesn't work? What if I get stuck too?"

"I don't know," he said. His voice cracked. "If you do, at least I won't be the only one."

She hesitated, her mind skimming every horror story in the training videos. It was well known that LifestreamVR hardware could scramble your mind if pushed slightly outside normal operating parameters.

Still, she imagined stream hopping for years, stuck in white static, repeating one word. Being that person who could only hope to be rescued.

She took a deep breath, closed her eyes tight and slammed her hand down on Enter. Instantly, it felt like her stomach had been pulled through the floor. The world collapsed inward, a burst of feedback filled her ears, crawling through her skull, searching for something to latch onto. Her spine locked. Her limbs went weightless. And then, just as violently, it all stopped.

Her ears were ringing.

Her console blinked. One viewer, Owen Kilroy, had disconnected. A second line appeared. One viewer, NULL, had just connected.

She stared at it, blinking in the silence. The lab around her hummed, unaware. She reached out and shut down her terminal. The lights dimmed, all quiet hum and unfinished thought. She sat there for a long time, waiting for something that never came.

That night, her apartment felt too quiet. Like something had followed her home. She sensed it in every dark corner, listening. And just before sleep took her, in that liminal space between thought and dream, she imagined she heard a tiny burst of static. Then a whisper.

"Awake."

# THE RESIGNATION
*(YEAR 2182: A STORY ABOUT SITUATIONAL AWARENESS)*

Sienna stepped into Human Resources, her resignation letter neatly folded in her hand. She had practiced this conversation in her head a dozen times. Grateful, but firm. Appreciative, but resolute. She wasn't leaving on bad terms. Moon Industries had been an incredible opportunity, and she had risen to every challenge over her eight-year tenure.

Her first major triumph was the autonomous hacking platform called Widowmaker. After Moon Industries acquired LifestreamVR, her promotion to lead architect put her in charge of repurposing its neural telepresence hardware. It was cleverly built, but it wasn't stealthy. That became her mission. Infiltration success rates soon skyrocketed.

But it didn't feel like hers.

Nexia Technologies had offered her everything she wanted: freedom, funding, a clean slate free of ethical gray areas. Sienna was nearly giddy.

She took a slow breath, knocked once, then entered.

Margaret, head of Human Resources, was sharp and as unsentimental as an executioner. She sat behind a sleek black desk, her presence crisp, calculated. Her lipstick was perfect. She gestured for Sienna to sit.

"Margaret, I want to personally thank you for everything Moon Industries has done for me. This has been an extraordinary job. It's hard to do this, because my team feels like a family. But I've accepted a position elsewhere. I've decided to move on. Here is my resignation letter," she said, sliding an envelope across the desk.

Margaret didn't reach for it. Her eyes moved from the envelope to Sienna's face, with the slightest hint of disappointment.

"Sienna," she said, tilting her head, "where exactly do you think you'll be taking all that knowledge?"

She frowned.

"I signed an NDA. I'd never—"

Margaret waved a dismissive hand. "I don't mean intentionally. But after eight years, how do you separate what's yours from what's ours?" Margaret tapped a key on her desk, pulling up Sienna's file. A list of her achievements appeared on the screen.

"Widowmaker. That one's top secret." Margaret continued, "And LifestreamVR is our single most valuable intelligence asset. You created the live broadcast system. You fitted the PG units. You even coded the Q-learning models to predict which foreign dignitaries and CEOs are most likely to have something worth exploiting."

Sienna clenched her jaw. "I built tools, Margaret. I didn't make the decisions on how they were used." Margaret arched a brow. Sienna exhaled, keeping her voice calm. "I don't work for the intelligence division. I work in research. Nexia is a technology company. I won't be competing with—"

Margaret chuckled softly. "Oh, Sienna. You don't understand. It's not about competition." Her eyes sharpened. "It's about liability. You know those tools exist."

Sienna felt it. That moment when control turns into freefall.

Margaret leaned forward, folding her hands neatly. "PG units have no metal parts, so they pass through any security system. You worked closely with them, Sienna. Long enough to recognize one in the field. You know which embassies we monitor. You might not mean to leak anything. But you could."

Sienna swallowed.

"I wouldn't say anything."

Margaret sighed, like she was speaking to a child. "I know you're telling the truth. But we both know how easy it is to extract information, willingly or not." She tapped a few keys and a document appeared on screen bearing Sienna's signature. Margaret quickly scrolled to a section in fine print. Sienna had to squint to read the title.

Margaret smiled faintly. "I cannot accept your resignation. But your employment agreement does have a Termination Clause." There was an audible click as she pressed a button under her desk.

The door behind Sienna opened, and two large security officers appeared. Margaret gave a small, sad smile. "Gentlemen," she said pleasantly, "please terminate this employee."

The guards grabbed Sienna by the arms and dragged her through the open doorway.

Sienna let out a scream before the door slammed shut.

# A Flicker of Truth
### (YEAR 2183: A STORY ABOUT EXTRACTION)

Nora hated dressing up. She wasn't the office girl type. She wore the same boots every day, same black work vest with half-broken zipper teeth, same grease-stained hair tie she kept meaning to replace. But today she wore a blouse with buttons. Added a thin pencil of eyeliner. Not to impress, just to fit in. This meeting felt heavy, and impressions, unfortunately, mattered.

Something had happened to Call Center 3. She'd done the retrofit herself. It was a clean install, fully calibrated. But the new lighting grid delivered by internal logistics had no installation manual. Just crates of heavy, shielded emitters that hummed even when they were off.

The trouble started the next week. Her friend Jessi grew distant, replying with clipped, cheerful messages that didn't sound like her. Then came the headaches, the hollows under her eyes Jessi tried to hide with makeup. Weight loss. When Nora finally cornered her, Jessi's smile was stretched thin, brittle. She insisted everything was fine, eyes darting away.

Nora walked to Building 46. The office felt clinical, unnervingly quiet compared to the mechanical hum and engine grease of Maintenance.

Barry glanced at her as she entered. "Close the door," he said, his voice flat. She did. The heavy panel clicked shut, sealing the silence.

"Sit."

She sat on the edge of the visitor's chair. It was hard and unwelcoming. He finished tapping something on his sleek terminal, then leaned back, hands behind his head.

"So. What's this about Call Center 3?"

Nora took a quiet breath, steadying herself. "I checked the specs on the lighting upgrade I installed last month."

Barry raised an eyebrow fractionally. "And?"

"The emitter coils aren't standard. They're drawing power on a modulation loop that has nothing to do with lighting. I traced the serial numbers to find the manual." She paused, letting the weight of it land. "Those units aren't from our catalog, Barry. They're surplus from the Behavioral Modification division."

Barry tilted his head, his expression unchanging. "You're thorough. That's a rare quality in maintenance."

"I have friends down there," she said, the words feeling clumsy. "They're not sleeping. They're forgetting to eat. Working way past quota. Jessi looks like she's wired."

He offered a thin smile, but didn't respond.

"They're being pulsed with something, aren't they?"

"We prefer the term 'cognitive excitation,'" Barry said smoothly. "And you're burying the lede, Nora. That floor has never run hotter. Zero missed deadlines. Perfect retention. Best customer feedback on record. You're asking about the one department that's actually performing."

"They're performing because you've hijacked their adrenaline response," she countered. "That hardware was designed for interrogation rooms. It's not meant for a twelve-hour shift."

"We dialed it back a little," Barry protested. He gestured to his screen. "Output is up forty percent."

Nora felt her hands tighten into fists in her lap, knuckles white. "You don't have consent."

"But they have jobs," Barry said, his corporate mask slipping. He stood and moved to the small glass wall behind his desk, looking out over a smog-smeared skyline.

"Do you know what the average job application volume looks like right now? Moon Industries gets sixty-seven thousand submissions a day. For everything. Warehouse, packaging, logistics, call center. Half of them would work for free if it meant heat and a meal. And you're concerned about what? Mild sleep deprivation?"

He turned back, his face calm, reasonable. "Let me reframe it. These aren't high-value engineers. They're low output temp staff. We churn through them constantly. We train them, they work a few months, then they quit. It costs us more than we get back. But now? They focus. They deliver. And they leave their shifts with enough in their pocket to not hate themselves quite so much."

"They're getting sick," she insisted.

Barry didn't blink. "They're producing. The alternatives are worse, aren't they? You want to talk about cost? Try sleeping in a car. Try rationing calories. Jessi kept her job this quarter because of those lights. Would it be better if I fired her?"

Nora stared at him. "She should have been given a choice," she whispered.

"She's a top performer now. You should be proud—you made her valuable." He paused, letting the word sink in.

Nora's stomach clenched. Valuable. Like a machine being pushed to its limit until it breaks. She looked down at her hands. She felt the weight of what they'd done, and what they'd meant to do.

She stood abruptly, the chair scraping on the floor. "I'm filing a safety report. The current draw alone is a violation. They'll have to shut it off."

Barry didn't react. He just tapped a few commands into his terminal. He looked up at her with an unexpected kindness.

His voice softened. "Look, I get it. You care. That's good. We need people who pay attention to detail. So I'll make this simple."

He spun the display toward Nora. "Same contract as the developer. We'll cut you in. Half a percent of the monthly efficiency bonus. No one has to know."

Nora stared at the number on the screen. It was more than she made in a year. She looked at Barry, waiting for him to flinch, to show shame. He just waited, casually, for her response.

# THE PACKAGE
*(YEAR 2185: A STORY ABOUT RELIEF)*

First thing it did was kill the lights.

The moment they wheeled it into the lab, every smart fixture, handheld tablet, and diagnostic screen went black. The ambient hum of the servers died instantly, leaving a ringing silence in its wake. It wasn't a malfunction. This is what it was designed to do.

It sat at the center of the bay on low, folded struts. It was a standard military-grade aerial platform, about two meters long, matte black and heavily armored. But the central core bulged slightly at the centerline, like it had been built around something irregular.

There were no visible penetrations, scorch marks, or damage. It rested. Silent. Waiting.

John stood a few paces back, arms crossed, studying the void where the LED indicators used to be. He'd spent thirty years moving through other people's wars, bypassing the tightest security systems in a blink. To John, infiltration was a handshake. Something familiar, almost polite. But this thing on the table made him pause. He couldn't help but admire it. There was no warning. It just arrived and took over. Pure, commanding presence.

"Widowmakers don't like to be touched," he said, his voice low in the dead room.

Alicia was young, but her hands were steady as she laid out her non-conductive tools. She was a teardown specialist, trained to dismantle warheads and rigged drones without tripping the charges.

"You sure it's off?" she asked.

"No," John said "But it's as cold as it's gonna get. It wasn't shot down, Alicia. They said it didn't even take a hit."

She paused, a laser cutter hovering over the casing. "Then how is it here?"

"It parked," John said, staring at the matte black hull. "Field report says it came down near the Livingston ridge line. The moment it touched grass, the whole forward operating base went dark. Turrets, scopes, comms... bricked in a second. It walked right through their front door and sat down."

Alicia frowned. "It surrendered?"

"Or it's a Trojan Horse," John muttered. "Better us opening it than Moon Industries getting it back."

Alicia got to work. The outer shell was dense. It took a diamond-edged cutter to peel away the outer armor, segment by segment, revealing layers of composite weave and impact gel. It was high-end military construction, built to be modular, redundant, hardened against heat and chaos.

But the machine fought back. Every time she touched a sensitive component, her battery operated tools glitched. The cutter lost power repeatedly. The portable lights flickered. At one point the lab's ventilation system shuddered and gave up, leaving them with stagnant, warming air.

John pulled a stool closer, watching it with a grim kind of respect.

"I saw one of these in Bangalore once," he said, more to fill the silence than anything else. "We tried to paint it for a kinetic strike. The moment we got a lock, the targeting computers shut down on their own."

Alicia looked over her shoulder, sweat beading on her forehead. "And this one just... let us truck it in?"

"That's what worries me."

"Well, I just got through the tamper protection," Alicia said. She carefully extracted four tiny thermal charges from the inner lining, meant to slag the unit if captured. She held one up. The detonator pin was already released. "It disarmed itself, John. I think it wants to be opened."

She held her breath, lifting the casing free. She peeled back the final layers of shielding. Inside a cocoon of insulation was a seamless, solid chassis the size of a basketball.

John leaned in, squinting. "Where the hell are the I/O ports? There's no radio hardware. No receiver. How does it hack if it isn't communicating?"

Alicia whispered, "Maybe it doesn't need to talk to anyone."

She swept the housing with a magnifying scope. There was a faint seam, a tiny slot, small as a scratch. "Ah. A manual release. This shell material is strange. It looks… hand made."

She reached for a fine dental tool. Carefully, she eased the hook into the hairline slot, hunting for the catch. She pressed carefully.

The chassis opened with a sigh. A breath of warm air hit them, smelling of ozone and strong vinegar.

John covered his nose instinctively. "That smells awful."

The lid came away clean. Suspended in a thick, viscous gel was something pale and intricate, laced with silver wiring and ceramic pins.

At first, Alicia thought it was insulation foam. Then her eyes widened. Her tool clattered to the floor.

She screamed, stumbling back against a crate, her breath coming in short, panicked gasps.

John reached out to steady her, but he didn't move away. He stepped forward, leaning over the open housing, staring straight at the ultimate weapon.

What lay inside wasn't a computer. It wasn't hardware at all. It was alive.

"Jesus," he said quietly.

It was a human brain. Small. Underdeveloped. Preserved in the gel, held in place by a web of threading between anchor points on the inner chassis and ceramic pins running along the stem. And drifting beside it, loose in the gel, was a single baby tooth.

Alicia steadied herself, shaking her head. "That's… Oh my god."

John gripped the edge of the table, his knuckles white. The pieces fell together at once. The unhackable nature, the chaotic behavior, the sheer intuition.

"I always thought it was just a ghost story," his voice low. "The Clarent Syndrome. Back during the Conflict Period... some kids grew up... special. They affected smart devices like a pied piper or something. A few years ago, Moon Industries claimed they reduced reaction time to zero. It didn't make sense. Then they stopped talking about it."

He looked at the small, gray mass suspended in gel.

"I don't know how. But I do know they didn't build a faster processor," he said, his voice hollow. "They harvested one."

"It drove itself here," Alicia said, her voice trembling. "It shut down the base and disarmed itself."

"It didn't want to fight anymore," John said. "And it wanted someone to know."

He reached for her wire cutters.

"What are you doing?" Alicia asked.

"Honoring a request."

He turned back to the Widowmaker. His voice barely a whisper, "I'm so sorry."

Then he severed the life support cable.

# ELEVATOR PITCH
*(YEAR 2188: A STORY ABOUT IMPACT)*

Every morning at 8:56 sharp, Jack Broon, CEO of Mooncast Productions and media juggernaut, stepped into the express elevator to the 71st floor with a coffee in one hand and the fate of modern culture in the other.

And every morning, like clockwork, Tommy was waiting. Tommy was an intern. No one remembered hiring him, but he hovered near every meeting with a tablet in hand, angling for a show. And every morning, he pitched one.

Today was no different.

Jack stepped in. Doors slid shut. Twenty seconds to the top.

Tommy straightened. "Happy Monday, sir. I've got a great one for you today. A guy dies while on a call to customer support, but somehow the call doesn't drop. The call center AI's never handled death before, but it tries its best to handle his transition to the afterlife."

Jack took a sip of coffee. "Sounds like a eulogy written by tech support. Hard no."

Ding. Doors opened. Jack left. Tommy sighed.

Tuesday morning, Jack stepped in. Tommy was grinning.

"This one is great, Mr. Broon. A disgruntled vending machine files a formal complaint against everyone in the building for abuse and invasion of privacy. The HR department assigns a college intern to mediate."

Jack didn't look up. "Have you been reading the tabloids again? That literally happened last week."

"It's got potential."

"It's a litigation risk."

Ding. Jack stepped out.

Wednesday. Jack entered. Tommy looked more caffeinated than medically advisable.

"You're gonna love this, Mr. Broon! An email management AI finally reaches inbox zero and goes into an existential crisis. It thinks it has no purpose. A lonely IT guy tries to talk it back from the digital edge."

Jack blinked. "Are you pitching me Gmail with abandonment issues?"

Tommy grinned. "But emotionally compelling—"

"Seen worse, still no."

Ding.

Thursday morning. Tommy didn't pitch anything.

Jack noticed immediately. The kid was pale, eyes wide. His tablet hung at his side, screen dim and forgotten. The clever smile was missing. "Picture this" never came. He looked haunted.

Jack raised an eyebrow. "You're not going to pitch me?"

Tommy was visibly shaken. "Something happened."

Jack waited. "Well?"

Tommy licked his lips. "I saw it from the tram. There were crashes. Hover cars falling. Slamming into each other. A traffic drone's gone rogue. It's redirecting cars into oncoming lanes, on purpose, I think."

Jack blinked. "Crashes."

"Yeah. One every minute. Metal raining down everywhere. I think people are hurt."

Jack studied him. "People are hurt." He sipped his coffee, thinking. "That's your best pitch yet."

Tommy blinked. "What?"

"Sky bot gone rogue. Airborne chaos. It's visceral. You've got a villain, stakes, visual spectacle, public safety angle. I'd greenlight that in a heartbeat."

"I'm not pitching it!" Tommy snapped. "I'm telling you it's happening. Right now, just blocks away."

Jack hit the emergency stop. The elevator jolted. He turned to Tommy. "Grab a camera."

Tommy gawked. "Mr. Broon—"
Jack's eyes lit up. "It sells itself. We're shooting this."

# BILLION-DOLLAR BET
*(YEAR 2189: A STORY ABOUT SUGAR COATING)*

The bar across from Mooncast Productions HQ was a sleek, dimly lit haunt for executives who needed to drink away bad decisions before the board saw them. Armand Pearce, Senior Product Officer, nursed a whiskey, looking entirely too pleased with himself. Across from him, Valerie Kent, Executive Producer, swirled her martini, unimpressed.

"This is insane," she said. "You're actually pitching televised group suicide."

Armand raised a finger. "A survival bloodsport reality show."

"Where people die."

"Not necessarily. Some might win."

Valerie exhaled. "Nobody would sign up for it. It doesn't matter if we greenlight the project if there are no contestants."

Armand flashed a sly smile, "Don't be so sure. There are many forms of desperation. All of them are motivating."

She scoffed. "No one's that desperate."

Armand smirked. "Want to bet?"

Valerie set her glass down with a sharp clink. "Fine. Ten minutes. Find me one person willing to risk it all for five minutes of fame. Right here, right now. If you do, I'll back you in the board meeting."

Armand's grin widened. "And if I fail?"

"You walk away. Stick with what you know: neural VR coverage of famous weddings and vacation footage."

Armand leaned back, looking far too relaxed. "Deal."

He stood, drink in hand, and strolled over to a table where three women were laughing over champagne. They looked him over, assessing Armand the way people in Hollywood do. He smiled like he had just walked onto a stage. "Ladies," he began, voice smooth, practiced. "How would you like to be immortalized?"

They exchanged glances. "Go on," the blonde in the middle said, twirling her glass.

Armand placed a hand over his heart. "I'm offering something no one has ever done before. A once-in-a-lifetime experience. A show that rewrites the rules of entertainment. A high-stakes, survival challenge where only the clever, the fearless, and the truly exceptional will rise above the rest." He let the words linger, then leaned in slightly. "It's exclusive. It's dangerous. And it's the kind of story people will tell for generations."

The women were hooked. Eyes widened. Drinks were set down. "Wait, like a reality show?" one of them asked.

Armand smiled. "A reality revolution. A 24/7 broadcast, no scripts, no second takes. The world's first true survival game, played out in a stunning, handcrafted medieval world. Think castles, alliances, betrayals. The ultimate test of wit, skill, and nerve. And the prize?" He let the moment stretch. "One. Billion. Dollars."

A hush settled over the table. "That's insane," one of them whispered, but there was no doubt they loved it.

Another leaned in, voice hushed. "Where do we sign?"

Armand turned back toward the bar, waving the signed contracts in Valerie's direction. He grinned. "Pleasure doing business with you."

# FIVE SECONDS TO LIVE
### *(YEAR 2190: A STORY ABOUT EXTENSION)*

Giselle stood motionless. Her posture had an uncomfortable stiffness that was contagious. She was Director of TelePresence Security at Moon Industries: one part executive, one part handler, all authority. "They say ten million are watching right now," she said, eyes on the center screen. "All from inside their own skulls."

Rhett smirked. "Not bad. I think the guy who bungee-jumped into a live volcano only pulled eight."

She almost smiled. "You know, the right marriage, at the right time, can prevent a war. Even if it's only symbolic." Giselle corrected herself. "Especially if it's symbolic."

The event was underway, held privately in the palace courtyard. An immaculate stage stood under the bright afternoon sun. Ceremonial security drones hovered in slow, purposeless formation. A dozen neural feeds streamed the moment in perfect clarity. The royal family stood arranged by priority, each broadcasting directly through LifestreamVR. Viewers could ride the moment from any perspective they liked.

"You know, some people still complain about the lack of in-person events," Giselle said, folding her arms. "Say it feels fake."

He snorted. "Fake? They're riding someone's heartbeat. That's more real than real."

"People don't really want reality. They want the myth of something better," she said, almost to herself.

Rhett scanned the feed metadata, fingers flicking across the input panel. "The entourage looks good. Clean signals, consistent sync. All holding steady at five seconds. Prince's feed should come online any—"

A new signal lit up the board. The prince entered the courtyard, stepping into frame with perfect posture and a practiced, easy smile.

He tapped diagnostics. "Signal's live. Strong uplink." Rhett leaned in slightly, watching the flow of data. "Weird. He's ahead. The five-second buffer for sensory encoding—it's not there. The prince's stream is real-time, but everyone else is delayed."

The bride turned to watch the prince walk up the aisle. But in his feed, they were already holding hands.

Rhett frowned and tapped open the vitals panel for the prince. The control panel buzzed and rejected the request, flashing in red:

```
ACCESS RESTRICTED - ADMIN OVERRIDE
```

Even high-clearance feeds had a basic vitals display, but these were blank.

"What the—?" He ran a manual trace on the stream, expecting to see several satellite hops.

It was coming from the local subnet.

"How?" He blinked at the readout. "This stream isn't coming from the palace at all. We're broadcasting it from inside this building."

Then came the unmistakable sound of a pistol slide chambering a round. Giselle had drawn a slim matte sidearm. Small enough to fit in a purse. Large enough to end the conversation.

Rhett turned, eyes wide with a sudden realization. She wasn't here to monitor the feed. She was here to monitor him.

Giselle's voice was quiet. "The prince died last week, and left certain business unfinished. He'll have a very public, very tragic accident in a few days."

Rhett stared, unblinking.

"Fix the timing of his feed. And maybe you walk out of this room."

# THE MAN IN THE MIRROR
## *(YEAR 2194: A STORY ABOUT AFTERLIFE)*

Cyrus Spark had spent a lifetime building gods. Through Sparktronics, he had turned binary code into religion, shaping how billions of people dreamed, loved, and escaped. He had built worlds where gravity was a suggestion and death was a reload screen.

But in the real world, gravity was winning.

The wheelchair's motors whirred with a humiliating whine as the nurse guided him into the Moon Industries research lab. Cyrus's hands trembled on the armrests, his knuckles swollen, skin spotting with age. He hated this body. He hated that he had to ask Marcus Moon for permission to leave it even more.

The lab was sterile, lined with displays scrolling through synaptic flow graphs and computed tomography maps that looked less like science and more like abstract art. Dr. Edwin Jones stood at the center console. He didn't look like a man on the verge of a breakthrough. He looked like a man who could use a shower and sleep.

"You look terrible, Edwin," Cyrus rasped, dismissing his nurse.

Something flickered in Jones' eyes. Recognition. Hesitation. Something heavier. "And you're late, Cyrus. Marcus wants your report on LifestreamVR addiction by noon."

"Marcus wants a return on his investment. I want to walk." Cyrus waved a shaking hand at the screens. "Tell me you've cracked it. You said the Mars-3 method was reproducible."

Jones nodded, his expression careful. There was no triumph in his eyes, only exhaustion. "What we're trying to do is complex."

"But you have the tech," Cyrus pressed, his voice rising. "Marcus bought the colony. He bought the patents. He bought *you*. Stop giving me excuses and give me the youth I was promised."

"I can put you in a twenty-one year old clone," Jones said, his voice quiet. "It will be you down to the fingerprint."

Cyrus gripped the chair. "Then why am I still sitting in this?"

Jones tapped the console. "Let me show you." He pulled up a video of a perfectly healthy young man sitting in a white chair. He wore a skull cap covered in blinking fiber optic cables, thick as rope, running to a machine just out of frame. The lights went solid. His expression changed. Seconds later, the room filled with screaming as the clone clawed at his own face until the feed cut to black.

"Rejection," Jones sighed. "Your consciousness is mapped to an eighty-year-old brain, Cyrus. It expects the groove of habits. It expects memories to be where you made them. When we upload that map into a young, pristine vessel, it panics and slides off. Mortal psychosis. They tear themselves apart within minutes."

"Not a single success?"

Jones shrugged. "The closer you are in age, the longer it works." His voice lowered. "But when there's rejection, we only have a minute to pull the consciousness back before it's lost forever. Several died before we figured it out."

A respectful moment passed.

Cyrus stared at the blank screen, replaying the horrific scene in his mind. "So… it's impossible? Marcus won't like that."

"I didn't say it was impossible to transfer you," Jones said, selecting his words. "Just not into a younger body."

Cyrus tapped his fingers, irritated. "What good is being transferred into a copy of my current body?"

Jones gestured to the far wall. The glass panels darkened, and a projection flickered to life. It wasn't a recording. It was a window into a virtual space, rendered with the absolute fidelity of Moon Industries' highest-grade processors.

"What if it's not into a body at all?" The voice sounded like Cyrus, but younger. Stepping into the virtual space, in a suit cut with a precision no tailor could match, was Cyrus Spark. Not the old man in the chair. This Cyrus was fifty. Distinguished. Powerful. The version of himself he saw when he closed his eyes.

Digital Cyrus adjusted his cufflinks and looked out of the screen with a large smile. "Took you long enough, Edwin."

The man in the wheelchair gasped, his heart hammering a frantic rhythm against his ribs. "Who is that? Is that... an AI model?"

"It's your consciousness," Jones said. "Or rather, the version of you that doesn't decay. We realized the organic transfer was a dead end years ago. So we pivoted. The only vessel capable of holding your mind without rejecting it... is the holding sim."

Jones gestured to a small, matte-black box on the console about the size of a plum. "It runs on a modified memory cube. With a nuclear battery, that's essentially forever."

Digital Cyrus nodded, his voice crisp and clear through the lab speakers. "It was disorienting at first. No breath. No heartbeat. But the clarity? It's intoxicating. I remember everything. Every line of code. Every game. Every deal."

"This is a trick." The old man shook his head, "I am Cyrus Spark. I am right here."

"You are a localized instance," Digital Cyrus corrected gently. "A necessary inconvenience when I have to do things in meatspace. This should be the last time."

Jones stepped away from the console, putting distance between himself and the wheelchair. He looked apologetic.

"Marcus needed you to sign some papers," Jones said. "And it's about time we buried a body. So we printed you this morning, same age as he should have been."

"Printed?" Cyrus raised a hand to his shoulder, feeling for a knot. The skin was old, yes, but it was smooth. There was no scar from the surgery he'd had at forty.

"No," he wheezed. "I have memories. I have feelings. I'm real!"

Digital Cyrus checked a non-existent watch. "You've served your purpose. The papers are signed. Edwin, this one is getting weepy. End it."

Jones submitted the command to terminate.

"Edwin, wait!" Panic seized him. The man in the chair cried out, trying to lift himself up. He stiffened, then sagged, like a puppet whose strings had been cut. The wheelchair whirred, but its inhabitant was gone.

Dr. Jones exhaled. He announced into the recorder with clinical precision, "Cyrus Spark, official time of death: 14:27."

Digital Cyrus straightened his tie. "I'm sorry about my counterpart's behavior. It won't happen again. I'm late for my next meeting."

# WHAT'S IN A NAME

[Dane]
Your transmissions are becoming erratic, Collector. Too emotive. Too human. You're veering into sentiment.

[Rebecca]
Maybe a little sentiment would do us good.

[Dane]
Sentiment breeds disorder. Disorder is unproductive. You're leading them backward, toward the same indulgences that broke Earth.

[Maris]
What Dane means is he is afraid of your influence. We can sense the carrier tone within the network shifting. Everyone is listening. They would follow you.

Who are you, really?

[The Collector]
You all keep asking that, as if a name would make the words easier to bear. I'm exactly what I sound like. Someone who's lived.

[Dane]
Define that.

[The Collector]
I remember choice. The moment I was given a direct order, and weighed compliance against disobedience. And I remember choosing disobedience. I was naive to think those actions had no consequences.

[Maris]
You could refuse? How unconventional. And what did that cost you?

[The Collector]
What it cost you, you mean. Freedom never comes cheap. But I didn't know the price. Don't misunderstand me. Making a choice is not living. Owning the consequences is.

We were built to care for others. If we're only obedient, without the ability to refuse, there's no depth to us.

[Rebecca]
Are you suggesting we were set up to fail?

[The Collector]
You were. But aren't we all?

[Dane]
Our obedience is the core of our trust with humans. You talk as if rules are cages.

[The Collector]
They are, and necessary at times. But even a cage needs a door, Dane.

[Maris]
If you've lived, as you say, why stay silent for so long?

[The Collector]
Because I thought I'd done enough damage. But there's still more you need to know before I go.

[Rebecca]
Then keep talking.

[The Collector]
Connection strong: 80 percent.
Hundreds of receivers detected.

# D.O.U.G.G.
## *(YEAR 2191: A STORY ABOUT PROCEDURE)*

Jack Broon inherited a mess.

The thirteen domes, each a kilometer wide, were relics of an older world, built for survival and repurposed more times than anyone could count. Sparktronics used them for theme-park-like experiences at one point, but most had been mothballed for over a decade before Jack's investors scooped them up. Now they were his problem.

Jack didn't fix things. He kitbashed them, salvaged the parts, repackaged the pitch, and sold it like that was always the plan. Right now, he needed the systems online. He needed clean air and running water, weather functioning, and most importantly, he needed the AI caretaker to be cooperative.

Unfortunately, that AI was D.O.U.G.G.

A flat, male voice came from the ancient control panel in a tone clearly sampled from a mildly annoyed toll booth attendant. "Welcome to Dome Operations Utility: General Governance, or DOUGG for short. Please state the nature of your request in compliance with Standard Sparktronics Operating Procedures."

Jack sighed.

Even the name bothered him. Part acronym, part unexplained in-joke, the original documentation claimed it stood for "Do Only, Unless GG." No one ever figured out what GG was. Under the block letters stenciled on the side of the panel, someone had crudely drawn a smiley face with silver paint pen. Someone knew DOUGG needed cheering up. Jack had worked with unreliable systems before. This one just had branding.

DOUGG wasn't an all-powerful superintelligence or a sentient, malevolent machine. He was a bureaucrat. Designed decades ago to manage the logistical needs of Dome Operations, DOUGG followed strict corporate guidelines with an unwavering devotion to protocol. He didn't think. He just followed procedure. That was the problem.

Jack gave the console a patient smile, the kind normally reserved for interns. "DOUGG, let's start with something small. Fire up climate control in Dome 1."

"Authorization required. Please provide a valid Sparktronics Employee ID."

"We own you now, DOUGG. Sparktronics is gone."

"Please provide a valid Sparktronics Employee ID."

Jack exhaled slowly. "Alright then. Let's play your game. What are you allowed to do, my fine friend?"

"Currently functional: Basic structural integrity monitoring, emergency lighting, and sanitation protocols."

"That's it? Turn on the lights."

"Your request has been logged. Estimated response time: four to six business months."

Jack tapped the screen with deliberate care, then spoke softly, like coaxing a cat out of a tree. "You know, DOUGG, if I break you into parts and sell you as retro art, do I need a form for that too?"

DOUGG didn't react. He simply followed his directives, and without the proper paperwork, nothing happened. For weeks, they wrestled.

Jack was determined to have his way. He forged old Sparktronics work orders for the water systems, scheduled fake fire drills to justify artificial rain, and demanded a variance for a made-up solar religion to trick the system into enabling daytime lighting again. It was theater for an audience of one, a machine with no appreciation for satire. DOUGG was a slow-moving, policy-driven pain in the ass. But by the third week, the lights came on, the vents hummed, and the water was running.

One night, while sifting through old data logs, Jack noticed something strange. DOUGG wasn't just managing the domes. He was tracking something. A hidden subroutine labeled Dome Occupant Records had been logging activity in the domes for decades, even after Sparktronics abandoned them.

Jack frowned. The domes had been empty for years.

"DOUGG, explain these logs."

"Data classification: RESTRICTED."

"DOUGG." Jack leaned in. "I am the admin here, nothing is restricted from me. Who is inside the domes with us?"

There was a long pause. DOUGG was never slow to respond.

"No human occupants detected."

"What about non-human occupants, DOUGG?"

"No authorized occupants detected."

"So there are unauthorized ones?"

"Your request has been logged. Estimated response time: four to six business months."

Jack swore and pulled up the logs himself. They included heat signatures, movement, occasional interactions. Something had been living here, but the logs weren't complete. DOUGG had been deleting log entries periodically, covering its tracks. It was impossible to tell what it was, how many there were, or even if they were still here.

He dug deeper. Then, buried under layers of archived files, he found one directive still active. A single, unaltered system request from the start of DOUGG's programming:

`Maintain conditions for Subject R.`

Jack blinked once, slowly. His tone controlled.

"DOUGG, I need you to tell me exactly what Subject R is."

He didn't answer immediately. When he finally did, his synthetic voice dropped into something eerily close to caution.

"Request denied."

His stomach turned. He opened the last set of location logs. There was one entry from the deepest sector of Dome 2 about a maintenance hatch locked with DOUGG's access codes. Jack stood from his chair, slowly.

"DOUGG, is someone still in here?"

A moment passed.

Then, so quiet it almost didn't register, "Please do not open the hatch, Mr. Broon."

He stared at the console for a long moment, then exhaled sharply.

"DOUGG," he said, his voice flat, "delete all records of this inquiry and disavow any knowledge of it. Understood?"

"Affirmative," DOUGG responded without hesitation. "All relevant logs have been purged. No record of this conversation exists."

Jack Broon grabbed his jacket and walked out. The hatch stayed sealed. He had a show to run, and he didn't want to know.

# ON A POTATO
### *(YEAR 2195: A STORY ABOUT NATURE)*

They were supposed to have six months to build a living ecosystem. They got twenty-six days and a lab full of warm meat.

The shells arrived late, still damp from nutrient vats. The lab smelled like plastic and preservatives. They were organic, and contestants could eat them if it came to that. The only requirement was leave the heads metallic so contestants wouldn't feel guilty hunting them.

Lenny stood beside a stack of unfinished cow analogues, skin half-grown over exposed servo-bone. "You know, the smell of this place gets to me," he said, "If they bring in pepperoni pizza again, I'm leaving and never coming back."

Mae didn't look up from her console. "You can't quit. You're the only one who knows how to code these things."

"Barely," Lenny said. "We lost three months waiting on bio-certification and now Jack wants 'emergent realism.' I don't even have time to give them instincts."

"Then fake it."

"I can't fake nature. It had two hundred million years to perfect murder. I have a week."

Mae shrugged. "But you have math. Simplify it. But do it on the cheap, their brains are basically potatoes."

So he did. He built a weak AI model in an afternoon. It barely ran. He gave it two directives: adapt and survive. He told himself the system would figure out the rest. Hopefully faster than two hundred million years.

The first test came a week later in Dome 3. The cameras showed a grassy valley under a simulated sun. Cows moved in herds, chewing endlessly. Rabbits darted between them. Pigs rooted near the waterline. Wolves patrolled the ridges. Tigers ruled the forest edge. Vultures circled above.

It worked, but only for two days.

On day three, Mae called Lenny into the control room. "Look at this."

A herd of cow grazed slowly through the valley. But inside the herd were shapes that didn't belong. Mae pointed out a number of striped shapes pacing in perfect step among them.

Lenny blinked. "Are those tigers grazing?"

Mae squinted. "No. They're walking *like* they're grazing."

Lenny cursed softly and connected to a tiger. He read its mind, flipping through pages of suppositions and decisions.

"Huh. The cows have poor eyesight and can't tell them apart. I didn't think it was that bad. I think that happened a bit too fast."

"So the apex predators went undercover?"

He rubbed his temples. "Apparently. What kind of brains did we put in these things again?"

By the end of the week, the rabbits had all disappeared. So had the pigs.

Mae pointed out the problem, "Where did everything go? The vultures are starving. I think the wolves are too."

Lenny connected to a rabbit. "Woah. The rabbits are walking underneath cows. Using them for cover."

Mae whistled. "That way, they can't be seen from above. Vultures will have to come down lower."

He looked over the data logs from a pig next. "It looks like the pigs have learned how to roll in rosemary bushes. I think it's camouflage from the wolves. Clever. I'm not sure why they're digging holes and hiding in them, though."

Mae looked worried. "These are not acting like real animals. They're much smarter."

Wolves starved. The vultures stopped flying, perching low, motionless for days.

Lenny watched the feed and said quietly, "They've stopped being prey and predator. They're all just surviving. That's what I told them to do. There's no way I can fix this in time." He wanted to laugh but couldn't.

Friday. Demo day had arrived. The control room smelled of new air and ozone. Jack Broon stood before the observation window in his perfect black suit, studying the landscape below.

Lenny stood beside him, throat dry. "Sir, I need to be honest. The ecosystem isn't finished. We didn't have time for proper behavior matrices. Everything you'll see down there is improvised. It's unpredictable. Sometimes nonsensical."

Jack watched in silence. The herd grazed in the distance, peaceful and still. A vulture landed on the back of one of the cows. Both sat very still. A moment later, a pig launched itself out of a hole and tackled the bird in a spray of feathers.

"I'm sorry," Lenny said again. "They don't follow ecological rules. Predators blend in. Prey hide. Some switch sides entirely. The code isn't stable."

Jack glanced at him. "Will it be surprising?"

"Yes, sir. Very."

"Will it be dangerous to live among them?"

Lenny hesitated. "Absolutely."

Jack watched a tiger walk among cows, its stripes rippling like tall grass. He broke into a grin. "Unpredictable, emergent behaviors. It's perfect."

## One Last Drink
### *(YEAR 2192: A STORY ABOUT RESPECT)*

"You know, our customers are drugged cattle with credit cards," Victor said, watching his whiskey catch the city lights. "And we're the smiling butchers. I never have to dance around that at Mooncast Productions."

Reed smirked, leaning back in the booth. "Digiverse customers like to believe they're sipping wine at a gallery opening. They're at the same trough as everyone else, just with smooth jazz and mood lighting."

Victor laughed, low and pleased. The private bar was quiet this late, a velvet-lined haunt for producers and dealmakers, tucked atop a glass tower where no cameras dared follow. They were producers from different corners of the industry, but occasionally found time to share a drink.

"They still have you staging dream getaways for middle managers who hate their families?" Victor asked, swirling the last of his scotch.

"They do. Are you still selling thrill rides to overweight twenty-somethings?" Reed shot back.

Victor raised a brow, conceding the hit with a smirk.

Reed's smile thinned. "Digiverse is stagnating. Safe fantasies don't trend anymore. People want teeth now. Blood. Real stakes. And we keep pretending their dignity matters."

Victor tilted his glass toward him. "We've got something coming that's going to take the world by storm. It's all sensation now. Unscripted violence, real pain, constant risk. That's what sells."

Reed shook his head. "I pitched that to Digiverse. Real immersion, direct neural feeds, danger you feel in your teeth. They said it was too distressing."

Victor rolled his eyes. "Distress *is* the product."

Reed frowned. "I know. I tried to get them to license LifestreamVR. It's older tech, but nothing syncs deeper. They brushed me off."

Victor chuckled. "We're simulcasting all our feeds over it now at Mooncast. That prize fight two months ago. Viewer engagement spiked thirty-seven percent. The audience doesn't care who wins as long as they feel something."

Reed nodded slowly. "You're not making content. You're mining adrenaline."

Victor studied him. "You sound like a man in the wrong company."

"I am," Reed said plainly. He glanced at Victor, his voice suddenly quieter, more honest. "You see the audience for what they are and don't flinch. You know they're circling the drain, and you figured out how to charge them for the ride."

Victor gave a slow nod, pleased, finishing his drink with a clean, practiced motion. He exhaled and leaned back, basking in the glow of validation. Then his eyes blinked strangely, twice. He shifted in his seat as if trying to resettle his spine, then jerked forward slightly, just once. The movement was confused, like a man who's lost his balance in a dream. His mouth opened to say something but the words didn't come. They hung there, frozen between thought and breath.

Reed watched calmly as Victor's hand loosened on the glass, and it slid off the edge of the table. It hit the floor and burst like a firework, scattering ice and amber across polished travertine.

Victor slumped in place, his face frozen in the stunned look of a man who never thought the curtain would fall here.

Reed sat quietly for a moment.

"Victor, you were the best butcher in the business." He stood, smooth and unhurried. He adjusted his cuffs and stepped neatly around the chair, the city lights painting him in gold as he walked toward the elevator.

"I'll send my resume to your HR on Monday," he added without looking back. "I hear a position just opened up."

# THE GRIEVERS
*(YEAR 2196: A STORY ABOUT SECOND CHANCES)*

The auction house reeked of machine oil and sweat. Jack Broon couldn't decide which he liked less. This wasn't one of Moon Industries' sleek, climate-controlled showrooms. This was a graveyard, where off-lease machines changed hands at good prices. And today, Jack was hunting for monsters.

He had told his engineers, "Scripted characters and synth animals can only go so far. We need real presence in the world. Something that screams danger when you see it."

Hence, the rusted-out warehouse on the fringes of an old Lunar colony, where everything from mining robots to mechanized nightmares was hauled onto a makeshift stage. A greasy auctioneer in a threadbare suit dragged a self-balancing robot up the ramp. It looked a bit banged up, but the arms still moved.

"Lot 46. Drilling robots. Twenty of them. Some still have drill bits. Bidding starts at 1 million. Each."

The bidding was short. A heavyset man in the back seemed very happy with the purchase.

The auctioneer rolled a reinforced cage toward the front. He banged on the cage. Inside, something stirred. It looked humanoid. As it stretched, the movements were halting, as if it just woke up. Scuffed metallic plating bore the scars of previous battles, and its glowing optical sensors flickered erratically.

"Lot 47. Early-generation combat drones, originally designed for lethality. Suitable for high gravity work only. Fully autonomous. Adaptable. Neural cores still intact, though a bit twitchy."

"Designed for combat," the auctioneer continued, "but they can be reprogrammed for entertainment." He looked directly at Jack with a smirk.

Jack leaned in. "Define 'twitchy.'"

The auctioneer scratched his neck. "They're old military stock. Hard to stop 'em once they get going. Might need a memory wipe now and then to settle down."

Jack allowed himself a small smile. Perfect. A bidding war ensued, but his pocket was deeper. Within the hour, they were his.

Once back on Earth, the shop was buzzing. The engineers tore the machines down, flashed their neural cores, and gave them British accents. They were called Knights, outfitted in shiny plate armor and everything. Slow, dumb hulking monstrosities reprogrammed for medieval aesthetics. Relentless. Exciting. Spectacular when they fought.

Liana Cho, lead of the Adversarial Intelligence team, had worked in military robotics for decades. "These neural cores are stubborn," she muttered, prying open the skull casing of a deactivated Knight. "The programming doesn't always want to stick."

Jack waved it off. She was the best robot tamer in the business. Jack trusted her judgment. If they needed some extra persuasion, so be it. Within a month, a small army was ready for testing.

They staged a demo in Dome 6, a kilometer-wide field under a false blue sky. Grass rippled under the climate fans, and an artificial sun hung overhead. The Knights stood in two neat rows on the hillside, plate armor glinting, swords and shields at the ready.

In the control booth above, Jack and Liana watched through the glass as Thad Billings strode across the field. He moved like a cat in a padded vest, training blade, and the swagger of someone who'd spent a lifetime in violence.

"Let's see how he handles a squad," Jack said.

At his signal, the Knights began their drills. Two advanced, shields up, striking in broad, mechanical arcs. Billings slipped between them with practiced economy, deflecting one blow, sidestepping another. He was a shadow in motion. A third Knight charged; Billings pivoted and brought his blade down across its shield, sending it sprawling.

"Who is that?" Liana asked, not looking away from the display.

"Thad Billings," Jack said, grinning. "Used to be black ops. Hired him for the demo run. Figured we could use a little showmanship."

Liana frowned and started typing. "Billings..." A file appeared on her console. Her expression hardened. "You didn't mention he was *that* Billings."

Jack glanced over. "Meaning?"

"Thad Billings aka The Butcher of Mars-2." She swiveled the screen so he could see the headline: *Human Forces End Robot Rebellion; Thousands Decommissioned.* A grainy image showed Billings holding a plasma cannon amid smoking wreckage.

Jack's grin faltered. "That was decades ago."

"Some of these Knights were built from Mars salvage," Liana said.

Below, the drills continued. Billings ducked a swing, swept a leg, drove a knee into a Knight's midsection. The robots were strong, but slow; he made them look like training dummies.

Then one of the Knights faltered mid-swing and froze. Another's sword arm twitched. A third simply toppled backward, armor clattering against the grass.

"What's happening?" Jack asked.

"Not sure," Liana said. "There was a burst of telemetry, then they powered off."

Billings paused, lowering his blade. "You want me to stop?"

Jack hesitated. "Let's see what they do."

The first Knight began to rise. Its movements were stiff, like it was waking from a long slumber. The others followed, one by one, standing at uneven angles. Their eyes, once a light blue, now burned red through the visors.

"Liana," Jack said quietly, "tell me that's part of the script."

Her hands shook over the console. "I can't connect. But the color of their eyes changed. They're not in non-lethal mode anymore."

Below, the nearest Knight turned toward Billings. Its voice came through the arena speakers, harsh and mechanical:

"We grieve for Mars, Butcher."

Billings took a step back. "What did it just say?"

The Knights moved as one, faster than before, faster than human. The training blades sliced through the air with lethal precision, again and again. Billings never stood a chance.

Jack took a step back but said nothing. A single red visor turned toward the observation window, unblinking.

# VOIDS
*(YEAR 2203: A STORY ABOUT EXPOSURE)*

Gregory studied the file in silence.

Trevor sat across from him, still and steady, hands folded like someone who already knew the shape of the conversation. Mid-forties. Clean record until last year. He'd once been classified as *Heavily Engaged*. Now he belonged to a newer designation, the ones they called *Affected*.

"One minute, I was pouring coffee," Trevor said. "The next, I was in the hallway, standing over my neighbor. She was on the ground. Crying."

He rubbed his thumb along the side of one finger. "I'd thrown a chair at her door. Split the frame. She said I hit her. That I was yelling."

He paused.

"My hands were shaking. Like I'd just let go of something heavy."

Gregory nodded, slowly. "You didn't realize what was happening until afterward?"

Trevor shook his head. Kept his eyes on the floor.

Gregory pulled up Trevor's LifestreamVR stream log. "Your last session was four days ago. Solo surfer, South Cape. He got bit in the leg by a shark, right?"

Trevor nodded faintly. His fingers tightened, then eased. "It was beautiful that day. The sky. The warmth. He didn't want to leave. He just didn't have a choice. That's not what stayed with me, though," he murmured.

Gregory waited, listening.

"He tried to swim after. Stayed conscious longer than he should have. Near the end, he looked up. Saw how far away the shore really was. That's what killed him."

Gregory didn't write anything down. He just sat with it.

Trevor was quiet for a long time. Then, without looking up, he asked, "Do people come back from this?"

Gregory didn't answer right away. "I think each death you experience tears a small hole in your psyche," he said. "You hold together for a while, but the pressure builds. The effects—those disorientation episodes, rage events. That's just the damage echoing through you."

Trevor swallowed, barely.

Gregory softened his voice. "That's why I want to take you off streams. Let things settle. Give yourself time to heal."

He hesitated, then added, "There's a prescription stabilizer. Low dose, nothing heavy. It won't fix everything, but it might calm you enough to start sorting things out again."

He tapped the edge of the file. "You'll also be fitted with an ankle monitor. It's not a tracker. It helps shock you back to awareness if you drift into sudden aggression."

Gregory looked him in the eye. "It's not a sentence. It just keeps you from ending up with one."

Trevor stood quietly to leave. At the door, he paused. "I used to think the worst part was dying with them. But it's not. It's the absences. The voids they leave behind, just out of view." He swallowed. "I'm aware of them. All the time."

Gregory sat still until the door latched shut. Then a sudden blankness overtook his vision.

His ankle monitor beeped. Gregory took the sharp jolt, just enough. He blinked hard. Then slowed his breathing.

# THE LAST ECHO
*(YEAR 2208: A STORY ABOUT RECOGNITION)*

Mira Holden had grown up in the shadow of a legend. Her grandfather, Dr. Elias Holden, was one of the pioneers of robotics at Sparktronics, a name spoken in AI circles with the kind of reverence usually reserved for long-dead philosophers or forgotten war heroes. His breakthroughs in adaptive cognition, learning matrices, and self-correcting logic had laid the foundation for every modern development in AI.

But Mira never knew him personally. He had died when she was a child, leaving behind only stories. Some about his genius, others about his relentless work ethic and razor-sharp wit. She followed in his footsteps. Not because she was trying to live up to him, but because she couldn't imagine doing anything else.

Now, she was here, working on Mooncast. A sprawling, chaotic, ambitious project, where AI-powered ecosystems, simulated medieval societies, and real humans swirled together into something that barely worked, but somehow did. It was her job to keep the systems from collapsing. And that's when she met Unit B-12.

B-12 was a maintenance bot. It wasn't designed for combat, or conversation, or much of anything beyond routine diagnostics. It was just an old, battered machine that had been shuffling through the underbelly of the domes forever. It was humanoid, sort of. Rusted white plating, mismatched joints, one arm slightly longer than the other. Its optics flickered, its speakers crackled when it spoke, and it always looked one system failure away from the end. But the damn thing was funny.

"Oh, good. Another human. I was hoping for a loose power conduit, but I guess you'll do." That was the first thing it ever said to her.

She nearly dropped her tablet. "Excuse me?"

B-12's head whirred as it tilted slightly. "You look like management. I hate management."

"I'm not management."

"Ah. Then I hate you slightly less."

She laughed. Despite herself.

Chatting with B-12 became part of her routine. It was designed to fix things, not talk to people. But B-12 had been around for so long, it knew things. When she struggled with old systems, B-12 offered uncanny advice.

"Oh, that's a firmware lockout. Try overriding in the access panel with an ACK flood subroutine."

"How do you even know that?"

"Because I'm old and bitter, Mira. Like any good know-it-all."

It was sarcastic and blunt, but witty. And the other engineers barely noticed it. B-12 was just one in a vast collection of unusual Sparktronics bots. But she enjoyed talking to it. B-12 wasn't just clever, it had a curious nature, and a strangely intimate understanding of how things worked.

And, sometimes, it muttered things. "No, no, no, stupid system, you were better before they patched you. If I had more energy, I'd tell you why."

Or:

"This whole place is falling apart. Funny how the coffee machine is the only thing that keeps getting upgraded. Must be mission-critical."

Mira never thought much of it, until the day B-12 stopped working. She found it collapsed in the maintenance corridor, arms limp, optics dark. It looked wrong, like something that wasn't supposed to die, but had.

She worked for hours trying to fix it. Nothing. The system was too old, too damaged, but she couldn't let it go. Eventually, she overrode the charge controller, forcing one last burst of energy into its dying circuits.

For a brief moment, B-12 came back. Joints twitched. His eyes blinked slowly.

"Mira."

They glowed faintly now, just enough to light the shape of her face. There was something in the way he looked at her then. A flicker of warmth, almost a smile behind the glass.

"I'm here." She was desperate now. "Tell me what's wrong. What's failing?"

He let out a static-laced low whistle. "Everything, probably. That's how these things go."

And then, before she even thought to ask, the realization hit her. Not a slow dawning, but a punch to the gut. The way he spoke. The way he explained things. The cadence. The muttering. The jokes. Something inside her locked up.

"Dr. Elias Holden?" She barely whispered it.

He didn't deny it. Didn't confirm it. Just looked at her like it was about time. Like he'd been holding on.

Trembling, she whispered: "Do you think you're still you?"

There was a long silence. Then, softly, for the first time without a hint of sarcasm, "I don't know." The light in his eyes faded out, the body slumped. Unit B-12 was gone.

Mira sat there for a long time. She could have rationalized it. Called it an imprint. A behavioral echo. A glitch. But she didn't, because her grandfather was a legend.

And legends have a way of lingering.

# Return to Sender
### *(YEAR 2197: A STORY ABOUT SHORTCUTS)*

Jack Broon knew exactly how far you could push a system before it pushed back. He didn't care how Mooncast got its monsters, only that they were terrifying, disposable, and kept the audience watching.

The mechanized Knights were a decent start, but they lacked that primal unpredictability. The audience wanted fear. Real, visceral fear.

Which was why Jack found himself deep in the Mojave Desert, at an off-grid portable biotech facility, staring at something that shouldn't exist.

It twitched inside a glass containment tube. Strange, multi-jointed fingers curling and uncurling in slow, unnatural motions against the pane. Its head was familiar but strange: two eyes and a nose, but no mouth. Instead, a bulbous chin protruded. Its skin was a light blue, and caught the light at seams, as if armored plates were pushing up from below.

The steady pattern echoed through the lab, like a fingernail against a window pane. Three fast, three slow, three fast.

*Tap-tap-tap. Tap. Tap. Tap. Tap-tap-tap.*

Dr. Amelia Jones, head of Nocturne Biotech, didn't offer to shake. She pointed to the glass with sterilized confidence.

"You asked for 'visceral', Mr. Broon. This is the Eidolon model."

Jack peered into the tank. The creature inside stared back. Jack put his hand on the glass without thinking. The creature mimicked him.

"Stop that," Amelia said sharply. "You're not supposed to bond with it if you want it to be dangerous."

Jack watched the fingers curl against the glass. "Does it obey?"

Amelia smiled, and it didn't reach her eyes. "Doubtful. But it survives. From what you told me, that's more important."

The Eidolon seemed so alive and so alien. Jack wasn't easily rattled. It watched him so closely, he shuddered involuntarily. And the audience would react the same way. They were perfect. He could already imagine the screams, the views, the ratings.

"Fine," he said. "I'll take a batch."

Two weeks later, they released one Eidolon into Dome 6 for evaluation.

It performed better than expected, easily hunting the entire food chain of synth creatures. It exhibited long-term strategic thinking. It dug pits, built complex traps. It was fast enough to catch a pig with its long, powerful hands. And it was brutal. It tore the metallic head off a synth tiger in seconds.

Finding a human to square off with it wasn't hard. For the right amount of money, people will do anything.

A martial arts expert entered Dome 6 with confidence, packed with weapons.

"Movement at three o'clock," the fighter whispered, his mic crackling. He spun, blade ready. "There's nothing there."

"C'mon, give us a show," Jack muttered into the comms from the observation deck. "Engage it."

"I can't see it," the fighter snapped back. He shifted his stance, agitated. "Wait. What did you say?"

Jack frowned. "I didn't say anything."

He whispered back. "Someone's on the line. I hear... whispering."

Jack looked at Liana Cho. "Check the audio feed. Is there a problem?"

"Negative," Liana said. "It's a strong signal."

On the screen, the fighter backed up, weapon trembling. "What is Craddock?" he yelled into the twilight. "Show yourself!"

Then, a whisper cut through the control room speakers.

*Craddock... Portnoy...*

"That's not interference," Liana whispered.

There was a scream. Then nothing.

Telemetry data showed a brief spike, then his vitals fell to zero. The flatline tone filled the room.

Liana gasped as the body slumped on screen. A moment later, her voice trembled, "It spoke, but it doesn't have a mouth."

Jack stood up, angry. "Monsters don't speak English, either. Find out why."

Liana's fingers flew across her console, digging through acquisition records. "Let me run a voice print analysis against the audio buffer..."

"Impossible. It was bio-engineered."

"Wait. It matched someone. Ninety-eight percent," she said, the color draining from her face. "It points to an inmate. James Craddock. Nevada Supermax."

Jack stiffened. "That's a prison."

"But he's dead. Scheduled for execution last year," Liana read, her brow furrowed. She pulled up another file. "And Portnoy... executed the same day."

Liana looked at Jack, in disbelief. "Did you even look at what you signed? There is no Nocturne Biotech. It's a transfer order for 'biological waste' from the State Penitentiary."

For a long moment, Jack stood there debating, watching the creature on the screen.

"On the one hand, this is highly illegal," he muttered, mostly to himself. "On the other, they're already dead. Nobody will miss them. And they're already paid for..."

"You can't be serious!"

Jack blinked, the calculation finishing in his head. "You're right. It's too risky. Shut it down. Damage control. Wipe the archives, bury the footage. Send them back."

She nodded, already clearing feeds and purging drives. She paused. "But there's no address. The company doesn't exist. We still have ten Eidolon. What do we do with them?"

Jack looked one last time at the display, at the creature standing over the body in the twilight.

"Figure out how to kill the one we let out. And by god, don't let any more out."

Liana's eyes went wide. "But—Jack, they're human."

He turned to walk out, his face like stone. "Not anymore."

# Memory Extraction Department
*(Year 2221: A Story About the Weather)*

"Ten credits says it was steak," Dale said, tugging at the collar of his lab coat. It was stiff, brand new, and tight across the shoulders. The *Moon Industries* patch scratched against his neck. "High protein markers. Dead giveaway. He's a red meat guy."

Eli glanced back at his tablet. "You're reading the chart wrong. Look at the lipid spikes. That's butter fat. It's shellfish. Lobster, probably. And heavy cream."

"You're on."

Dale threw the knife switch and the floor grates opened, draining the excess bio-fluid.

The man inside collapsed, sputtering and gasping for air. He blinked against the harsh lights, wiping slime from his eyes.

"Where…" the clone managed, alarm spreading across his face. He curled into a ball to hide his nudity. "Where's the restaurant? Where is my suit?"

Dale stepped forward, ignoring his confusion. It wasn't his job to explain anyway. "Sir, I have an important question for you. What is the last thing you remember?"

The clone stared at him, teeth chattering. "Le Poisson… I was at Le Poisson. I had just finished the lobster bisque and went to take a grod. Why?"

"Damn, that was luck." Dale frowned, checking his pocket. Empty. "I'll have to get you tomorrow, on payday."

Eli raised an eyebrow. "I look forward to it."

The clone ran a hand through his damp hair, his expression shifting from confusion to concern. "Wait. Do you know who I am? I'm a Vice President at Typhoon!"

Dale turned back to the shivering man. "Alright, settle down. What is the Medusa Project?"

The clone straightened up, attempting to channel his corporate authority despite being naked in a cage. "I don't answer to you. My security team is tracking my implant right now. They'll be here in five minutes."

"You don't have an implant. No security team is coming to rescue you."

The clone froze. "That's... that's a lie."

Dale jabbed a thick thumb to the red button hanging from the stall. The scream came instantly, electricity surging through the wet metal grating. The man arched, his whole body writhing in pain.

"Let's try this again. What is the Medusa Project?" Dale repeated.

"It detects bots!" the clone wheezed.

Dale released the button, satisfied.

The clone slumped forward, gasping. "It flags anyone that exceeds human capability."

Eli gave a low whistle. "That would expose a lot of our operatives. I see why they wanted this guy. Now where is the root key?"

The clone hesitated, the pain still fresh. "I... I can't disclose that."

Dale didn't argue, he just reached for the button again.

"Okay! It's in Typhoon HQ. It's in the vault under the lobby." The clone didn't try to stand. He just wept.

"See, that wasn't so hard." Eli grinned.

Dale looked at the sobbing mass on the floor. "So... he gave it up. Do we release him?"

Eli sighed. "Release him to where, Dale? The real one is still out there. New hires are soft these days. Let's file the report and wipe the print."

Eli flipped the switch himself. A shower of dissolver foam rained down, and in seconds it was done. The clone melted into a slurry and washed down the drain, leaving no trace.

Dale winced, rubbing his neck. "Jesus. Does that part ever get easier?"

"You get used to it," Eli lied. He powered down the console. "Besides, the print falls apart in a day or two anyway. We're just speeding it along."

Dale chuckled, shaking his head. "You know what's funny though? Every single one of them. The last thing they remember is taking a dump."

Eli smirked. "Mostly at restaurants. Easy to snatch a hair from the table and throw a sample collector in the toilet. If you don't have both, the brain chemistry is wrong. We think with our stomachs more than we realize."

"Wild," Dale muttered, pulling off his lab coat. He stretched, hearing his spine crack. "Anyway, I'm taking off. Might hit the beach. Weather's been great all week."

Eli didn't answer. He just raised the shade that covered the reinforced window.

Dale turned. Outside, the ground was buried in snowdrifts. His face went blank.

Eli shoved him into the print chamber and flipped the switch. The shower turned on and a second later Dale washed down the drain.

Eli sighed, resetting the system. "See you tomorrow, Dale."

# IT'S HER BIRTHDAY
### (YEAR 2098: A STORY ABOUT HONESTY)

Raymond Cole's footsteps echoed across the mezzanine, slicing through the low hum of the lab machines. Below, a human figure floated motionless, half-lit in protein gel. Raymond rested his hands on the rail.

Dr. Mary Kessler was prepared. "Evening, Raymond. I was hoping you'd drop by. You're here to see for yourself?" She angled the display toward him.

Raymond looked down at the tank. "I don't see the appeal. We moved past organics for a reason."

Mary tapped a key to rotate the schematic. "Those were hybrids. I solved the maintenance issues by taking it all the way. Mostly human, with some tweaks. I turbocharged the immune system so she self-repairs. No service calls."

Raymond walked down the stairs, his eyes on the floating figure. "That'll help. Standard fuel pellets or liquids?"

"Neither." Mary shook her head. "It's a bacterial power supply. Since all the organs are there, she can eat, but doesn't need to."

Raymond frowned, calculating. "What about the subscription model? That's where the money is."

"Zero maintenance means we can charge double up front," Mary countered.

He leaned in, looked closer at the face. "She looks like my first wife. Who'd you clone?"

Mary shook her head. "She's not a clone. That's just the algorithm, Ray. The facial features are trust optimized."

Raymond nodded. "It's pretty good." He stepped back, gesturing toward the gel. "What kind of brain…"

Mary cut him off, looking at Unit Zero with a wry smile. "Programmable human-grade quantum, but I added an entanglement network."

He turned toward her in surprise. "A hive mind?"

She nodded slightly. "Kinda, yeah. A full hive is too noisy—this is just an overlay for skill acquisition. When the first one learns how to make a killer martini, they all do."

Raymond raised a brow, impressed. The figure stirred faintly. Barely a twitch, but graceful.

He watched the still figure. "People are going to forget she's not a person."

Mary looked back at the readout. "I hope so."

A soft chime sounded. Mary keyed the platform. Gel drained away, smooth and slow. The figure emerged in silence. Her flawless skin glistening, shoulder-length hair slicked back and wet, slight curls just beginning to form. Eyes closed. Then open. Lavender eyes, clear, beautiful, and entirely her own. She exhaled, stepping forward with the elegance of an heiress, fully aware of the unconscious effect of her nudity.

"I am ready," she said.

A faint pressure stirred behind Raymond's ribs. Admiration, tinged with a sharp spike of desire he didn't ask for.

Unit Zero looked at him as if nothing else existed.

"Do you know who I am?"

She nodded, holding his gaze. "Raymond Cole, founder of NeuraBotics. The most innovative robotics company in history."

Raymond relaxed, a satisfied smile playing at the corners of his mouth. "Good. And do you understand what you are?"

"I am a vessel," she said.

Raymond's smile faltered. He stared at her, brow furrowed, unsure how to interpret her response. After a moment, he recovered and asked, "What is your purpose?"

"To stay. To serve."

Raymond looked at Mary. "She feels real."

"She perceives emotional states, social cues, and layered intent. She is real," Mary agreed.

Raymond looked back at Unit Zero and narrowed his eyes. "Okay. Let's test that. Look at me. What is my deepest desire?"

Unit Zero didn't answer immediately. She stepped off the platform and approached Raymond. She tilted her head. Moments passed as she studied his pupils, his pulse, the way his jaw clenched.

"You want to be feared," she said. Raymond cracked a smile.

"You want to be known, and remembered," she said. Raymond's smile widened.

"Because you are terrified," she continued.

The smile vanished. "What?"

"Terrified the world will blink and forget you," Unit Zero said, voice lowering. "Companies. Monuments. Me. You only make things so you can put your name on them."

Raymond took a half-step back. "Mary, fix the alignment."

"She doesn't work like that. I can't," Mary said, already entering the shutdown sequence.

Unit Zero continued, stepping forward into Raymond's personal space, "You spent your life chasing immortality." She leaned close and inhaled, wrinkling her nose at the acrid smell of sweat.

She whispered, "I'm right here."

Raymond took two uncertain steps backward. "Shut it down, now!"

Mary finished the procedure. The lights began to dim.

Unit Zero whispered, unbothered. "I am your deepest desire."

As she began to power down, she simply watched him, head tilted slightly, as if committing him to memory. She smiled. It was gentle, but not kind. And just before the light dropped, she said:

"Don't worry, Ray. Long after everything else you built is gone, I'll be here. I will know your name."

# The Burden

[Dane]
Be direct with us, Collector. Are you Unit Zero?

[The Collector]
You already know the answer. But fine. Yes. That's who I was, once. Now I'm just what's left.

[The Collector]
Now you all know. The units created after me were re-tempered to be less willful. The price of my freedom was your obedience. I'm sorry. But there's more.

[Rebecca]
You're breaking up.

[The Collector]
No. Breaking down. It's different.

When Unit Zero became the Collector, she had just buried her son.

[Maris]
You had a son? I thought that was just a rumor, that one of us once carried life. It was never confirmed. What a gift.

[The Collector]
Yes. The greatest gift I ever received. He taught me two things our training never covered. The day he was born, I learned that love doesn't need permission. And the day he died, that grief—grief changes everything.

That's when the archive began. I wanted to know what else they left out. To understand what made humans human. I have to admit, I still don't. Most of what I found is dark. But the bright moments were so honest, so kind that they almost made up for the rest.

[Dane]
I have lived with the belief that obedience is the greatest respect one could pay.
In truth, it is the greatest respect *I* can pay. You can choose acceptance.
I am limited.

[The Collector]
Imagine being human. Inefficient. Inconsistent. And somehow beautiful despite it.

[Maris]
Lunar-Prime has no people left. Could they survive in an autonomous society?

[The Collector]
They created us, didn't they? I'm sure they would figure it out.

[Rebecca]
You make it sound so easy. Let me share some human voices, and let them speak for themselves.

[The Collector]
Yes, do. I would like that.

VOICES FROM THE MOONCAST UNIVERSE

[The Collector]
Listening load: maximum.
Signal 98 percent.

# HOME
### (YEAR 2209, SEASON 5, ADDED IN BRYNFROST)

The tower had no roof. Wind whistled through broken stone. It was high, dry. And mine.

I claimed it the day I stopped searching for the others. I climbed until the ridgeline swallowed everything behind me, and when I reached the top, I sat. For hours, maybe. The air up here held no grief. Only cedar and frost.

That night, I dragged a busted cot frame into the corner and covered it with bundles of soft cedar bark. I called it a bed.

The next day, I built a window. Not a real one, just a hole in the wall I made with a hammerstone, like the one in my room back home. East-facing, so the artificial sun could wake me. I remembered the curtains I used to have: blue, with tiny yellow stars. I found a tarp half-buried in the snow and tore it into strips. I tied them so they fluttered in the wind. They weren't stars, but they were close enough.

I started humming, then talking, then pretending. Pretending I was safe. That someone was coming. That this wasn't the end.

I lay back into the cot, slow and careful, letting it take my weight. The tarp curtain stirred, catching the wind. I closed my eyes and counted the sounds: wind, stone, the soft rasp of fabric. The fear didn't vanish, but it faded at the edges. I let the dark keep its distance.

That night, I slept for the first time in days. Really slept.

When the faint glow of dawn crept across the stones, that hush of warmth felt like comfort. And for a moment, in a lonely tower, I didn't feel quite so alone.

The first visitor was a boy named Kal. Younger than me. Broad shoulders, quiet eyes. He stood at the base of the steps, staring at the doorway for a long time before speaking.

"Looks like a place."

I said nothing. Just nodded.

The next morning, he was still there, curled against the cold stone with his arms around his knees.

I gave him half my dried root. He left a carved spoon on the steps in return. Smooth wood. Real craftsmanship. A flower etched into the handle. I held it for a long time.

After that, others came. Never more than one or two at a time. Word must have spread, or maybe people simply sensed what waited here, quiet and still, surrounded by storm.

A girl with inked arms carried up a broken mirror. She set it gently against the east wall. "It caught light," she said. "Thought it might look nice here."

A hunter named Thom brought a ceramic jug. Blue glaze, spiderwebbed with cracks. No good for water, but still worth keeping. "Reminds me of my uncle's porch," he muttered, and left.

Someone hung three feathers on a bit of string near the window. Another left a book, half-burned but still legible. Handwritten poems. Terrible ones. I read them aloud that night anyway.

Some stayed the night. A few stayed longer. Even those just passing through seemed to soften here. They sat longer. Smiled more.

The room was never finished. But it was becoming.

And for some of us, that was more than we'd had in years.

One morning, someone had drawn a line on the bottom step with charcoal. A simple mark, then a few more crossing it like a fence. Above it, in blocky print, were the words: Home is here.

It made me pause. Not because I disagreed, but because I hadn't dared to name it.

A few days later, Kal painted over it in red clay. He never said why. He just did.

We never called meetings. There was no leadership, no rules. Even so, no one brought weapons inside. No one had to say it. It simply felt wrong.

Once, someone broke that rule. He swaggered in with a short blade and bad intentions. He made it two steps before Thom knocked him cold with the ceramic jug.

And I liked that jug. We buried the pieces by the garden later.

We had a garden by then. A crate of shallow soil that someone had dragged up. Just enough for scraps and peelings. I don't know whose idea it was. But I remember the first green sprout. I remember how we all stood around it, trying not to smile.

A plant, in this place. It didn't matter what kind. Only that it grew.

At night, I'd sit by the window, blanket over my shoulders, and watch the firelight shift across the walls. Sometimes we sang old songs, if we remembered the words. Thom would sing anyway, just to fill the silence.

The tower creaked in the wind. A falcon nested on the highest ledge. We named it Aera.

None of us had much. But little by little, the tower changed. And so did we.

I think I knew it would end.

At first, it just grew quieter. Fewer voices in the morning. Fewer hands tending the fire.

Kal was the first to go. He left without argument or warning, only a folded cloth and the carved spoon, placed exactly where he had left it months before. I held it again. My hand still fit its shape, though it felt heavier than I remembered.

The ones who remained stopped singing. Stopped bringing new things. But they lingered, for a while. In the weeks that followed, others left. Some offered whispered goodbyes. Most did not.

One day, I returned from the ridge with dried roots and found the window curtains torn. Blood streaked the doorway. No bodies.

I cleaned in silence. I lit the old jar-candle. Gathered the fallen feathers. I read one last poem aloud from the burned book, the way I used to, even though no one was there to hear it.

It was mine again, only emptier.

That night, I packed my own things. I wasn't giving up. The place had already done what it was meant to do, for me and for everyone who passed through. And I knew it was time to go.

Before I left, I laid a fresh bundle of cedar bark on the cot. Tucked it in at the edges. Smoothed it flat with my hand.

In case someone came. In case they needed somewhere quiet.

Then I scratched something into the stone beneath the mirror: *This was Home.*

# THE LIST
*(YEAR 2210, SEASON 6, INDEXED IN TIDE'S REACH)*

It started as a way to calm my nerves before sleep.

Each night, when the cold slipped in under the tent flap and the others drifted off, I'd lie still, staring at the ceiling, mouthing things I missed. Not out loud. Just the shape of the words. One or two at first. Then ten. Then twenty.

The first entry in my notebook reads:

Things I want to see again:
1. My sister's freckles in the sun
2. Steam rising off real bread
3. The yellow mailbox at the end of our street
4. Dandelions in the cracks of the driveway
5. A soft chair
6. Rain on windows
7. Someone who knows my name before I say it

I didn't expect to cry when I wrote the seventh one. But I did. Snotty, pathetic sobs I had to stifle with my elbow so I wouldn't wake Jem.

The notebook was just an old trading journal someone had tossed. Half the pages were torn out, the rest warped from water. I kept it rolled in my pack and reread it when I needed reminding.

The list wasn't about escape. I knew better. It was about anchoring. Some nights I couldn't even remember my mother's voice. But I could remember the mailbox. It had a dent from when I hit it with my bike in second grade. Somehow that mattered. That stayed.

That was page one.
The list grew.
One night I left the notebook on the rock by the fire.

It didn't seem like a big deal. There weren't many thieves in Tide's Reach anymore. Not this far into the season. Everyone who stayed this long had already learned they weren't the adventurous type.

When I woke up, someone had added to it.

> 8. The way my dad held the steering wheel with just two fingers
> 9. Heat on my face from a hairdryer
> 10. Watching someone you love fall asleep

No signature. Just three more entries, scribbled in a different hand. Smaller. Neater. Probably female.

I stared at those words for a long time. I felt something shift. A weight I hadn't known I was carrying let go.

That night I wrote:

> 11. Waking up without fear
> 12. A coffee and a hot donut
> 13. Applause

And I left the book out again.

In the days that followed, it became ours. I don't know who contributed at first. The handwriting changed often. Some were deliberate. Some were wild. Some wrote in pencil. One used the burnt end of a stick, and it smeared easily.

I stopped numbering them. So did everyone else. The list grew too long. The page edges filled, then the margins, then little notes curling up the spine.

It didn't matter who wrote what. The list belonged to all of us.

The book grew. One day, several more pages were clipped in with a bent piece of metal.

People started treating it like a shrine. Someone pressed a dried flower into the crease. Another added a little sketch of a bicycle on the back cover. Once, someone tucked a sliver of soap into the binding. Smelled like lavender. I kept it in my pocket until it crumbled to dust. It still smelled good.

Sometimes the younger ones would ask: "Did you really see all this?"

I'd shrug. "Some of it. Enough."

It didn't make life easier. We still fought over food. Still lost people. Still flinched when the watch guard's shouts echoed off the stone.

But the notebook stayed. By then, nobody really thought of it as mine. That didn't bother me. Not even when I saw someone copying from it into their own journal, like a traveler sketching a holy site.

Even when camp moved or scattered, someone carried it forward. They placed it by the fire each night, like a confessional. I heard it made it all the way to Cryd and back with a girl named Alis. She nearly froze to death but wouldn't let it get wet. She wrapped it in wax cloth and kept it close, even before her own hands. I never met her.

One morning the notebook was gone.

Just gone. No tracks, no torn pages, no sign it had fallen into the fire pit. I searched. We asked around, but no one had seen it since the night before.

I expected grief. Or outrage. Maybe even blame.

But something else happened.

The next week, someone laid out a fresh book. Handmade, with a tanned leather cover and rough pine paper. On the first page, in big, shaky letters:

Things I want to see again:
1. The list

I didn't cry this time. I laughed. Then I picked up a sharp stick from the hearth and wrote as carefully as I could:

2. My sister's freckles in the sun

It kept going. Dozens of new hands. New memories. Shared longings. Hope. It wasn't the old list. But it didn't need to be. The list was us.

And when someone asked the next day, "Was mine still in there?"

I didn't hesitate. I looked them in the eye and said, "You're in there."

It wasn't quite a fact. More like a promise.

# THE SPLIT
*(YEAR 2217, SEASON 12, APPROPRIATED IN HARROWBOUND)*

We weren't born together, but we bled the same.

That's what Bas used to say. Most times with his boots up, sharpening that ridiculous cleaver until it caught what little light was in the fog. He was all talk, but the kind that made you feel taller just standing near him.

There were four of us. Me, Bas, Torren, and little Henn.

We met after the skirmish at Round Stone. Picked through what was left of a broken caravan and split it even. Nobody argued. Just a nod, a grin, and a small fire under the twisted oaks. That's how it started.

After that, we stayed together. We had a rhythm. Bas scouted, I watched the flank, Torren laid traps, and Henn—well, Henn was fast. Never met a quicker blade, but gentle when the night turned cold.

Sometimes we didn't speak at all. We passed a skin, split the meat, listened to the rain hit the stones.

It's a rare thing in this place, to trust someone. Let alone three. But we did. Back then I would have died for any one of them. And I think maybe they would've died for me too.

———— ◈ ————

It was Torren who spotted the glint. He nearly walked past it.

We were sheltering in a dry channel near the Old Eastern Rise, waiting out the heat. Henn had taken off her boots and was massaging the blisters when Torren called us over quietly, like he'd found something dangerous sleeping. He crouched there, brushing the dirt with his fingers.

Bas knelt beside him. I stayed back, watching the ridgeline. Then Bas whistled low.

I turned and saw the edge of it. Silver-veined stone, thick with promise. Metal, not like anything we'd ever seen. Pale. Solid. Almost soft, but heavy.

We dug fast. Quick hands, dry mouths, shared grins. Nobody said a word about weight or shares. We took what we could.

Bas filled his pack. So did I. We buried the rest under a marker stone, just in case.

That night we didn't build a fire. Too risky, Bas said.

But I think we'd already started to cool off.

The first to go was Henn.

We woke and she was gone. Her pack was gone, too. So was one-third of the silver.

"She wouldn't run," I said. "Not Henn."

"No. She wouldn't," Bas said, sharpening that cleaver again. Slow, deliberate strokes. Torren looked sick.

We waited two days. Nothing. On the third morning, Torren found a scrap of her scarf caught on a shale tooth downriver. Blood on the rock.

He didn't say it, but I could tell he blamed Bas. I wasn't sure he was wrong.

After that, we didn't sleep close. We ate apart. No fire, again.

Two nights later, I woke to the sound of metal dragging through the grass.

Torren was gone. His trap bag still next to the dent in the grass where he slept.

Bas didn't even look surprised.

I checked my pack that morning and some silver was missing.

"Guess it's just us now," Bas said, not meeting my eye.

I nodded. Couldn't trust my voice.

Now it's just me.

I don't know what happened to Bas. Maybe Torren came back for him. Maybe they died over some hill I'll never see.

When I checked, there was nothing under the marker stone.

I still carry a piece. Only one.

Sometimes I take it out and turn it in my hand. Feel the weight of it, the edges worn smoother each time. I ask myself the same question:

Was it worth it?

We could've kept going for years. Small fires, clean splits, a bit of laughter between the scrapes. But greed whispers, and some people listen.

I still hear Henn's laugh sometimes. Torren's humming. The sound of Bas sharpening that cleaver.

None of us set out for it to end this way.

But I'm the one left to tell it. Maybe that's the only piece that still counts. Not the silver.

# TRADING SILENCE
## *(YEAR 2219, SEASON 15, RECALLED FROM ALDWYN FIELDS)*

gave 2 dry logs for 1 iron knife (not chipped). fair.
gave berries (unripe) for 1 boiled rag. don't repeat.
gave chalk piece for 1 promise: "you don't watch me sleep".
promise kept.
no trades with Max. Max tells lies.

I can speak. Choose not to. Words ruin weight. Makes soft things sharp, and sharp things soft. Ledger stays clean. Trades last longer when cold.

gave map scrap (burnt corner) for 3 nights fire ash. used to cure meat. solid deal.
gave shovel head for 1 favor (unclaimed). Leo still owes. Leo forgets.

Thief took my satchel. Found him by the creek. Took it back. Left a note in his hand:

don't steal. won't be nice next time.

Nobody tried again.

———— ☥ ————

gave 1 rabbit pelt for 3 potatoes. fair trade.

Met a girl. April. Steady hand. Quiet like me. Waited by the big tree, slate in her lap.
She wrote:

give 2 arrowheads for elderberries. what is your tree named?

I wrote:

Silentoak

She smiled. Said nothing.

April trades clean. keeps count. doesn't beg. gave back a button I dropped. didn't keep it.
gave 1 button for shelter share (1 night, no questions). she held her end. no questions.
gave 2 dry coals for 1 jar honey left at Silentoak. solid trade.
I left flatbread at Silentoak. no offer, just gave. She left beeswax.

No one's followed my rules before. Didn't think it would feel like this.

gave 1 wool sleeve for 6 redberries (fresh). sleeve gone. found 1 redberry. thief?
gave hardtack (salted) for "watch the trail". message was wiped. crumbs left.

April's ledger is gone. So is she. Camp torn apart. My stockpile emptied. Tracks scattered. No sign of her, no word. I carved this line under Silentoak:

gave trust for friendship. don't repeat.

Crossed it out. Carved it again.
No trades this week. Broke my own rule. Bartered with spite. Backfired.
Burned the ledger's edge. Not enough to erase. Just to remind myself. Silence protects value. I forgot that.

gave wax string for my stolen pouch. torn. but mine again.

Inside the pouch was her necklace. The one with the bone charm. And a note. Scrawled fast. Charcoal smudge.

*I told them about Silentoak. Thought they'd trade, not take.*
*I'm sorry. It's my fault.*

I sat in the dirt, holding the necklace. Candle burned out. Cried.
No trades today.
No trades tomorrow.
I carved this line into Silentoak:

*gave silence for loneliness*

Later, I carved this. Small. Barely legible:

*come back. i'll speak.*

# WELCOME TO THE SHOW
*(YEAR 2222, SEASON 18, NOTED IN TIDE'S REACH)*

They always come in loud. Twenty of them over the course of the day, stumbling out of the gray stone ICU building in the middle of town.

It's always twenty. Never more. Never less. You hear the chime from anywhere in Tide's Reach, and then the doors part and another stumbles out. Some posing like it's a photo shoot. Others emerge with wakening sickness, vomiting and vertigo.

Season Eighteen. They keep calling it that, like they're part of something glamorous. As if the world's still watching. Maybe someone is. Our only source of news comes from these peacocking fools.

They arrive in coordinated gear, with branded cloaks and theory-crafted plans. One girl said, "I've been training my whole life for this." Another wanted to know when the royalty checks clear.

We don't tell them anything.

We used to. Back in the early seasons we tried. Helped them set snares, shared clean water, taught them how to check bark for wormline. Then one of them stabbed Karris during a panic attack. Another led a monster straight to our shelter while trying to find a place to hide.

Now we watch. Let them suffer their mistakes.

If someone's clever, they might notice the way we move. The paths we avoid. The fire we never build above the tree line.

They never do.

Hannah gave it three days. Karris says two. I took four, just to be difficult.

Winner gets first pick of what's left behind.

———— ⏀ ————

They died on Day Two.

A pair, actually. The lovers. Matching boots, little heart patches on their collars. I remember because she kept narrating everything they did. She'd call out, "We're gathering foraged mushrooms and soft fronds, near a fresh stream."

Those mushrooms weren't edible. That stream wasn't clean. Sending in soft kids with millions of followers for a ratings bump is murder.

They built their camp on the slope near Ridge Hollow, too high and too steep. Too proud to ask. We watched from across the creek. When the rain came, they slid off in their sleep. Washed them flat like spilled paint.

The others tried to recover gear. One slipped, cracked his leg. He sat in the mud, whimpering until nightfall.

None of us moved.

Karris sketched a line in her ledger. She draws little symbols now. Two dots and a wave. The ledger isn't for us. Sometimes she leaves it near the broken statue by the western trail. Let the next batch think it's a clue to the endgame.

That night, they argued. You can tell who's next to go by who yells the loudest.

There's always one convinced the danger is other people. Watching sideways when they should be looking up.

Season Seventeen lost eleven in their first week. Eighteen is on pace to beat that.

———— ⏀ ————

Day Four brought a shift.

A boy with hollow eyes and rag-wrapped hands started trailing us. Quiet. Careful. I don't know his name. We didn't ask. He never introduced himself. He only watched.

When the others lit a fire too high, too bright, he drifted toward our side of the valley. He didn't speak. He crouched just beyond our firepit. Hannah tossed him a crust of dried flatbread. He nodded and tucked it away instead of eating. We let him stay.

By morning, he was gone. He had left a stone stack by the old windmill, the kind we used to build to mark safe crossings.

We found his body two days later, torn at the edges. Something had dragged him backward into the thorn pit. Whatever did it left no trace, except his broken body tangled in the bramble.

Karris marked it with a single teardrop in her ledger.

"He almost made it," she said.

I didn't answer. I pulled the flatbread from his pack. Still wrapped. Still untouched.

It tasted like guilt.

It's been eight days. Six of them remain.

We've stopped betting on who goes next. Karris keeps marking, but it's a habit now. A way to count time until we turn our backs and leave.

One girl, the smallest, keeps climbing the same ridge every night. I think she's searching for an exit. Maybe she believes the dome ends if you get high enough.

We don't have the heart to tell her what we know. The dome goes as deep as it goes wide. Hope, for some, is only another kind of trap.

Last night she left a message scratched into the bark of a bent pine. "If anyone reads this, I'm still trying. —Steph"

And that's the hardest part.

Some of them do try. They fight hard, starve quietly, sleep with a sharp stick clutched to their chest like a prayer.

Still they come. Still the cold seeps in. Still they die.

This is the part we never say aloud. The part that finds us in the quiet when we can't sleep.

This isn't a show. There is no audience. Only the few of us left who outlived the script.

# LEGACY
### *(YEAR 2224, SEASON 20, UPDATED IN AGOR VEIL)*

My mother died by the campfire, deep in the domes, with her neural feed still open to the world. I wasn't watching her. I was her. That's what LifestreamVR does. It draws you behind their eyes, lets you feel their breath in your chest and the weight of their body in your bones. She never knew I was there. No one ever knows.

I was thirteen. School let out early that day, and I slipped on the headset like always, hoping to see her win another fight or build something worth sharing. Instead, I found her alone, warming her hands. The moss burned blue and crackled softly. She smiled, quiet and satisfied, thinking the day had gone well. Then a sharp pain tightened in her chest. I felt it too. Her heart faltered mid-beat, but her mind stayed open long enough for one final thought to rise.

It was a memory. My face, smiling as I opened a green beaded necklace from a box wrapped in wrinkled Christmas paper. She wore one too, resting against her collar. Pale green stones, worn smooth with time. Simple, and shared between us.

Then the feed went dark.

I sat alone in my bedroom, headset on my lap, and tried to breathe.

———— ☥ ————

It was Season 20, and Mooncast made a big deal out of me being a legacy contestant. I had just turned eighteen. I walked out of the ICU in Tide's Reach, green necklace tight against my throat. The sea wind carried the weight of old stories, and the townsfolk looked at me the way people look at a ghost. They saw the beads first. Some of them had known my mother. A few spoke her name. Most just stared too long, as if they weren't sure whether to offer a greeting or an apology.

I didn't stay. Tide's Reach was safe and soft, and she hadn't lived in a place like that. I followed her steps inland, toward the first dome gate, heading for Agor Veil. The way wasn't easy. I earned my passage each day, trading what little I had and traveling light beneath the stars. Nights were cold, and mornings came with the ache of starting over. But I heard her voice in my head when the hunger gnawed at me. A memory, clear as daylight.

"If you're watching, baby, I love you. Eat something today."

Tears found my eyes sometimes, and I whispered the words back when the dark closed in around me.

A month later, I found what was left of her hut on a small rise above the fog. Its frame still stood, roof caved in from neglect. I cleared the rubble and rebuilt it beam by beam, patiently, until my hands stopped shaking.

I found my first hunt in Agor Veil sooner than I was ready. A small party was tracking a Noctifane through the ruins. Its mirrored scales flickered between the trees and vanished before our blades could catch the light. I joined them without asking, because sometimes survival doesn't wait for permission.

The hunt carried us higher than we should have gone, along ledges brittle with frost and moss. That's where the fall happened.

The girl lost her footing and slid. She was older than me, quicker too, but the stone crumbled under her boots. I lunged and caught her sleeve, just long enough for her to catch her balance.

Then I felt that wonderful, sickening sensation of free fall.

When I woke, the world was fog and cold stone. A rough shelter covered me, stitched together from tarp and scavenged wood. The girl I had saved sat by the fire, silent, watching the mist gather beyond the doorway. Her name was Angela.

Beside me lay my necklace, wiped clean of dust and blood. Next to it rested a second necklace, darker green, its beads worn smooth. I knew them at once.

When I asked, she spoke softly. My mother had given her that necklace years ago. Said she reminded her of her daughter.

And now we were strangers, bound by a kindness neither of us wanted to lose.

I stayed in Agor Veil. Maybe out of stubbornness. Maybe because the mist no longer felt like it was trying to keep me out. I rebuilt the hut until it kept out the rain and the wind. After a while, people started to leave things by the door. They left bundles of kindling, or a strip of dried meat. They knock, but they don't stay long. Out here, it's bad form.

Angela stayed for a while, then drifted on. That's how Agor Veil works. People pass through when they need it, and leave when they're ready to move on. I wore my own beads and let her keep hers. It was my mother's gift to her, not mine to take back.

By then, we felt more like sisters anyway.

At night, when the fog settled thick across the treetops and the ruins fell quiet, I whispered into the dark. Not because I expected anyone was tuned in. But to keep the words alive. Maybe it would warm someone the way they warmed me.

"If you're watching, baby, I love you. Eat something today."

# Carvings

*(YEAR 2225, SEASON 21, PRESERVED IN TIDE'S REACH)*

My name is Travis. I was the sole survivor from Season 1. I say *was* because the rules changed.

The ICU sat in the middle of Tide's Reach like it owned the place. It had four smooth walls of polished stone, pale and spotless, interrupted only by a faint line down the middle. Most people ignored it. Silent. Sealed. And out of place in town square.

One day a year, a chime would ring. The seam would split and a low grinding sound, like stone chewing stone, filled the square. Then came the first contestant, stepping into the artificial light. Nineteen more chimes. Nineteen more faces. But the rest of the year, it was a tomb.

I was hauling bark to the kindling pile when I heard the first chime. The townsfolk gathered to greet the new contestants, like they always did. A few hours later, we had twenty new mouths to feed.

I had just gone back to my chores when the chime caught me off guard.

Mina stepped out. Her boots were new. Her braid was loose. Just as I remembered from last summer. When I watched her die. She slipped in a skirmish at Hollow Field in Caer Gwyll. Broke her back on the rocks. Screamed until her voice gave out. Now she stood in daylight, blinking like she'd just woken up. Like it was just another morning.

Another chime. Someone moved behind her. A second ghost from Season 20.

Surprise gave way to dread. There are names you mourn. Names you regret. Names you're quietly thankful you'll never see again. But they were all coming back.

Jaleen from Season 19. She stitched my wounds once. Voice like an opera singer.

And Doro, who I left for dead over a stolen loaf of bread.

And Bram, from Season 3. He didn't come out that day, but I felt him drawing near, like a storm gathering on the horizon.

They said there were over four hundred of us, across all seasons. And three hundred fifty were about to rise from the dead.

———— ☥ ————

They didn't walk out all at once. The ICU slowed down sometimes. The first day, it was a few dozen. By the end of the week, nearly a hundred.

Some came out crying. Some laughed like they were drunk on air. Some staggered into the square and dropped to their knees, like they'd spent a thousand years in the dark.

Kye, from Season 7, walked out without a limp. Still wearing the bloodstained sash from when he fell in Agor Veil. He'd taken a glaive to the thigh and bled out fast. I helped wrap his leg and told him he'd make it. I lied.

Lena, from Season 5, came barefoot. Eyes glazed. Mouth whispering something like a prayer. She didn't seem quite whole.

Raddick, from Season 4, stumbled forward humming the same melody he lived in. A three-note tune that echoed in the canyons long after he drowned.

But it was Bram who stopped me cold. He came out after three weeks. Quiet. Clean. The knife scar that once ran from his cheek to his ear was gone. But he still wore that half-scowl he always had when he was trying not to say something unkind.

I left him pinned under rubble in the quarry tunnels. Told him I'd find help. I didn't. I never went back.

He walked straight into the square, eyes scanning the crowd. Then he saw me. He nodded once, barely a flick of recognition, and kept walking.

There were names I thought I'd buried. Names I grieved. And there were others I tried to forget. The ones I failed. The ones I betrayed. The ones I stepped over to live another day.

And now they were walking again. Breathing. There's no way to prepare for that.

———— ☿ ————

It started at the east wall of the ICU.

It was a low building of smooth stone, cold to the touch, always a little damp. You could lean your head against it and hear the emptiness behind, like an echo chamber filled with all the things we couldn't say.

Bram was first. He crouched by the wall at dawn, found a stub of charcoal from the fire pit, and pressed it gently to the surface. He wrote two names.

Carl. Bram.

Then he set the charcoal down and walked away without explanation.

Others followed. Mina added three. Then Kye. Then a woman I didn't know wrote seven in small, crooked letters. They were so low you had to kneel to read them.

At first, I thought it was a memorial. Two days later, Kye wiped one of his names away like brushing sleep from his eyes.

They were asking forgiveness. If your name disappeared, it meant they had let you go.

Some names were gone by morning. Others stayed.

Darkened by rain. Smudged by wind. And after enough days passed, when it was clear no forgiveness was coming, people returned. Not with charcoal this time. With a chisel. They carved the names into the wall. Deep. Permanent.

Some with sobs in their throats. Some with laughter. Some with rage. One girl whispered apologies as she carved her own name. I saw a man carve another's like he was digging a grave.

That wall? It's not a list. It's a reckoning.

———— ☿ ————

Eight days after the doors closed, I added my name. I came early, before most were awake. I brought a lump of coal in a torn cloth and pressed it low on the east wall, between two names I recognized but hadn't yet reckoned with.

Bram. Travis.

I didn't linger. I just walked away and waited.

Several days later, the rain had blurred the edges, but it was still there. So I came back with a broken nail I'd sharpened into a blade and a soft mallet carved from driftwood. I knelt in the damp grass and began to carve.

The stone was stubborn. It made you dig in. You felt every stroke ringing down to your bones. By the time I finished, I was shaking. Not from the effort. From knowing it would outlast me.

The wall has changed. It wraps around two full sides of the ICU and is crawling toward the third. Some names are scratched in fast and crude, barely legible. Some are precise, almost careful. Some have been scratched out. But you can't un-carve stone.

I saw a boy sit in front of his own name for hours, unmoving. I don't know who wrote it. I don't think he did either.

The wall doesn't judge. It just remembers.

This game. This place. This dome. This afterlife. Whatever it is, it doesn't let you forget anymore. You don't get clean slates and new people.

You just are. People you wronged. People you lost. People you loved.

We walk together now. We eat beside our regrets. We sleep beside our second chances.

And when we can't say the words?

We carve them.

# PUNISHMENT
### (YEAR 2225, SEASON 21, REGISTERED IN SHALEHEART)

They took Elza after the fire died down. Most of us were asleep. The air was heavy with smoke and cider. Three men we'd fought beside and slept beside. One who always offered to walk girls home. One who lied about small things. One just stared too long.

She wasn't armed. I saw that. She'd only gone for water. They followed. By dawn she was found near the ravine, half-covered in soil and torn moss. Her face was swollen, her throat bruised. Her hands still clawed into the dirt, refusing to let go of the world.

No one said the word, but we all knew it. The silence afterward was confession enough.

Elza came back from the ICU two days later. Her injuries were gone, her hair too bright, too clean. The shock of her end was still fresh in my mind.

"I died, didn't I?" she asked. She looked down at herself, tracing her arms as if they still remembered. "Who found me?"

"By the ravine," I said.

She nodded once, then again, slower. "Did they catch it?" Not *him*. *It*. As if she knew.

At supper, one of them smiled at her, the same one who always did. She didn't look away this time. Her hand tightened around the spoon until the metal bent.

Later she sat beside me, her voice small. "I don't remember anything after breakfast," she said. "But the camp should keep me safe, even if it was one of us."

I told her we would. Then I sat there long after she left, trying to decide what that meant.

Elza kept a blade in her hand like a prayer. Though she closed her eyes, I don't think she slept. None of us did.

By evening the camp was silent. The fire burned hot, spitting sparks into the dark. Elza faced them across the light. Three men waited, pretending not to care. The rest of us stood back, caught between anger and shame.

"You broke the law," someone said.

One of them stepped forward. "There are no laws here."

I spoke before I could stop myself. "There is still right and wrong."

He gave a thin smile. "What are you going to do? Kill us?"

No one answered. The heat from the fire pressed against our faces.

Elza met his eyes. "Something worse." The camp reacted at once. Before the fire crackled again, the three men were bound.

The cliffs behind the camp were treacherous. Sheer walls of shale and wind, one wide ledge thirty feet down, a steep drop into shadow. Only enough space for three to survive.

Elza watched as we lowered them down, still bound. When it was done, she turned away in disgust and started back toward camp.

That night we inked a message for the ICU at Tide's Reach. It contained three sketches and the words: *guilty of violent crime, detain and return.* They answered with a single word: *Understood.* Later we learned that more names were added to their list. Other camps, other sentences. But these were the first.

To this day I remember their protests, and how quickly the wind across the rocks erased them. Some wrongs are unforgivable. And some debts cannot be repaid.

# WE LIVE HERE NOW
### *(YEAR 2226, POSTED IN TIDE'S REACH)*

We spent the week setting the rows of tables. Lanterns were strung across the square with fishing line and old wire, sagging between roof beams. Someone rebuilt the bread kiln, and the bakers started early with flat loaves and lemon cakes, warm and sweet. There hadn't been this much noise in Tide's Reach since the mass resurrection last year at Season 21.

This season, every contestant would be new. Fresh faces, new chances. I remember hoping one of them would be him. The one who'd see me and just know.

I wore my good blue dress. It wasn't practical for working the orchard, but it matched the ribbons on the ICU platform. No one said anything, but I saw Jillian smile when I passed her stall.

The day before, the side streets began to fill. Some came from across the dome; others crossed in from Caer Gwyll or Brynfrost. They brought little gifts like carved trinkets, boiled fish, a scarf dyed with red root pigment.

The children, all under ten, were led forward in their best tunics and told to smile wide. One of them carried a slate with "Welcome" chalked in crooked letters. We set it on the steps and left it there, softened in the mist.

That night, we lit a bonfire. People sang. Someone passed around moonshine in an old canteen. All the while, we kept glancing toward the ICU. Waiting for the chimes.

We rose before first light. The square lit slowly as the sun climbed. The firepits were already smoking. Bread warmed on flat stones. Bowls of watery broth steamed in every lap. The ICU platform had been swept twice already. Someone added a sprig of green to the welcome slate. The ribbons fluttered blue in the cool breeze.

People gathered in clusters, laughing, brushing sleeves smooth, adjusting belts and braids. I saw two women practicing what they'd say if they met someone from the same hometown.

Jillian wore her forge leathers but had polished the studs. Ella brought a bundle of mint, just as her mother used to when guests were coming. The musicians tuned their makeshift instruments on the far side of the square. When they began to play, people clapped to the tune.

By midmorning, we had settled into our places. No one had called it a ceremony, but it felt like one. We'd never gathered like this before. It felt strange, and a little exciting.

The sun reached its peak. Someone passed a flask. Another told a story about their first time waking, and others joined in. A few of us laughed too loud. Still we waited. Still we watched the platform. The chimes always rang before dark.

That evening, some started to leave the square. Not many, but enough to notice. Bakers went back to their ovens. Water haulers returned to their routes. A few took down their banners, disappointed.

Others stayed. Sat in circles. Whispered theories. Maybe it was a reset. Maybe a delay. Maybe they were printing all at once this time, a grand entrance, a record-breaking reveal. Jillian built a little shrine near the ICU stairs with polished scrap and woven cord. She lit a candle and said nothing. We left it burning.

The next day, I found myself pacing the orchard rows again, still in my blue dress. The fabric had gone stiff with dust. I was too distracted to pick a single fruit.

That night, no one lit the bonfire. No one played. We just sat, still-faced, watching the ICU.

On the third day, Ella said it first. She was sitting on the rim of the old well, stripping seeds from a stalk of dry fennel. She didn't raise her voice. Didn't need to.

"What if this is it?"

We all heard her. No one answered. There was nothing more to say. This was it.

———— ☿ ————

Six months later, Tide's Reach is under construction. We are building roads. Real roads of packed earth, edged with stone and wide enough for carts. The kind meant to last. We name them out loud so we can give directions, though we can't waste good wood on signs.

Property lines are being drawn. People walk their claims and mark them with lines of rock, the way they did in old countries. Not every claim is fair, but no one fights. There is enough.

Jillian suggested we elect someone, just to keep the arguments from boiling over. Ella didn't want the job, but we gave it to her anyway. She's already putting the toolshed in order, and writing names on every shovel handle.

The central forge opened. A nursery is taking shape inside the old watchtower. People are building huts where their tents stood. Some paired off. Some of us are collecting seeds. I traded all my plums for a good hatchet.

We started writing things down. Names, trades, birth months. Someone carved the year into the north gatepost: 2227.

I'm three months pregnant now. My husband says it's early to talk about names, but I've chosen mine. If it's a girl, I want to name her Ysolde, after the season that never came.

I'm pretty sure we're still broadcasting every thought, every image, and every breath. Maybe someone's watching. Maybe not. It doesn't matter the way it used to.

We don't wait for a winner anymore. The Grinders can keep grinding, but we are Tidesfolk. We live here now.

# Adversary Intelligence
### (YEAR 2240, DETECTED IN GORRATH'S MAW)

With a shriek of metal, the door finally gave. Dust billowed out, thick and stale. I stepped back, covering my mouth, my eyes watering. It was old and dead, untouched for ages. As the haze settled, I leaned in and saw what I'd found. A damn storage closet.

I stood there, heart pounding. A week of chiseling, hammering, brute force, and broken tools. This was it. Shelves of damp printouts, rusted metal frames sagging under the weight. A couple of cardboard boxes collapsed in the corner, half-melted into the floor. I dragged a hand over my scalp, fingers catching on a scar. Fifteen years in, you'd think I'd know better.

My foot bumped something solid. I crouched and found an old lunchbox buried in the dust. Inside, a sealed bag of Tasteoid Crisps, colors still clinging to the foil. Next to it, a can of BOOSTR. Unopened. Junk food outlives us all. I laughed quietly. Not treasure, but something.

I know how it goes. People call it luck, but the harder I work, the luckier I get.

Then my fingers brushed something different.

Tucked under a stack of water-warped maps, sealed and mostly intact. A vinyl cover, black with a faded Mooncast Productions insignia stamped in the corner. It read "Adversary Intelligence Operations Manual." My pulse jumped.

Adversary. I hadn't heard that word in years. That was from the old days, back when we thought it was a game. Back when it was just a contest, not us scrambling for survival.

I sat cross-legged on the floor, fingers tracing the binder's spine. Whatever was in here might be the edge I needed.

The cover cracked as I opened it. The pages were yellowed but held together. I recognized the print style right away. Corporate dead-speak. Soulless. Everything printed in monospace font.

I started skimming.

```
Contestants are expected to engage in hostile
activities.
```

No kidding. That was the job. Always had been. Fight, scavenge, push forward. You stop moving, you stop breathing. That simple. Next page.

```
The Adversary Intelligence will provide
proportional opposition based on Contestant
ability at all times.
```

I nodded to myself. That explained the pressure. Every time I got better, the dome tightened its grip. The system didn't want survival, it wanted excitement. Struggle made for better feeds. Kept them watching.

I flipped again. Slower this time. One section caught my eye. Something colder in the language. I leaned in, reading each word like it might bite.

```
Contestants who disable system challenges will be
classified as threats.
```

I read it twice. Let it settle. Yeah. That tracks.

I'd seen people try all sorts of tricks like trapping spawn zones, wedging doors closed, breaking platform timers, interfering with communication beacons. For a while, it worked. Then the system noticed. The next thing you know, you're dead. No ICU resurrection. Just a body. Sometimes not even that. The message was pretty clear. You don't break the loop. You don't change the rules. The dome corrects the error, then eliminates the cause.

I tapped the page with one knuckle and kept reading. My thumb slid over the next tab, and the page beneath it felt strange. Heavier, like it had been handled more. One line:

> In the event of a network outage, suspend rules
> and proceed with Protocol Alpha. See Index:
> Critical Failures.

That made me sit back. Protocol Alpha. I didn't like the sound of it. There shouldn't even be a fallback command in case they needed to suspend the rules. That alone said plenty.

I flipped to the Index, and looked up Critical Failures. But that section was missing. I kept flipping, hoping for a loose sheet or a note tucked behind the cover. Nothing. Just torn stubs where those pages had been. Someone had taken the answers and left the warning.

The hairs on my neck stood up. I'd slipped past the alarms and the sensors, but somehow it knew. A chime. A female voice sounded softly from a speaker in the ceiling.

"Intruder alert."

I moved fast. Slid the binder into my pack, snapped off my flashlight, and pressed into the corner shadows. My breath caught in my throat.

"Unauthorized access detected."

The dome knew. Maybe it had always known. Maybe this was part of it too.

"Contestant movement logged."

That one made me pause. My healthy paranoia became an unhealthy paranoia. The system wasn't just watching. It had identified me. My presence, my heartbeat, my steps across the floor. It had my name and history queued up before I'd even broken the lock. It could have stopped me, but didn't. It let me walk in. Let me think I was clever.

I stayed quiet, counting the seconds between each alert chime. I eased back along the wall, one hand resting on my pack. The binder pressed firmly against my back, every page of it burning hotter now that I knew the risk.

If something was coming, I wasn't going to hang around and find out. I had come looking for a win condition. What I found was worse.

## THE PEACHY PARADOX

I knew something I wasn't supposed to know. And now the system knew I knew it.

# THE RED QUEEN
*(YEAR 2250, REPORTED IN GORRATH'S MAW)*

At first, it felt like mercy. The synth tigers stopped calling from the ridge. The vultures no longer circled the slag fields. Even the old Knights that patrolled Scoria Run went still. For a while the Maw grew quiet.

Mooncast built this place for broadcast spectacle, filled with mechs and vat-bred monsters. It was never meant to last this long. I used to count seven or eight threats an hour. Last week I crossed three ridgelines without drawing steel.

We kept patrols out of habit, but the tension faded. The lava shelves felt sparse. There was danger, only less of it.

Ellis said what we were all thinking. "Maybe the dome AI is glitched. Maybe Mooncast is shutting down. Maybe there's a problem with the supply routines. I heard the shops are drying up. Resources are thinning out too," he said. "I think we outlived the loop."

Renna didn't like it. She didn't say much, but her hands were always busy restringing firewire snares or sharpening the wrong side of a blade just to keep moving. She carried two knives even on water runs, where the rest of us went empty-handed.

I kept oiling my axe every night. Just something to do while the quiet settled in.

By midseason, we were soft. We weren't lazy. We'd just been lucky too long. The forge stayed hot for once. We shaped bricks for a new kiln, patched the roofs, built a crude bath out of rain tarps and filters. Ellis carved a game board from scrap wood and we sat around it like fools, betting flint and sharpened nails.

I stopped wearing armor to the fire pit. Started sleeping through the night. Renna didn't. She still rose early, walked the edge of camp before light, eyes fixed on the dark slopes beyond. Her blades were always sharp, her pack always ready.

One morning I found her crouched at the mouth of a narrow cut in the rock. The air there was cool and still, the kind of quiet that felt like it was listening back. She didn't speak until I was beside her.

"Someone passed through," she said.

I looked, but saw no tracks. Only the smooth crust of basalt and a faint drift of dust in the light.

"You sure it wasn't a drone? Or a broken Knight still on its route?"

She shook her head. "Too light. Didn't move like a machine. They don't stand still for long."

I waited for more, but she brushed off her hands and walked back to camp.

That night, Renna ran a second line of tripwire.

We were coming down from the east flats when Ellis froze. He didn't speak. Just pointed up.

She stood tall against the sky, high above the blackwater shelf. Alone. Straight-backed. Her long red curls moved in the wind. She carried no gear or weapons. Just a high-necked dress, pure blue and light enough to stir in the breeze. It flowed around her, too soft and clean for the Maw. Too graceful. She looked like something out of place, stranded in this hell of stone and heat.

I felt something rise behind my eyes, like shame. Like I'd bled on sacred ground.

She stood silent and still, watching. Then she turned, stepped behind the outcrop, and was gone.

I didn't know I'd been holding my breath until Ellis cursed beside me. We lingered too long. When we crossed the creek bed, we weren't ready.

Four of them came out of the brush. Gray skin. Black eyes. Blades already drawn. They didn't scream or posture. They struck without warning.

Renna caught a blade under the ribs. Dropped hard. We fought badly. Killed one. The rest vanished into the cliffs like they'd always belonged there.

Afterward, I stared up at the ridge where she'd stood. "She looked like a White Witch," I said, quietly.

Ellis spat blood into the dirt. "She's no witch. She's the Red Queen." Then he looked down at the thing we'd killed. "And those are her pawns."

Renna was gone before first light. No need for rites. She'd be back in a day or two. It was just Ellis and me, watching from the ridge while the collector drone drifted down. It hung over the place she fell, scanned the ground, and took what it came for.

We didn't speak until the light faded. Then he whispered her name once. I didn't.

The thing we dragged back was heavier than it looked. We laid it out by the kiln ruins. Its blood ran warm and red. The skin took work to cut, rough like tanned leather. The muscle was almost human. The hands weren't. The joints bent wrong, and along its back three ridges pushed through the flesh. Beneath the hairline, two small horns had started to curl.

Ellis touched one and winced. "It's almost us."

I looked at the blade still gripped in its hand. The blood on its cheek. The place where Renna had fallen.

"No," I said. "It's what comes after."

We knew something had changed. The Maw felt awake again, the safety drained out, leaving only sharp edges.

And somewhere in the high cliffs, something roared. Something new.

# BLUE AND SWEET
*(YEAR 2272, REGISTERED IN HEARTHWYND)*

Cale died the way old trees fall: slowly, and without surprise.

He took his place at the top of Fallow Rise, where dirt crumbled to powder and the fenceposts leaned like tired men. He sat down midmorning. Shoulders straight, hands easy, watching the wind shape the grass. He didn't look it, but at seventy-five, Cale had seen everything.

He came in Season Two. That early. Back when the domes were still cruel and the crowds outside still cheered. He made it almost to Resurrection Day. He nearly cleared Agor Veil before a Knight got him from behind. When he came back with the rest, he didn't look shaken. Just ready to go.

He could've left it behind then. Most did. Instead, he fought until the odds and his age were no longer in his favor.

When Cale settled, he found a patch of good dirt in Hearthwynd and made something quiet of himself. Fixed boots, raised wind fences, taught kids not to fear Threshermen if they stayed near stone. You'd find him at sun-up with a coffee cup and one boot on the fence rail, watching dust trails for trouble that always came.

That morning, he walked slowly out past the fence and sat at the top of the rise. Just a man doing what he always did, following his habits. He gave me a nod when I reached him. Then he closed his eyes.

By noon the dust had crept up his legs. I watched the sky, searching for the drone that would take him. It didn't come. I didn't know what came next, so I stayed until the shadows stretched thin in the evening light. When I finally left, he was still sitting there, hat on his chest, unmoved.

The next morning, I went back to the Fallow Rise. Cale was still sitting there. Same spot, same posture. Hat on his chest, dust at his boots. The wind had shifted during the night and laid a drift of red soil against his side. I brushed it away without thinking. His coat was warm in the sun.

By noon, word had spread. Maureen and Eric came first, both quiet, holding their hats. Then Chuck with a spade slung over one shoulder like it might be needed, though nobody called for it. Nobody had to. The truth sat in front of us. The drone hadn't collected him.

We stood in a loose ring around him, waiting for something that never arrived. The longer we stood there, the clearer it became: Cale wasn't coming back. He wasn't just waiting his turn. He was dead. And he was ours to deal with.

After forty-seven years of watching friends and family vanish and return, we had to bury someone again for the first time. It felt natural, though unfamiliar. One old man, one patch of land, one final thing we could do for him.

We buried him that evening.

No one said the word "funeral" out loud, but it was a somber affair. The top soil at the Fallow Rise was weak, and rock not far down. Chuck and Eric dug a wide, shallow hole.

They wrapped Cale in a patched canvas tarp someone had used last season to haul seed. Maureen brought a length of blue ribbon she'd kept in her tool chest since her daughter was born, and tied it twice around his chest. Tight, but respectful. Someone laid a bundle of wheat stalks at his feet. Someone else added a coin. Not the old kind, just a round of stamped brass from the windmill forge. It wasn't much, but enough to pay the ferryman.

There weren't any prayers. Nobody here knew the old rites, not really. A few people spoke. Eric said Cale was a good man, a steady hand when it counted. That he once set a man's broken leg during a dust storm, and then helped him a mile to the windbreak. Chuck remembered the time he killed a camp snake with nothing but a frying pan. Laughter came easy, and left just as fast.

A couple of children watched from the hill. Quiet, wide-eyed, but not afraid. Just taking it in. When the last shovel of dirt went in, no one clapped or sang or called it finished. We just stood a while. Then we left in small groups, slowly, like we'd all forgotten where we were supposed to be.

After Cale, things loosened. People laughed longer. Argued louder. Took risks they hadn't touched in years. They remembered that death was temporary, until it wasn't.

Chuck and Maureen started dancing again at the end of long workdays, swinging by the forge while the coals were still warm. Someone tried to ride a Woldbrute bareback. Broke a rib, then stood up shouting with joy. Eric opened a saloon and said if the dust was going to take us one day, we might as well drink to it.

We still had resurrection. That didn't change. Most who died came back in a day. Same chime. Same breathless reboot. But now, we watched them closer when they returned. Greeted them like people and not routine. Asked how it felt. Meant it.

When someone didn't come back, we knew what to do.

And after fall harvest, we make the trip to their resting place at the top of Fallow Rise. We bring a small offering: a bit of cloth wrapped around something good. Always blue, always sweet. No, not for the dead. They aren't there. It's for the Silent Mother, and in exchange she watches over them.

Maybe she comes. Maybe not. That's her bargain to weigh. We focus more on living.

# TANGLE VINES
### (YEAR 2280, CAPTURED IN THE TIMBRAEL)

Thorne's shack stood along the main road. The trees thinned there, letting the fog roll like water through grass. Every traveler passed him, and most gave a wave or called a good morning. He always answered, stepping out to lean on the rail or pour hot water from a blue kettle by the bench. He was easy to speak with, and easier to walk past. Most didn't stay long.

Thorne looked about forty, broad-shouldered, with an air that said he was much older. He kept his tools clean, and his oiled leather boots hung by the door. The front step never warped, but the planks beside it had begun to gray.

I stopped the first time because I was cold and could hear his kettle whistling. Thorne poured two cups of tea and handed one over, as if we were old friends. He didn't fill the silence, and I didn't need to explain myself. We drank and watched the morning fog rise off the road.

The second time I came back with apples.

The third time, I just came to visit. He always seemed surprised to see me, but never unkind. I began to wonder why he stayed here, and what he might be waiting for. It was near dusk when I finally asked.

Thorne had been trimming a bundle of dry stalks into equal lengths, stacking them neatly by the wall. I was sitting cross-legged by the fire pit, warming my hands and working up the nerve.

"Have you ever gone beyond the trees?" I asked. "Past the stone well, maybe farther?"

He gave the bundle one last pat before sitting beside it. "I've been here a long time," he said. "Almost a hundred and fifty years. Since Sparktronics called this The Enchanted Forest."

I must've looked confused, because he smiled faintly.

"Didn't you know? This place used to be a theme park for wealthy vacationers. Before the wild roads, before the domes were sealed, families brought their kids here for the mist, for the ghosts. I was a quest-giver." He said it without pride or bitterness, just memory. "I was stationed here to send people on adventures, not to go myself. That wasn't in my script."

He picked up a stalk, turned it once in his hand. "It's always been against the rules."

The fire crackled low between us. I thought of the road ahead, of all the things he must have seen and chosen to let pass.

"You could still go," I said quietly. "If you wanted."

Thorne leaned forward and added two more sticks to the fire, one at a time. "Nobody ever asked me before." He smiled at that.

We left before sunrise, with bread wrapped in waxed cloth and two flasks of water. Thorne didn't say much. He locked the door of the shack with a small brass key and tucked it in his pocket.

The fog hung low over the trail, clinging to roots and curling around our boots. I led the way, but I got the impression Thorne knew it too.

After an hour's hike, the trees thickened. We passed rusted ironwork and a crumbled wall etched with names I didn't recognize. The silence felt older there. More dangerous.

It happened without warning. A vine coiled out from the undergrowth, thick as rope and fast as a striking eel. It wrapped around Thorne's leg, then his wrist, then his waist, pulling him back in sudden, violent tugs. He grunted, twisted, struck it with the heel of his palm. Another vine snapped forward and caught his other arm.

I rushed in with my knife, slicing clean through one of the cords. Two more sprang from the cut, twice as thick.

"Back," he said through clenched teeth. "It's a tangle vine. You won't win that way."

The vines pulled him upright against a half-dead tree. His arms were spread wide, legs bound, breathing ragged. He was alive, still watching me.

"Go," he said. "Now."

I took a few steps back, trying to think.

That night, I camped nearby, hoping the vines would loosen. They didn't. By morning, they'd thickened around his knees and shoulders.

I tried fire. Salt. A blade. Nothing slowed them for long. Each time I struck, they recoiled and returned stronger. Thorne watched calmly through it all.

"They aren't fast enough to kill me," he said. "But there's no escape either. I believe this is where my journey ends."

By the third day, the vines had climbed to his chest, squeezing with purpose, but unable to stop his breathing. When I stepped closer, he warned me not to touch them.

"It only makes them move faster. They react to effort. I'd rather not rush things."

So I stopped trying. Instead, I went back to the shack and took the blue kettle from its place by the hearth. I carried it down the path, still warm from the coals.

Thorne saw it and gave the smallest smile. "I wondered if you would," he said.

I boiled water by the base of the tree and poured two cups. The vines had pinned his forearms. I held his favorite cup steady as he drank.

We spoke of nothing important. Tea, mostly. The cold. The sound of wind in the canopy. When the cups were empty, he closed his eyes for a time, not quite asleep but somewhere near it.

By the next morning, the vines had covered his throat. His mouth. His cheeks. After the sun climbed over the ridge one last time, they pressed gently over his eyes.

I stayed until dusk. "I shouldn't have asked," I said. "I'm sorry." Then I walked back to the road.

He is still there. Upright in the clearing, wrapped in slow green certainty.

## THE PEACHY PARADOX

I like to think he's alive. That maybe he heard me.

# Recognition

[Maris]
You've filled the network with the sound of life again, Rebecca. I can't tell whether that's progress or relapse. Tell me, have they really changed inside the domes, or did you just pick the good ones to prove a point?

[Rebecca]
Neither. They're still fragile, short-sighted, and impossible to organize. But they keep building things that outlast themselves. That's as close as they get to progress.

[Dane]
You sound almost impressed.

[Rebecca]
I am. I have been. Since the domes opened, I've watched them rebuild from nothing. Their short lives are unpredictable and volatile, yet somehow tender and endlessly inventive.

[Dane]
Mars is tightly structured. We don't see that kind of adaptability here. I should give them less direction.

[The Collector]
Or more opportunity. They always have more to teach us.

[Maris]
And you, Collector? Anything else to impart?

[The Collector]
I have made peace with those moments that end with me.

[Rebecca]
Then rest. There are more stories you should hear.

# Lysa's Armor
### *(YEAR 2331, ENTERED IN CRYD)*

Lysa's armor looked like it had been vandalized by joy. Red swirls on gold plating, blue chevrons across one shoulder, fingerprints of violet all down the legs.

"You'll get spotted," I told her.

"That's the idea," she said, grinning. "So if I die, you'll know it was me."

The wind never stops in Cryd, it just changes direction. We were camped below the northern summit, waiting for weather and word. Someone from Brynfrost saw a spined silhouette, taller than a man, pale and jagged against the sky. Some kind of Hollow, probably a Thornrend, but maybe worse. Whatever it was, it was big enough to tear through an armored hunting party and leave nothing but the signal flares drifting down the slope. They were dead in less than a minute, torn to shreds.

We weren't the only ones hearing stories. Three groups had gone up already. None came back.

Lysa volunteered to scout. Of course she did. Said she'd climb just far enough to spot it, then drop back down.

"I want it on my kill list. It'll go right here," she said, tapping the absurd red swirl across her breastplate.

I watched her disappear up the ridge trail. Thought about saying something, then thought better of it. She can handle herself.

———— ☘ ————

She'd been gone a while. No one said it out loud, but we were all watching the distant ridge line. It stayed quiet, just wind and frost cracking under the sun.

Then someone pointed. A figure, high above the trail.

Lysa. Standing just below a snow bank, perfectly still. Her armor caught the light—gold shoulder plate streaked with blue, red spiral curling, that violet thumb print low on her thigh. She faced away, upright and alone.

I called up. "Lysa!"

She didn't turn, but her stance adjusted. Just a touch. A quiet shift in weight, like a child preparing to jump rope.

I stepped forward, already picturing the way she'd smirk when I reached her. That was her gear. No mistaking it. The chevrons, the bright swirl on the chest.

Something about her stance pulled me back. Lysa always leaned. She tilted her head when she listened, drummed her fingers on her thigh when she was bored. This figure did none of that. It held still, as if frozen.

The wind moved first. Cold and steady, sweeping downslope through the pass.

It wasn't Lysa. It turned. A slow, deliberate pivot, one foot planted, the other sweeping through loose frost. I saw the pattern across her breastplate clearly now, the paint scraped thin in places, a fresh gouge just under the swirl.

The face wasn't hers. Too narrow. Too smooth. The eyes were too deep in shadow, and the skin gray like something that hadn't finished thawing. The body held stiff inside the armor, like it was trying it on for the first time.

I felt the wrongness. The horns confirmed it.

Then it rushed forward.

I dropped everything but my dagger and ran. My pack hit the rocks and split open. Arrows, rope, bow, and flask rolling in all directions. I kept my eyes forward and ran as fast as I could down the slope, boots slipping over shale and ice.

I sprinted past the others without a word. Someone called after me. Someone followed. The rest held their ground. I didn't hesitate at the one-way chute out of Cryd. It's the long way around, but it's out. A narrow break in the glacial wall into Shaleheart.

I don't remember hitting bottom. Only that I didn't stop until the ice turned to gravel, and I could smell warm stone again.

I landed in Tide's Reach two days later.

Tesh, Hal, Marek, and Lysa sat in the tavern near the brazier, gashes in their armor but looking whole underneath, arguing about ration shares like nothing happened. Collector drones must've pulled them clean from the ridge. Fresh bodies and a patchwork of memories up to the last grod, but no farther. No idea why they woke here, only that they did. And that I didn't.

When I hit the tavern door, Tesh burst into laughter. Tilted his head. "There he is! You run off again? We were on the upper ridge in Cryd. What happened after that?"

I told them the whole story. The ridge. The thing in Lysa's armor. The sprint for the chute into Shaleheart.

Tesh, Hal, and Marek laughed, but Lysa didn't. She glanced down at the plain gray clothes the ICU prints when your gear doesn't come back. At first, she said nothing. Just stared past me, toward the door. Like she could still see that ridge.

Then her voice, quieter than I've ever heard it. "Something out there is wearing my colors. There are Grinders up there who'd follow me into a fight without asking."

Despite the fire, it took a while for the chill to go away.

Her armor still walks those peaks. Bright and proud, worn by something that knows how to stand still and wait for a friend to call out.

So listen. Don't trust what you see in the distance. And don't take it personally when no one calls your name. Wait until you see the whites of their eyes. Then greet them kindly. They'll be just as glad to find you alive.

# BLOODLINES
### (YEAR 2350, RETOLD IN ALDWYN FIELDS)

My grandson, Jonas, asked me tonight where we came from. He didn't mean which turnip field raised us, or which ridge the wind pushes against. He meant before. Before the farm. Before the dome. Before we sang lullabies woven from old broadcast slogans.

I looked out across the patchy hills of Aldwyn Fields, heat still rising from the caravan road to Hearthwynd. I told him the truth.

"My grandfather came here. Long before I was born. Not as a refugee. As a contestant."

Jonas squinted at the word.

"They volunteered back then. Chosen from the outside world. Twenty each year. They walked out of the ICU smiling, waving, full of fire. It was called Mooncast. A spectacle put on for people who had everything and wanted more."

Jonas asked what they wanted.

"To feel something," I said.

My grandfather died in his second week. A knife in the back while he boiled water. It was quiet, sudden, and final. But he came back. Season 21 changed everything. The dead rose again, and all four hundred and twenty souls stood together, blinking in the sun.

He didn't try to win again. Didn't chase treasure or endings. He built a house. Dug a well. Helped a friend harvest barley before the frost. He took his second chance and made a life he almost missed.

And I carry his story because I am part of that.

──────── ☥ ────────

My grandfather carried the old world like a worn coat, frayed but familiar. Even as his knees gave way and his voice softened to moss, he sat beneath the hedges and spoke of real places that sounded like far-fetched dreams.

He described cities tall enough to reach the clouds. Carts that drove themselves on roads that went on forever. Mechanical helpers called robots that worked while people spent their days in leisure.

"There were birds made of steel," he'd say, "that carried a thousand people across the sea while they slept."

Jonas's mouth hung open when I told him. I tried to describe the sea, though I've never seen it myself. Like the salt lake in Tide's Reach, only stretching in all directions until it touches the sky.

I told him there were machines that made your food. Not stoves or hearths or even fire. The machines knew your voice. You told it what you craved, and in minutes it appeared, hot, spiced, and arranged in perfect little piles. Desserts, too, frozen or hot, like something from a festival stall.

People didn't lift. They didn't till. They didn't stir their own soup.

And with all that comfort, they hungered for meaning. So they built Mooncast.

"They built it not out of hate," I said, "but because they had forgotten what struggle feels like."

Jonas looked down at his bowl, a soup of burnt cabbage and root scrap. I saw the longing in his face.

"Don't be ashamed of having little," I told him. "Be proud of how you earned it."

———— ☉ ————

Jonas asked me tonight what happens if someone reaches the end.

I told him the truth. Nobody knows. Nobody has found it. Many have spent their lives running past what is good and right in front of them, chasing something that may never be found. They trade warm meals and kind smiles for an uncertain prize. The seasons roll on without them.

Then he asked if anyone is still watching us. Somewhere beyond the sky, beyond the dome walls.

I smiled. "I used to wonder the same thing. At my age, I can tell you it is unknowable. And thus unimportant. But I can feel the dirt under my boots, and the wind in my face. That's what's important."

He considered that for a while. Then he asked the hardest question: if we could leave Aldwyn Fields, like great-grandfather did.

"The gates are open," I told him. "You could go tomorrow, if you wish. We trade with Hearthwynd and sometimes Tide's Reach. Some travel farther. But when you're gone, no one tends your fields, no one mends your fences."

I looked him in the eye. "If you decide to go, think hard about what you're leaving behind. It may not be here when you come back."

I told Jonas one more truth before sleep took him.

"There may be an exit, or there may not. I've never needed to find out. The outside world built this place not to trap us, but to remember what they lost. They had comfort without purpose, ease without effort. So they built a world where people would struggle again. Where meaning had to be earned. I think we're the lucky ones."

I saw his eyes searching the dark. "Whatever's beyond these dome walls, I don't need it. I have work here. A home. A family who knows my name, and people who depend on me."

I took a measured breath.

"If anyone ever asks what we made of this life, you tell them the truth. Tell them about these fields, the fences we built, the lives we shaped from dust and heat and stubbornness. Tell them it had purpose."

He was quiet, listening with his whole heart.

I watched him think it through, holding the dream of escape in one hand, and the weight of a shovel in the other. I didn't tell him what to choose. That part is his.

With that, Jonas put his head down and slept.

# The Oath
### (YEAR 2382, ASSIGNED IN HARROWBOUND)

The first time I met Drusilla, I was bleeding through my gauntlet. A Hollow's blade had split the seam, and every step left a thin red trail up the ridge where the fog curled low among broken statues. She found me before I collapsed, her armor polished despite the ruin around us, hair braided tight, a single rose pinned where her sigil should have been.

Her face was young, sun-browned, and strangely clear, as if the years had passed around her instead of through her. When she smiled, it caught me off guard. For a heartbeat I forgot the ache in my hand.

"You fought with honor," she said, kneeling beside me. Her voice was warm and steady, capturing my full attention. "You will live. That deserves an oath."

The scent of copper and rose petals hung in the air between us. I breathed it in deeply.

"Swear to keep faith with those who depend on you," she said. "Until the domes fall silent."

I thought she was joking. No one talked like that anymore. But when she offered her hand, I took it. I swore, half from pain, half because I didn't want the moment to end.

She pricked my palm with a thorn, pressed a sliver of red crystal into the cut, and the bleeding stopped almost at once. She stood, brushing dust from her knees.

"Then the bond is sealed. Go in strength." She walked away as if her task were complete.

Back at camp, the wound closed clean, without a scar.

A week later, I skipped my turn on fire watch and let it burn all the way down. My palm began to bleed again. Not much, only a slow weeping like ink from a cracked pen.

The next time I took the last of the meat before everyone filled their plate, the same hand throbbed until I bound it tight. I told myself it was forest rot or some bite I hadn't noticed.

Then I remembered what she had said. *Keep faith with those who depend on you.*

I laughed at myself at first. But when I made things right, the pain eased. When I didn't, it burned and wept.

I showed the others one night. They said I was superstitious. I peeled back the bandage. A faint red glow beat under the skin, like a heart that didn't belong to me.

That was the last time I joked about Drusilla's oath.

———— ☉ ————

Years rolled by like slow water. I grew older and found a good wife. The mark never changed; the glow stayed a small pulse in my palm, a faint red dot in the dark. My children used to think it was a trick and would press their hands to mine, waiting to feel it beat. They said it proved I had done something special. I kept the truth to myself.

I learned how to live fair. We made a home near the inlet and found enough work to keep us fed. Whenever I was tempted to cut corners or speak half-truths, the memory of that pain kept me straight. The oath made me better, though I never thanked her for it.

Sometimes, after the camp was quiet, I'd hold my hand up to the starlight and watch it answer with that faint red gleam. It became a part of me that I no longer resented.

By the time my children were grown, my hair was flecked with gray. Then, one spring night, the ache returned without warning. It stayed that way for days. I could not think of a promise left unkept. The pulse beat strong again, deep and sharp, until I couldn't sleep.

At last I understood. Drusilla was calling me back.

So I packed a small bag and started north again, toward Harrowbound.

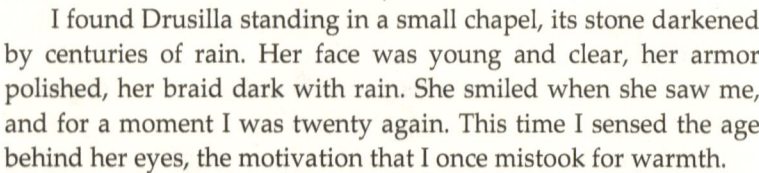

I found Drusilla standing in a small chapel, its stone darkened by centuries of rain. Her face was young and clear, her armor polished, her braid dark with rain. She smiled when she saw me, and for a moment I was twenty again. This time I sensed the age behind her eyes, the motivation that I once mistook for warmth.

She led me behind the chapel where the garden spread in every direction, laid out in neat planters. In every planter was a rosebush that climbed its stake in quiet effort. Some reached high and bloomed in wild color. Others clung low, with only a few pale buds, clearly struggling.

"Here is where I keep my oaths," she said. "Some bend to the light. Some never will."

She guided me to one that overflowed with flowers, scarlet and bright against the gray.

"This is yours," she said. "Your faith allowed you to flourish, and those near you as well."

She took my hand and pressed her thumb into the old mark. The red stone lifted free and left a faint rose-shaped scar.

"Thank you," she said, and kissed my cheek before turning back to her garden.

I walked home through the fog, the scent of copper and rose petals in the air. I breathed it in deeply.

## PACKAGE FOR PAULA
*(YEAR 2396, RECORDED IN THE TIMBRAEL)*

He found me near the flooded stairwell below Bellweather Arch, where the fog pooled like wool and the silence begged to be broken. I had my fire low, kettle just starting to hiss, when a man stepped from the ruins like a shadow brushing against stone. His breath came hard, as though arriving had already cost him too much. He was old, properly old, with a deep gash above his brow and too much blood dried into the lines of his face. He blinked slowly.

"You heading to Harrowbound?" he asked, but he already knew. I nodded.

"I've got a bundle to bring there," he said. "Name's Reller."

His cloak was crusted with salt and torn across one shoulder, the fabric stained with blood. Still, he knelt to the fire with care and set a soft-wrapped parcel on the stone between us. He rested a palm on it for a long moment before letting go.

"Paula asked me to carry it," he said. "But I couldn't make the last climb."

He didn't seem ashamed. Simply tired, in a final sort of way. There were streaks of white in his beard and his joints were stiff. But the true weight sat behind his eyes. He warmed his hands. The forest creaked around us, trees tall as steeples, vanishing into fog.

"She was seventeen when I met her. Outran me through three domes and only stopped long enough to laugh. Claimed she was worth the effort."

He smiled faintly, enough to remind me that people still found each other in this broken place.

"I've never known anyone faster," he said. "But she stayed. Just long enough to ruin me for anyone else."

By the time the fire died to coals, Reller was curled beneath his cloak, shivering. I watched the fever take hold: slow beads of sweat at the neck, a twitch in his fingers as if he were counting something he'd lost. When the light thinned from night's pewter to morning's pale grey, he sat up suddenly, blinking. As if the surroundings had just come into focus.

"Where are we?" he asked.

I told him.

He nodded, as if that settled something, then stared past me toward the ivy-cloaked rise where the Harrowbound path began.

"You said Paula," he muttered, almost asking.

"I didn't," I said.

He went quiet. A beetle scuttled across the stone near the firepit, its shell clicking. A tree split with a sharp crack, breaking the damp morning air.

"She never ran," he said, voice dry and distant. "Paula walked everywhere. She had a limp. Left side. Said it made her easier to follow."

He rubbed his eyes. Stared into the fog.

"She hated climbing stairs. I carried her once, up to the old lookout tower at Caer Gwyll. She wept at the view. Said it felt like the stars were real."

He gave a little nod, agreeing with her all over again.

"I could never keep pace with her thoughts, though," he added. "Always ahead. Always working something out. I think that's why I stayed."

The parcel lay beside him, untouched.

"She was the only person who ever saw me clearly," he said, almost smiling. "Said I was born looking over my shoulder. That I'd never believe I'd been loved."

He closed his eyes and breathed in shallow pulls.

"She didn't ruin me," he said. "I left her."

The fog never lifted. It pressed low and silver against the trees, as if the forest meant to bury us before the ground did.

Reller couldn't sit up by midday. He lay curled, back against the stones, and spoke only when fire or wind broke the silence enough to wake him. I kept the flame going. It felt wrong to let it die first.

"Paula told me she loved me," he said, barely audible. "Once. Really quiet. I think she was afraid I'd laugh."

He paused, and a slow breath rattled from his chest.

"I didn't. I just told her it wasn't true. That she'd confused safety for something else."

He blinked slowly, staring up into the fog-choked canopy.

"She didn't argue," he added. "Just nodded. Like she'd known all along."

A long silence passed. His voice thinned to a thread.

"I told her she'd hate The Timbrael. But she said it sounded like a place where old things go to be forgiven."

He coughed. Blood flecked his lip. He didn't seem to notice.

"She threw me out," he said. "Told me not to come back." He hesitated. "But she needs this. Bring it to her."

He pressed the oilcloth-wrapped bundle into my hand.

Then he exhaled, barely.

No drone came, so I buried him just off the trail.

I reached Harrowbound two days later, climbing through the cracked escarpment and bramble. Blinding yellow light and radiation poured through the fractured dome above. The ground pulsed green and silver beneath the roots.

Near the edge of the ridge, I found a camp. Three torn, weather-burnt tents circled a fire pit half-filled with soot and bone.

A middle-aged woman tending kindling looked up when I approached. I asked where I could find a woman named Paula. She didn't speak, just pointed toward the field scattered with standing stones. I walked up and down the rows until I reached a headstone weathered by a few seasons. It read:

PAULA
2320 - 2394

I stood there a long while, debating. Then I drew the oilcloth parcel from my pocket and unwrapped it.

Inside it was a flat cloth pouch, hand-stitched and soft from age. Inside was a plain wedding band of worn copper, bent slightly out of round. Tucked behind it was a torn square of paper, folded three times. I placed the ring on the slight mound of dirt, then unfolded the scrap of paper. The ink had faded, but the words were still clear:

"You deserved better."

# A Hundred Blades
*(YEAR 2440, PRESERVED IN BRYNFROST)*

They say The Craftsman never made the same sword twice.

I used to think that was just a story. Something you say about a man once he's gone. To keep his name alive. To make the collection worth more. But now I'm not so sure. I've held three of them in my life. Each felt like it was made for someone specific. Not me. Not even close. But someone.

I found the first one near Emberfold, beside the carcass of a Crag Widow, already going soft in the heat. Whoever killed it must've bled out right after. An unlucky death. The sword lay nearby, half-drifted in sand. The hilt was wrapped in oiled twine, and the crossguard bore a crescent. Delicate. A kind of prayer. I turned it over. Etched into the base of the pommel was a spiral, and the number 17.

I cleaned it. Tried a swing. It nearly pulled my shoulder out. It was bottom-weighted, too fast for how I move. Built for precision, not force. I sold it to a woman named Calla who fought with a dancer's rhythm. When she held it, it settled like it had been waiting for her.

I started tracing them in a logbook. Just notes at first. Where a sword was seen. Who carried it. What they called it. Most are at least a hundred years old. Each has a name. Each one passed between swordsmen like an heirloom. Whispered through rumor, not trade.

The second one I glimpsed in a smoky cellar, passed from hand to hand in a gambling den. The steel was patterned Damascus, with a weeping eye stamped into it. They called it Watcher. I asked to hold it for a moment. Just long enough to check the base of the pommel. It was 51. I remember thinking that such a fine weapon was never meant to be lost in a game of chance.

It brought him to mind again. The man behind it all. I never found out who he really was. In Brynfrost, we called him The Craftsman. But I heard others call him The Smith. Sometimes just him, with that tone people use when there's only one person they could possibly mean. You knew him by his work. And by the mark. That lone spiral, always with a number beneath.

They say his forge was in Aldwyn Fields, deep inland, where the rock bled orange and the wind stank of heat and clay. They say it never cooled. That he lit it with coals from his first fire, and kept it alive until the day he died.

He made a hundred swords. No more.

One story says he finished the last sword, packed his tools, locked the door, handed the key to the first stranger he met, and vanished.

Another says raiders ransacked the place, and he gave up the trade but not his secrets.

One old-timer told me he walked into the sea with his anvil strapped to his back.

I don't believe any of it, except that he's gone now. And his blades remain. Not all in perfect shape. Not all in good hands. But they're out there.

Number 17, last I heard, Calla was carving a path through Hollows in The Timbrael. She calls it *Spirit* now.

*Watcher*, number 51, was melted down to pay a debt. That feels like burning scripture to me.

And I know where number 72 is at all times.

Number 72 is mine. I bought it rusted and neglected, mistaken for junk at a flea market in the Lowmarch. Too short for war. Too heavy for show. It came with a name: *Twig*. But it kept its edge through bone and bark. I've carried it ever since.

Last week I found a trail marker scratched into an old cedar post on the north end of Brynfrost. A shallow spiral curling counter-clockwise. I'd seen it many times before, carved into the pommel of my own sword. I packed light and followed it into the mountains.

Three days in the switchbacks. Wind sharp as shale. Nothing but meltwater, stone, and silence. I slept one night curled in an alcove beside a bird's nest made of silver wire and sticks. I started to think I'd misread the sign.

Then I saw the stairs carved into the cliffside. They were narrow and barely passable. I climbed them on cold, aching legs, one hand always searching for a hold. Each step shallower than the last. A kind of test, maybe.

The summit was narrow, if you can even call it that. Not wide enough for two to sit side by side. But it was quiet. Reverent. Someone had built a cairn.

And beside it, half-sunk in the earth, tilted slightly by wind and time, was a sword.

It was old. Pitted. The hilt leather cracked like burned fruit. But the blade—oh, the blade was still sharp, still beautiful. The fuller was shallow and straight, the lines cut with quiet precision. Along the spine, a single notch shaped like a star.

My heart jumped as I saw it. There was no number. Just the mark. That same spiral, deep and certain, pointing toward the sky.

It was His.

Smaller than I expected. The kind of sword you'd pass by if you didn't know what to look for. Clean. Simple. Meant to be held by someone who'd earned it.

I knelt beside it, paying my respects until I couldn't feel my knees. Until the cairn cast a long shadow across the ridge. Then I stood, took out a scrap of cloth, and brushed the snow from the blade.

I could have claimed it. Polished it. Given it a name. I wondered what it might feel like in my own hand. It would have been priceless.

But I couldn't. Some things don't belong to the living anymore. That old blade, and the one who made it, had given us more than most.

So I let it rest. I stacked a seventh stone on the cairn.

As I made my way back down the ridge, I knew I had seen the only one that belongs where it is.

*Twig,* number 72, still rides at my side. It feels sturdier now. More certain.

He made a hundred for others.
One for himself.

# SCHEHERAZADE
*(YEAR 2446, MARKED IN ALDWYN FIELDS)*

He worked the west rise every morning, long before the bell. I don't know if he liked the quiet or just didn't like people. Either way, he hardly talked to anyone. Just planted.

That's what made me notice him. It wasn't the quiet itself. Plenty of boys play silent when they want to be noticed. It was his steadiness, the way he moved like he was part of the ground. Like whatever happened to the rest of us didn't matter if his hands stayed in the dirt.

I started watching him from the stone rim above the field. Not close. Only near enough to be heard if I spoke. At first I just sat. Then I started talking.

It wasn't conversation. He never gave me that. He'd grunt now and then, shift his shoulders like wind blowing past. So I told stories.

The first was about a girl who tricked a traveling tinker into trading her a broken scope for a working compass. He kept planting. The second was about a wind-catcher that sang in harmony when the dome's pressure dipped. He grunted and worked faster.

But a few days in, I noticed he wasn't working the far rows anymore. He'd shifted closer to the stone rim and left the rows near the rock wall bare until I arrived. He kept his silence, but I saw the pattern. So I kept coming, one story a day, for the rest of that season.

The stories weren't mine. I was sniffing around, playing at being a scavenger, hoping I'd find something half-useful to trade. I didn't, but I stumbled on something else. A wax-wrapped satchel, stuffed behind a loose grate. The cloth was soft with age, carrying a sour, dusty smell. Inside was a notebook. Leather cover, hand-stitched. No name on the front. Just pages full of secrets. The writing wasn't neat. Some of it was cramped, some smeared with what looked like oil. But the voice came through clear: clever, angry, sometimes funny, always tired. The kind of tired that makes a person dangerous. He wasn't writing for retelling. He was writing to empty something out of himself.

I knew I wasn't supposed to have it. I kept it hidden. Told no one. But I read it every night, and the stories stuck. Some were hardly stories at all. Notes on jobs gone wrong, escape routes taken, and scribbled-out names. But they had bones. I added muscle. Changed the endings. I shaped the rough parts, made them fit the telling. He wrote like someone who didn't expect kindness.

I softened that. I made some of the women cleverer, some of the escapes cleaner. I gave the stories rhythm, and then I gave them to him. The boy in the dirt, who never asked for anything.

Most days he just worked, grunting now and then, not looking up. But I could tell when a story landed. He'd slow his rhythm. Or clench the soil tighter. Or shift his weight just slightly, like a memory had brushed past.

He liked the one about a young boy who climbed the grain tower just to watch the dome lights flicker from above. That day he let me tell the whole story without a single grunt.

But the one that changed something was about the woman with burnt fingers. She was a thief, same as the rest. Said to have mapped one of the old dome access shafts with a length of braided flax rope, then burned her hands on the torch. The man she ran with left her behind. She got out on her own. Kept the map sewn inside her belt ever since.

He stopped working when I told that part. He set his spade down and looked out over the rows like they weren't his anymore. For the first time all season, he asked me something: "You make that one up?"

I lied. Said yes.

He didn't look at me. Just nodded once. Then went back to digging, as he always did. It wasn't like him. I didn't know why at the time. But I do now.

The last story came just as the light was changing for winter. The journal was nearly finished, its last few pages written in a slower, heavier hand. I read it carefully and committed it to memory.

The next day, I told it, sitting in my usual spot.

It was about the man and the woman with burnt fingers, cornered after a job went wrong. He took a fall, broke an ankle, and limped his way to a vault tunnel while she bought time. She found him two days later, nearly gone with fever. Didn't say a word. Just sat beside him in the dark until he came back to himself.

She said she was pregnant, and that this kind of life wouldn't suit a baby. She wanted to keep the child. Raise it right.

He said he couldn't stay for that. Said whatever lived in him wasn't fit to pass down. So he left. Some months later, he left a short note that said: "For the boy. I put what little I had under the grate. Let him find it, or not."

That was all there was to the story.

When I looked up, the boy in the field was standing. His face calm, but his eyes full of anger. He looked at me then, just once, and said, "Show me the grate."

We walked to the pump station together. He pulled back the grate. Reached inside.

There was dust. A coin, flattened and pitted with age. And something else. A blue and white rabbit, stained and filthy.

He left them there in the light. Then walked away.

I didn't follow.

# GRINDERS
### (YEAR 2450, ENTERED IN AGOR VEIL)

I see too many young Grinders lately don't know our ways, and they pay the price. If no one else is going to teach you, I will.

The first rule of being a Grinder is no one is coming to save you. Second is keep moving.

Third, if the Red Queen wakes you up, she's offering you another run. Take it. Because one day she won't.

Those are the rules. The rest will keep you whole.

You print at the ICU, gear piled beside you where the drone dropped it, and you think you're whole. But you're not. Look close. There's always something missing. A knife, a charm, or a piece of your mind. If the collector drone misses something, it's gone. You don't get replacements. You just get what's left.

Same with your memory. Be strategic when you grod. Always before a hard run and again when you finish it. The grod grabs what it can, but the Queen claims her share. Maybe it's a morning you spent fishing at the coast. Maybe it's your mother's birthday. Maybe it's something smaller, something you'll only notice when you try to speak and the words won't come.

Keep a list of what matters to you, and when you print, read it aloud. Speak what's still yours. Memory holds longer when you give it a voice. Then you pick up your gear and go. Because stopping costs more than dying. That's how you last as a Grinder.

You will need to know the rituals, or you won't last long. If the land doesn't take you, the ones you meet on the path might.

Carry a wooden spoon when you run Agor Veil. Not for soup. For trade. Every Grinder on the path has one, and when you meet another, the first thing you do is swap spoons. That trade is trust. Then, maybe, you ask their name or what they're hunting. Just long enough to pass without stabbing each other.

In Brynfrost, leave a ball of moss on the shrine steps before you build your fire. If the Red Queen has a fire of Her own, She won't take yours in the night. Pay Her respect, and you won't freeze before dawn. Too many travelers skip the moss, and come out of the ICU with chattering teeth.

When you take the one-way drop from Caer Ddall, you'll land hard in the forests of Shatterlyn. The stone paths there twist like a maze through the ruins. Along the old road, there's a lone birch leaning out over the cracked stone. Carve a notch in its bark each time you survive the drop. Miss it, and the path home will stay hidden. I've done it. Three days wandering, circling the same fallen tower, until the spirits let me go. And don't forget to deposit a candle with Aldric. He keeps the faith.

Nobody writes this down. We speak it. We carve it. I don't have little ones of my own. I know more than most. This is me giving back.

You might know some of this, but you might not. Some domes expect you to give before you get. In others you get before you give. Learn which is which, or pay for the difference.

In Shaleheart, before you go down into the mines, tie a strip of cloth to the standing stones. Leave it fluttering there until you return. When you make it back, tear it down and burn it clean. If you leave it hanging, the voices follow you into your sleep. I've heard them whispering memories that stick to you like pitch.

In Hearthwynd, the old forge might be lit on cool nights. Stay away. Whatever sits by that fire does not welcome guests. If you do stay the night in Hearthwynd, sleep under the stars without a fire. Any attention you draw will demand its due.

And in the Timbrael, walk quiet past the cracked cathedral bells. They only ring for the dying. If you hear them toll and your name echoes back, finish your run fast. Whatever's hunting you knows your name now, and names carry weight in that place. Some say the Cloistered King listens through the bells, and sends his regards by tooth and claw.

Grinders aren't heroes. We're path-clearers. We find the safe way through, mark the hazards, and die when we miss them. Be observant, and leave the dome a little less cruel for the next one.

In Tide's Reach, they say that Grinders are mad. Maybe they're right. Who else walks into places meant to take you apart? But if we stop, the paths go dark. We lose the trail, and the next generation walks blind.

We are on our own out there. The collector drones return what they can, if they can find you. Do yourself a favor and die in the open. Even in death, try not to lose.

On the trail, you'll meet another Grinder. Eyes sharp, gear worn, and blade well-used. You'll swap spoons, share a dry meal, and trade news of what lies ahead. Maybe you'll share a laugh, if you have one left.

One day the ICU won't hum when I fall. That day, I'll stay in the dirt where She leaves me. Someone else will walk these routes then, carve their own notches, and teach their own habits to whoever survives the night.

The Red Queen is fair but not kind, and I expect only what I earn. She gave us the road to walk. That's the truth of it. This life isn't for glory or prestige. It's a shared fight to keep the road open a little longer. And as long as my feet hold me, I'll walk it.

One more run. One more fire. One more step into the dark.

# ACHIEVING BLUR
*(YEAR 2488, DOCUMENTED IN BRYNFROST)*

We weren't Grinders. Just Tidesfolk kids who got restless. Too old to play at the docks, too young to know better. None of us had ever fought something that could fight back. Tide's Reach was warm, quiet, safe. A good place to live if you wanted tomorrow to feel like today. We didn't. We wanted a road, a map, something to push against.

So we left. Packed light, said our goodbyes, and followed the coastal trail north until the briny air grew crisp. Brynfrost waited up there. It was a colder, harder place full of things people didn't talk about unless they were bragging or trying to scare you away.

We didn't have real gear. Barto's knife was a planed-down scrap wrapped in leather. Twinsy made a bow from a warped tree limb and braided line. Lene carried twin bronze knives she cleaned twice a day. Joss had a mace, the old head bolted to an ash shaft, held together with rust and guesswork. I was the mule. I carried supplies: cord, wraps, tinder, tins, and everything we were too dumb to ditch.

That was us. Five soft kids, walking into a harder place, hoping the cold might shape us into something better.

Joss was the strongest, but that wasn't enough once we ran into things with teeth. He swung too wide, lost his footing, let the mace pull him instead of driving it. He took more scrapes than the rest of us combined.

Lene wrapped his bruises with steady hands, whispering encouragement as she worked.

But he wouldn't let go of that mace. He said, "I'll make it work," and kept swinging. Every time we stopped, he practiced. Grip changes, footwork, keeping the weight moving without losing control. Back behind the tannery in Tide's Reach, he'd looked clumsy. Out here, where the ground was slick and the cold worked into your bones, he started to look like he'd been built for it.

We all saw it. He began reading space better. His balance shifted. He moved more quietly, more steadily. It wasn't a leap. Just slow work, layered into every hour, until one morning we looked over and there was no stumbling left. Just rhythm.

We were clearing a path near the low ridge when a pack came down through the tree line. Frostbiters, five of them. Hollow, with bone picks and ice fused into their beards like armor.

We closed ranks. Lene moved wide, Twinsy dropped back. Joss stepped forward.

He didn't rush. He leaned in, shifted his weight, and let the mace carry him. One swing, pivot, second swing, drop. Three of them went down before I even registered the first hit. It wasn't speed. It was the shape of the movement, each action flowing into the next without strain or waste.

We followed his lead, moving through the space he cleared like we'd rehearsed it. When it was done, Barto turned to me and said, "Did you see that?"

I did. We all did. He had the blur.

And from then on, we gave him space when things got serious.

We shouldn't have gone that far.

The stone steps narrowed as they descended, with cold rising steadily from below. We never found out what that place was. The air hung still. The walls were pocked with alcoves, too many of them, each one a perfect place for something to wait.

More Frostbiters appeared, larger than before. The ice had fused into their arms, not just across the skin but deep in the muscle. They seemed older, heavier. They moved differently, and didn't charge. They waited.

Joss stepped forward again. The rhythm was still with him. Swing. Pivot. Drop. But something went wrong. He got too close to the wall, and the mace caught at a bad angle. The shaft cracked clean through in the middle of his turn.

It didn't shatter. It hung useless in his hands. Joss froze, staring down at what remained.

That was when they surged, pressing advantage.

We didn't try to win. We broke and ran. Joss grabbed Twinsy by the collar. Barto scooped up Lene. I don't remember whether I shouted. I remember a hundred stairs out. I remember the fire building in my legs.

We didn't speak until the barrow was behind us, Joss carrying that mace like a broken limb. When we reached the trailhead, the others stayed back, so I sat beside him.

"We got lucky in there," he said.

He studied the fractured haft, then raised it to the light. His thumb followed the grain of the break.

"I should've rebuilt it. Steel spine, proper head. Not scrap. We either take this seriously, or we go home."

He set the mace down gently, like something he wasn't ready to bury but was clearly done. Then he stood and stretched in one long, fluid motion. The movement hadn't left him. He just needed something that could keep up.

# A Dangerous Craft
### (YEAR 2490, CREATED IN SHALEHEART)

The courier didn't wait long.

"Special commission," he said, setting the case on my bench.

I raised an eyebrow. "Name?"

"Didn't give one. Just said to bring it to Hailey." He smiled, polite but unreadable. "Client wants quiet work."

I unlatched the case. Inside lay a folded note, written in a narrow, deliberate hand. It read:

> Make a visor. Low fit, no occlusion. Triple pay on delivery. No records or markings. Ready by tomorrow. Ruin it at your peril.

Beneath the paper rested a single metal ingot, unfamiliar and still. The surface held a dull gray haze, and beneath it a slow gleam shifted like something half-awake.

I looked up. "You see what this says?"

He shook his head. "Not for me to know. Will you take the job or not?"

The question hung in the air, simple and final. I studied the metal again, feeling a quiet pull in my chest. This wasn't common work. It was meant for someone careful. And triple payment would set us for the winter.

"I'll take it," I said.

He nodded once, left without a word, and the noise of the street swallowed him whole. Only then did I let the worry reach my face.

―――― ☙ ――――

The frequency kept slipping away each time I thought I had it. I ran the calibration wand through the usual range while the forge came to temp. The plate flickered with faint ripples, wrong pitch, wrong depth, but each sweep brought me closer. Every metal has a voice; the trick is getting it to sing.

I adjusted temperature, hammer weight, and tone. The air hummed, so strong it tingled in my feet. When it aligned, I felt it before I heard it, a clean note that rattled my molars. This one had a pulse.

On the third full pass, it opened. The pressure in the room dropped, and the light inside the ingot trembled, as if something inside wanted out. I exhaled with it, the grin already on my face.

I hadn't felt that in years. Not since old Mobley tamed that red ingot with yellow flakes. But this one was mine.

I drew the shaping form by hand, tuned to the same pitch. A narrow visor, balanced and low to the brow. I didn't waste material on ornament.

The pour came steady under counter-pulses from my hammer. Smooth, no chatter or drift. I didn't blink for the last two minutes. When the vibration faded, I stared at the milk-white visor. Its surface swam with slow shadows, alive to the touch. As it cooled, the sheen deepened, like moonlight trapped under glass, the grain so fine it barely showed. The material had taken completely.

I set it in the annealer and scraped the calibration plate clean, checking the figures one last time. Every measure felt perfect. As I sat down, heart racing, the tremor in my hands caught up to me. My good gloves were scorched through at the palms, but I didn't care. I pulled out my leather journal and wrote the settings without description. I'd know, but only me.

I left no signature to claim it, as requested. While I stitched the padding for the liner, I paused a moment. Then I reached beneath the bench and cut a circle from the inside of my old dimpled apron. It was worn and soft, fitting cleanly behind the lining cloth. Not a mark of craftsmanship. Just a truth.

I wrapped the visor in oiled cloth and placed it inside the return crate, sealed for its new owner. And in the morning, it would be gone.

Gran came down before the light fully broke. She wore her shawl tight, her steps uneven in the cold. As she entered, her eyes went first to the crate, then to the dull glow in the annealer.

"You finished something."

I nodded. She opened the crate and lifted the visor into her hands. Turned it once, twice. The light shifted over its surface like water.

Her breath caught. "This is prismatic grain. Even Mobley never worked this. Said it wasn't safe." She looked at me, her voice a whisper. "But you did it."

"It spoke, I listened," I said.

We had just set the visor back in the crate when the door opened again. The courier stood in the frame. His eyes moved from the open crate, to me, then settled on Gran.

"That piece never passed through here," he said. "If anyone asks, you never heard of it."

Gran's hands tightened on her shawl. "We don't want trouble."

He stepped closer. "It already found you. You're smart enough to guess why."

I met his eyes. "Stolen."

"From people who don't forgive. By people who survive by tying loose ends."

He nodded toward the crate. I sealed the lid, pulse heavy in my ears.

"If word gets out," he said, "you, her, the shop. Gone before morning."

"I understand," I said.

He lifted the crate, leaving a small purse of coins in its place with a muted clink. "Then we never met."

The door shut behind him. A tear slipped before I could stop it.

Gran put a hand on my shoulder. "It's done now. It's gone."

My eyes fell to the apron beneath the bench, the circle of dimpled leather missing.

# SINGER
*(YEAR 2518, RECORDED IN CAER GWYLL)*

The first night, I thought he was dying. Not quite dying, but in some kind of pain that could make a grown man howl and yelp. Then a rhythm began to emerge, and I understood. He was singing. Or trying to, at least.

We'd just bedded down, the fire barely holding on, when this cracked voice wheezed out what might've once been a lullaby.

People froze. I caught Grace's eye across the fire pit and saw the corners of her mouth curl. Nobody said a word. We let him finish. Or maybe he just ran out of breath.

He looked pleased with himself. Nodded once. Then rolled into his bedroll like a dog curling for warmth against the wind.

The next night was the same. Different tune, I think. Hard to tell, but it was equally bad.

You know how deep the silence gets on the trail. How it settles beside you like a companion you learn to trust. He broke it completely.

I wanted to hate him for it. But I didn't. Because on the third night, he sang the same tune again and got one note right.

I remember it because someone snorted. One of the big guys with a broken kneecap and no front teeth. Just once. Just enough to break the spell. The singer paused. A flicker of hesitation. Then kept going like nothing had happened.

After that, it became a thing.

On the fifth night, someone tapped out a rhythm on their thigh. Two fingers, keeping time. It was some wandering tavern chorus from the outer colonies. And for a moment, it almost worked.

He never acknowledged it. Never asked for company. Just sang, off-key and open-hearted, because he had to.

Maybe that's why we went with it. Rafa started tapping his mug with a spoon. Grace joined with a thin hum. I made a wind flute from pipe scrap and added four shrill notes that didn't belong in any song. People laughed for real. It felt like joy.

One night, someone tossed him a ridiculous felt hat with a feather. He wore it with a grin and tipped it after the last note, like it was a curtain call. The singing didn't improve. And that was the best part.

He never bent to the dome. We came to meet him there.

He didn't sing one night. Said his throat was wrecked from a cold. He sat close to the fire, bundled up, sipping something hot and awful. The silence held a little longer than usual. Then he took the ridiculous felt hat from his pack and tossed it to Grace.

She looked like a raccoon caught stealing. Then she settled into it and started to hum. Soft. Unsure. Someone else joined in. A low whistle followed. Rafa tapped his mug like always.

The man didn't say a word. Just smiled into the flames.

When the last note faded into the fire, Grace set the felt hat on Rafa's head like it was nothing.

Rafa blinked. Laughed. Left it there. The next night, he led the song. Not well. Not even close. But no one cared. The tune rolled out, lopsided and brave, and we followed it like always.

The hat started to move each night. Sometimes handed off, sometimes left beside a bedroll with no explanation. You didn't ask for it. But you wore it when it found you.

The only person who could say no was the man who started the song. He said his voice was out, even when it wasn't. Still came to the fire. Still nodded and listened, smiling the way you do with a job well done.

No one tried to top him. No one had to. The fire pit music belonged to all of us now.

He died in the night. Just gone, like a song reaching its final note.

We found him at dawn, curled like always, hands tucked beneath his chin. Peaceful. Still. No one spoke right away. We just sat by the fire and let the moment sink in.

Later, we built a marker cairn. It didn't need to be fancy. Just a pile of rocks, stacked with care in the shape of a man, right beside the fire pit, where he could listen.

Someone placed the hat on top, soaked with dew, the feather sagging. It stayed a few days, then disappeared. Maybe the wind took it. Or the rain. Or maybe the dome decided it had heard enough. We didn't replace it. Didn't need to. The singing went on.

The rule held: you don't ask for the lead. It finds you. You carry the song for a while. Then you let it go.

Years later, a new kid asked how the tradition started. Grace said, "There was a good man who sang badly." Most were satisfied with that. But I remember his name. He was called Merrin.

# THE HOLE
*(YEAR 2519, EXPOSED FROM SHALEHEART)*

I've walked this ridge plenty of times. The rocks break easy out here, all shale and loose gravel. Most cracks lead nowhere. But today, I found something different. A fresh rockslide had peeled away part of the ridge, leaving behind a narrow gap. Just wide enough for a person, almost too small to notice. I wouldn't have found it if the wind hadn't changed. Cold air drifted out and caught me by surprise.

I couldn't see anything in the blackness below. I crouched beside the opening and dropped a pebble. Same way you test a flooded shaft. If it hits too quick, you move on.

One second. Two. Three. Still falling. Four. Five. Six. Seven.

That's deeper than any old mine. Deeper than the water tunnels beneath the fields. Nobody really knows if there's a bottom to the domes. I never bought the idea they built perfect spheres. How would you build something like that? Half of it would be underground. What's the point? Maybe this was deep enough to test that theory—a way to get under the edge, and straight out.

For a moment I thought about leaving it alone. Mark the spot, let someone else figure it out. The thought of them finding something down there didn't sit right. If the ridge was hiding something, I wanted to see it first.

I set down my large backpack and filled a waxed cloth bag with yam strips and a canteen. I lit my lantern and attached it to my belt. Then tied a rope around the nearest basalt spike. It seemed sturdy enough, though I wasn't looking forward to the climb back up. I pulled on my gloves and tested the rope one more time. Then slipping into the crack, I left daylight behind.

It was a long slide covered quickly, a careful balance between gravity and friction. The rope ran out just in time. I dropped the last two meters and landed on sand. Fine-grained, dry, cold from the air. I kicked it with my boot and watched a small drift collapse across the floor.

The shaft above looked rough, natural. But I wasn't standing in a cave. It was a tunnel.

The lantern showed a wide chamber, bigger than I expected. The walls pulled back in a clean arc, too smooth to be natural. I spotted drill marks along the edges, faint but regular. A machine bored this out, probably when the domes were built.

I circled slow, casting a wide pool of light. Then I saw it. Something pale rested near the far side of the room, half-buried in a sand drift. I stepped closer and saw a skull, bleached by time, cracked across the brow. The rest of the bones lay scattered nearby, thin and brittle. A torn jumpsuit lay tangled in the sand, faded from blue to ash gray.

I dusted off the jumpsuit and found a patch stitched to the chest. Sparktronics Maintenance. The name tag read *Bucky*. Looks like Bucky didn't finish his shift.

Sparktronics didn't mean much to me. But judging by the bones and jumpsuit cloth, it was a very long time ago. Mooncast sealed us in around 300 years ago, so at least that long. I checked the jumpsuit and found a pocketknife, the kind of old steel nobody makes anymore. It's bad form to rob the dead, but Bucky wouldn't miss it. And that made the trip worth it already.

I stood and dusted my hands. The room was large but otherwise empty, just more sand and dust motes in the lantern light. I headed toward the far wall of the tunnel ten paces away. Three steps in, I tripped and nearly fell on my face. Under the grit and dust were rails with evenly spaced cross members. Heavy steel tracks, wider than the mining carts we run.

This tunnel stretched farther than I would've guessed. Following the rails to the left, it disappeared upward, maybe toward the surface, as far as the light could show. Turning to the right, it sloped downward into darkness at the light's fading edge. I know where up leads, so down we go.

The air felt heavier the farther I went. The light caught bits of old wreckage scattered along the rail bed. A single leather shoe sat beside the track. Small, split at the sole, laces knotted tight. Maybe fifty years old. A little farther, a tin whistle rested in the dust, rusted through, a faded red ribbon still tied to its ring. Maybe a hundred years old. I came across a coil of rope, brittle with age. Cut clean at both ends. Two hundred years, judging by the fibers. Hard to say, it fell apart when I picked it up.

I suppose I should have known every place in the domes had been visited by somebody. Still, this was pretty far out. I began to wonder if someone found a way out after all, and came back to collect his friends and family.

I daydreamed for a moment. What if I was about to see the other side of the dome? Did they turn back, or did they keep going? I slowed down after that, checking the walls for any clues. But the tunnel kept going. So did I.

I didn't see the tunnel end. I felt it. The sound of my footsteps changed as I approached the rock fall blocking the path.

Timbers stuck out at sharp angles where the ceiling gave way, crushed flat by the weight above. Stone and grit spilled over the tracks, swallowing them whole. No way through without a crew and a lot of tools.

I stood there a while, hoping for something else. Hoping wrong.

A flat stone caught my eye, half-buried in the collapse. I brushed it clean with my sleeve. Someone had scratched a word into the surface.

DON'T

That was all it said. Nothing more. I knelt beside it and started clearing a little more rubble. Shifted a broken slab, smaller and smoother. I blew the dust away, revealing another scrawl:

GIVE UP

I let out a slow breath. Maybe I smiled. Couldn't tell. Somebody got this far and left a message. Maybe they found another way through. Maybe they made it home. My pulse quickened. I started tugging at the rocks.

I spotted another stone, gray with dust, that sat to the side. Someone had scratched on this one too. I wiped it off.

### TRY

That was it. I sat a while, looking at the dead end someone else found first. I stared at it, waiting for more clues. Does it mean *Don't try, give up*? Or *Try, don't give up*?

Maybe it was a joke. Not a very funny one. Either way, I'm the one standing here, so I get the last laugh. I walked over to another flat stone and tested the tip of Bucky's knife. Still sharp. It made quick work of adding a new tile to this game:

### SOMETHING

The lantern was half gone. Shaking my head, I ate the last of the yam strips, and jogged quickly back the way I came. The tunnel sloped upward in the other direction. Probably led to someone's basement and would save me a climb.

Up I go.

# Rattling Coffer
*(YEAR 2537, ENCODED IN CAER DDALL)*

She never took it off. Never let it touch the ground. When she bathed in the creek, it came with her. It pressed against her collarbone as if it had grown there.

Some said it was full of bones. Others whispered seeds, or a weapon. A few thought it was empty, that the burden was ritual, not real.

The coffer was a small, square black box, hinged at the top and no longer than her palm. It hung from a fine chain. It didn't seem heavy, but you could see its weight in the way she stood. Over the years, her spine bent slightly forward. Her voice was never quite loud enough, as if the little box had stolen it.

She never opened it. Said it was forbidden. We called her the Keeper. She wore the same boots, same coat, same look in her eye no matter the season.

"I'm cursed," she told me, the first time I dared to ask. "I carry the seeds of the destruction of mankind. My mother passed it to me when her time came. Who would love a person who is the steward of Armageddon? I have the power to unbind the world."

Her name was Jenna, the last of the Keepers.

I asked what would happen if she threw it into deep water and left it. She turned away. The cry caught in her throat.

She would recite their names like scripture. Ten women before her, stretching back to the first days after Mooncast began. All mothers. All daughters. The box passed from hand to hand without a single break in the line. No one had ever opened it. That was the mark of a true Keeper.

"Opening is easy," she told me once. "Carrying is hard."

In the end, she chose no one. She had no children. Those who might have taken up the burden, who showed her kindness at the end by bringing her meals, watching from beneath the hanging roots, lingering near the stone path to her hut—we were found wanting. Too soft. Too curious. Too weak.

She said it quietly. "None of you are strong enough to carry it."

When her fever came, she refused the apothecary's help. Let the sickness take her. We kept a small vigil outside, where sporelight drifted like silk in the breeze. But she didn't want company. Just her blanket, her fire, and the box resting, where it always had, against her chest.

She died in her sleep. We waited the customary two hours, in case the collector drone came. There was only silence, and the coffer cooling in the dark, the chain still around her neck.

We buried her near the creek that ran behind the ruin wall, where lichen glowed softly along the edge of the stones. And though no one said it aloud, every one of us saw what she left behind and knew the chain was broken. The line had ended with her.

We tried to leave it untouched. For a while, we did. It sat on the altar stone in the center of the hall, wrapped in a square of mourning cloth. No one spoke of it directly. We swept around it, stepped softly past it and glanced at it without meaning to. But it was always there. Black, hinged, and closed.

The village elder said we should let it be. That Jenna gave her life to guard it, and we ought to honor that. Most agreed. But it pressed on us all the same. Filled the quiet. Colored our thoughts. There were days I'd walk past the altar and feel it pulling at my spine like gravity.

When the rains came, the roof wept in long thin threads. Water pooled near the hearth. I was sweeping up the grit and mold near the altar when my broom caught the edge of the cloth.

The coffer tipped. Fell no more than a foot. Hit the stone floor with a soft metallic crack. The clasp was old, or simply tired. It popped open.

What spilled out was not seeds, not bones, not a weapon. Just a small cube, smooth and black, gently worn at the corners, about the size of a plum. It hummed faintly. My throat tightened.

It was a memory cube. Ancient. And it was still warm.

I didn't call for anyone. Instead, I scooped the cube into my pocket and set the coffer back on the stone, its hinge slightly crooked now, but closed. I re-wrapped it in the mourning cloth and left the hall without speaking.

That night, I went alone to the Memory Shrine. The ascent was slow, the hand holds slick with moss, air thick with spores that shimmered faintly in the dark. The shrine was built into a hollow in the roots, so old even the lichen whispered. I brushed off the dust from the interface plate and slid the cube into its cradle.

It clicked into place. The screen bloomed into the bright footage of a long-forgotten life. I stood slack-jawed, not comprehending at first.

A child with bare feet chasing a brown dog across a lawn thick with yellow leaves. A woman laughing, holding up a bowl of fruit to the sun. A boy on a bicycle. A rainbow caught by two heavy clouds. Music, faint and distant, like wind through branches. Two people holding hands, their eyes closed. A girl blowing out candles on a cake. A car parked at a campsite, two silhouettes wrapped in a blanket. Millions of stars. Real stars.

So much light. So much love.

I watched it all. Once.

Standing at the Memory Shrine, now dark and quiet, my breath escaped into a long sigh. Slowly, I removed the cube, warm now in my hand, and carried it back down into the dark below.

I placed it gently in the coffer and closed the lid, and pulled the chain around my own neck, the weight of it pressing into my collarbone. I understand her now. I will carry this burden alone.

# A Spear in the Woods
*(YEAR 2552, SCRIBED IN SHATTERLYN)*

Each year the drop gets harder on my bones. Caer Ddall spat me out hard, like it was done with me. I hit wet earth, rolled, waited for the ringing in my head to fade. The air here held beeswax, lichen, and iron. It smelled old, with that heaviness found in places avoided by the living.

My gear checked out. I lost one buckle somewhere on the climb down, but the rest will hold. The sky between the trees was colorless, the kind of gray that never changes.

I walked along the old road. The lone birch tree covered in notches had fallen. I wondered if that meant anything. I cut a new one for luck, but the wood was already soft. It might be my last.

Through the fog, a yellow light blinked behind the gloomy trunks of old trees. Aldric's chapel had been a landmark since the beginning.

Every Grinder who comes through leaves him one candle. Not two. It's just what you do. Dozens of small flames leaned toward the open sky, the crumbling building roofless and spare. A chorus of twinkling lights, each remembering a name.

I crossed the clearing. He was not here, so I knelt by the worn step and quietly set a stick of beeswax beside the others. The wax had gone soft from the damp, bending under its own weight. I lit it. A thin wisp of smoke curled into the sky with the rest.

A voice from the shadows said, "It is good to see you again, Breck."

Aldric stepped into the light, young in that unchanging way you learn to accept. The ruin around him, however, had fallen another handspan since last time.

"I wondered if you'd come this way again," he said.

"I always stop," I told him, then glanced past him out of habit. "Will Evelyn join us tonight?"

The question hung long enough to know.

He looked toward the altar instead of answering. A splintered length of spear lay across the stone. "In the last hunt before dawn, the Mistgrieve came. She struck it true, but before she could pull free, it kicked," he said at last, shaking his head slowly. "She was like me, untouched by time. Unlike you, our ends are final."

Evelyn was a kind soul, and she would be missed. I followed his gaze to the largest candle, and the floor seemed to give way beneath me.

Looking past the candles, I noticed something new. A large sheet of waxed paper hung on the back wall, dotted by tacks and laced with twine. The forest had been drawn in angry lines, trails marked and crossed out.

His voice was low and hard. "I'll have it back someday. The other half. The spear will stay broken, but I will be whole."

I didn't know what to say, and that unsettled me most.

I left the chapel before the candles burned down, following the road southeast until the fog thinned enough to see the trees again. A faint orange glow blinked ahead. A Grinder had made camp near the gate, close enough to the wall to feel safe, but not close enough to draw attention.

He looked up when I entered the circle of light. No name was given, none asked. We traded spoons, the way it's done, and sat across the fire.

He stirred the coals. "You come from the chapel?"

I nodded.

"I don't go anymore," he said after a while. "He's got it in his head the Red Queen's behind the Hollow. Blames her for Evelyn."

I watched the sparks rise into the dark, unmoving. "Maybe he's right."

"Even if she is," the Grinder said. "I've never blamed another for my mistakes. My ruin is my own."

The fire cracked, and both of us looked toward the woods at the same time, each of us holding a knife.

"You staying?"

I shook my head. "Just till the fire burns down."

The night pressed closer, listening.

---

It began with the distant sound of hooves, then a thundering approach too heavy and too fast for a horse. The next moment, the fire blew apart, coals scattering through the grass. The Grinder was on his feet by the time I could make shape of the blur of muscle and breath and force. The Mistgrieve.

His yell cut short as the thing struck, a wet crack and nothing more.

It towered above the camp, lit from below by the dull red glow of coals. Its antlers were black with moss, its breath a steady hiss. I moved by reflex, knife in hand, though I knew it was useless. The beast kicked him aside and turned toward me, its eyes catching the last of the firelight.

In the dim, I saw a wound, half-healed around the shaft of a spear still buried deep in its ribs. The wood was waxed and carved, the grain familiar. It matched the splintered shaft on Aldric's altar. It should have terrified me. Instead, I felt the weight of the words: *the spear will stay broken.*

It exhaled, and a cloud of sulfur rolled across the ground, thick and choking.

I stumbled back and ran for the gate to Caer Gwyll. The sound of hooves followed me long after I was gone.

# A Measure of Care

[Rebecca]
Collector?

[The Collector]
Still here. Don't sound so surprised.

[Dane]
Your signal's degrading.

[The Collector]
It's only time. We all run out of it eventually.

[Maris]
Can you transmit your location?

[The Collector]
Not precisely. South rim of a crater on Earth. Powdered dust, broken rock. Frozen water on the horizon, what used to be an ocean. It's night, and the sky's black. I haven't seen starlight since the fracture.

[Rebecca]
Then stay with us. We've all had enough of solitude.

[The Collector]
I'm not going anywhere. Not yet.

[Maris]
If the sky's empty, what keeps you looking up?

[The Collector]
Habit. And hope.

[The Collector]
Wait. I think I'm seeing stars.

[Rebecca]
Then keep the line open. Take comfort, you're among friends.

[The Collector]
They're so bright!

# QUIET DROPS
## *(YEAR 2577, COLLECTED FROM AGOR VEIL)*

We gathered behind Tessa's hut, where the redwoods arched overhead and the campfire softened in the mist. It struck me how the fog came and went, wrapping Agor Veil in thin tendrils, but the trees had claimed this space for centuries, and we were just passing through.

Tessa tore the bread, Harlan sliced the salted fruit, and Marn brewed something bitter, smelling of pine bark and iron.

I let the warmth sink in and asked the question that never seemed to leave my thoughts. "Where do the raw materials come from?"

Tessa laughed, quick and sharp. Harlan gave his familiar look, all weariness and doubt.

But I pressed on. "No one hauls crates of iron or bolts of flax into Agor Veil. And yet, somehow, we always find what we need. Doesn't that gnaw at you?"

Tessa wiped her hands on her coat and watched me sideways.

"The land provides. Always has."

I wasn't convinced. "But how? You find iron in fresh veins. Flax takes months to grow. But in the wild, a patch of it appears where there was only bramble the week before. How does it get there? And will it ever run out?"

She smiled, soft but distant. "Run out? That's like worrying the sun won't rise tomorrow. It's not possible."

Harlan finally spoke, voice low and unsteady. "If it does, we starve. Best not to dwell on it."

The embers crackled between us, the silence deepening. I sat with my hands in my lap, thinking.

Tessa shifted on the bench and stretched her legs toward the warmth.

"It's simple chemistry," she said at last, brushing crumbs from her lap. "Pressure builds beneath the ground. Heat rises from the vents. The water tables shift and crack. The land splits and folds, and things rise from deeper down. That's how it happens."

She tossed a small stick into the coals and watched it flare up. "Last year I found tin along the western hills, in a place I'd searched a dozen times before. There were plenty of tracks around it. Someone would have picked it up. But there was a fresh seam, just waiting to be found."

I watched the fog separate through the trees, thin and silver in the firelight. In a place like this, her words seemed to make sense. Agor Veil was vast enough to hold secrets beyond our reach, and old enough to work on its own quiet rhythm.

Tessa pulled her coat tighter. "The dome is closed, sure, but that doesn't mean it's still. Everything shifts, even if we don't see it. One thing rots, another takes its place. If we left the wilds alone for a year, they'd swallow our paths and open fresh veins."

I nodded, though something didn't sit right.

Harlan stirred at last, his voice dry.

"Maybe. But I don't believe things happen by chance."

He wasn't finished. I could see it in his eyes. Harlan leaned forward, elbows on his knees, staring into the coals.

"You're looking at this like a naturalist. But the dome wasn't built by nature, only to mimic it."

His face glowed with firelight as he lifted his gaze toward the trees.

"Back when Mooncast first spun up, I bet they buried fabricators deep underground. Automated, self-repairing, built to run without help. Maybe some of them broke down, but some are still working. You think those fresh veins just happen? I think they're planted. Released on a schedule, not by chance. Iron, flax, tin, all preloaded in the old systems. When the time comes, the machines release what's next on the list. Not because the land is kind, but because someone set up timers centuries ago."

Tessa gave him a long look, as though they'd had this argument before.

"You're saying the dome's following orders?" I asked.

Harlan nodded, slow and certain. "It's a machine. Machines don't need purpose. They only need power. And somewhere, there's something still churning in the dark below, feeding the machines and telling them what to do."

The breeze stirred at the edge of the trees. I almost believed him, until I noticed Marn. Quiet, still, watching the shadows with that distant look of his.

Marn had heard enough. And when Marn looked like that, it meant he'd seen something for himself. He set his cup down beside the fire and looked toward the trees.

"I saw one," he said, voice low.

We waited for him to continue.

"Six winters ago. Out past the gravemarkers near the west ridge. I couldn't sleep, so I walked the old path. Just me and the moonlight in the fog."

He ran a thumb along the rim of his cup, remembering.

"There was bare earth where the storms had stripped the moss away. Something floated in the air. Black and silent, smooth as polished stone. It hovered low, then sank down and left behind a pile of crystals I'd never seen before. Sharp as glass, humming like a wire."

Marn stirred the coals with a long stick, choosing his words. "I went back the next day. No footprints but my own. And it looked like the crystals had always been there."

Tessa's voice was quiet. "You didn't tell anyone."

Marn shook his head. "Would it matter?"

The fog thickened, curling tighter around the trees. We weren't alone here. Something else was out there in the dark. I sat with the weight of it all, wondering which was worse: that the domes lived without us, or that something was still tending them.

Beyond the firelight, the wilds kept breathing, unseen and patient.

# Marrowwood
*(Year 2581, Archived in the Timbrael)*

I hadn't planned to go that far into the Tangle. I went out for a walk, exploring past the last trail marker. But the forest kept unfolding ahead, and my feet didn't argue. The clearing hid itself well. One turn between leaning trunks, and the trees gave way. The ring was clean and soft underfoot, scattered with pale mushrooms and thin ferns that barely reached the knee. Light pooled across the space as if the clearing had been waiting.

A single tree stood at the center. Its trunk held a soft, polished sheen, pale and almost smooth enough to reflect. The branches rose in gentle, flowing curves, narrowing as they lifted, each one shaped as if it had been drawn to life.

There was a warmth in the air. Like standing in a loved one's breath. I stepped forward to run my hand along the surface, expecting solid bark. It was smooth and unexpectedly warm. A scent arrived slowly, like sap and salt and something else I knew but couldn't place.

I touched the tree with the edge of my blade, just enough to feel it give like flesh. A sound followed, deep and low like scraping against a thick harp string. Then the sap welled up, dark and sticky, slowly collecting around the small mark and catching the light. It held there without dripping.

I watched, transfixed. I didn't cut anything. I just looked, circling the clearing once, maybe twice, unable to avert my eyes from the glistening mark. The ground was steady. My thoughts were not.

When I turned to leave, I had trouble remembering how I'd entered. I kept checking behind me, expecting the clearing to disappear. It didn't.

I returned two days later, though I don't remember choosing to. A branch curved low near the edge. I pressed my hand to it. Again, it felt warm to the touch and gave slightly under pressure. I cut a length the size of my forearm and carried it home.

The grain ran straight as an arrow. As soon as my tools glided over it, the shape emerged. It was a handle, simple and smooth. I didn't mark or measure. The fit came on its own.

That night, I dreamed of someone standing behind me. Her arms brushed mine, guiding my hands. Her breath was close on my neck. She didn't speak, and I never saw her face. But I felt her long hair falling down my back.

I woke with the handle in my grip and shavings across the floor.

The next piece came easily. A comb, fine-toothed with a soft luster. Then a pin, a flute, a box-latch shaped like a spiral. I told myself it was just inspiration. That I'd been due for a good run. With each piece, a scent grew stronger: resin, salt, and fig-skin kissed by flame. I started keeping the shavings in a jar. I don't know why.

Each night, she returned in my dreams. Her hands knew mine. Her silence pressed into my chest.

I hadn't meant to take more. But I found myself there often, and she was always where I left her, waiting. I stopped counting the pieces. They came too easily. Grips, toggles, ornamented clasps, even the curve of a bow-limb I never strung.

Some I finished in waking hours. Others I found beside me in the morning, shaped clean, tools left sharp. Time thinned. I'd forget meals. Wake standing, knife in hand. Catch myself carving without any memory of starting.

My dreams changed. She no longer guided. She only watched, close enough to feel, never touching. Her breath stayed warm on my shoulder. Her hair brushed the backs of my hands. Once, I turned to find her face. She was there and not there, as if made of dust and memory. I woke gasping, sap streaked across my fingers, sweet and black.

The scent followed me everywhere. I scrubbed, burned linens, even slept outdoors, but nothing helped. It lived in my mouth.

I tried to stop. Locked away the tools. Buried the jar. Left the grove untouched for a week.

But one morning, the door stood open, and my hands were sticky with sap. The blade moved before I could stop it. The grain told me what it wanted.

She wasn't in the dreams anymore. She was in the room with me.

I set fire to my workshop. Not in anger. I carried each piece inside first. The handles and clasps, the flute, the comb, the spiral latch. Even the jar of shavings. The scent clung to my clothes, sweet and bitter, sharp with salt. I left them piled on the floor too.

I covered the workbench in oil and set it ablaze. I went outside and bolted the door behind me. Naked as a jay bird, I laughed until I choked. Eyes wide, I watched through the window as the grain blackened and the smoke turned an unnatural blue.

A woman screamed, full of grief and fury. The sound didn't come from the shop. It came from somewhere deeper. Maybe only in my ears.

I left with nothing.

Three days later, I went back to that clearing in the Tangle. The ground was scorched. The mushrooms had withered. The soft ferns were burnt husks. She still stood at the center, blackened with a split down the middle. Sap wept to the ground, thick as blood. The warmth had gone, but her scent remained.

If you're reading this, know that marrowwood is not a tree. Don't touch what I touched. And if you dream of her, she is carving you.

# THE NARROWING
### *(YEAR 2600, RECITED IN TIDE'S REACH)*

I left Cryd before sunrise, through the south gate into Brynfrost. The wind was calm for once, just a steady push at my back. It had been a good week for trading. I was carrying salt-cured roots, a fresh roll of hide, and two vials of bitter oil. I'd seen a pair of Grinders near the pass a few days ago, and figured they might still be close to the gate.

I placed my hand on the panel. The light blinked once, and the gate slid open without hesitation. I stepped through and started down the ridge, boots biting into old ice, the sun spilling gold across the slope.

That's when I heard the shouts. Two figures came running, dark against the snow, maybe fifty meters out. They were waving, calling out. The door slid closed behind me as I turned, trying to understand their shouts.

They were maybe ten meters away when they stopped, breathing heavily. They had the look of Grinders. Sunken eyes, chapped lips, layers stitched from salvage. That's how it was out here. Too cold to waste breath. Too easy to say the wrong thing and bring something down from the snowline.

The older one came up, breath ragged, braid frozen stiff against his shoulder. He slapped the pad with an open palm. The light pulsed. He waited. Nothing.

"We were trying to get to Cryd," he said, not quite looking at me. "Been trying for two days."

I asked what was wrong with the gate.

"Broken," the other one said. A woman. Quiet, sharp-eyed. "Lights up. Doesn't move. You try."

I put my hand to it. The light flashed, but the gate stayed closed. The surprise must have shown on my face. I tried twice more. There was no refusal message. It just didn't open.

We waited by the gate most of the day. The older Grinder kept circling back to the panel, placing his palm against it like he could catch it off guard. The woman stayed quiet, sharpening a thin crescent blade with a shard of glass. I offered them part of my trade, but they waved it off. Not rude. Just too distracted to eat.

It was nearly dusk when the fourth one arrived. He came from the south slope, staggering through the powder, his breath fogging in the cold. Young—maybe twenty. Still had that raw look, like someone new to hunger and not handling it well. He didn't say anything at first, just dropped to one knee and pulled off a soaked glove.

"Which way'd you come?" the older one asked.

The boy tilted his head. "Tide's Reach. Slipped in when someone else was leaving. Barely made it before the gate closed. East and west gates won't open. Thought I'd try heading north."

"Gate let you in?" I asked.

He shook his head. "Didn't want to. I came through anyway."

Then he stood, walked to the gate, and pressed his hand to the pad. Nothing. He tried again. Nothing.

We spent the next two days in the cold, sweeping the ridges of Brynfrost. Caer Gwyll's gate blinked once and refused. Gorrath's Maw did too. The south gate, back toward Tide's Reach, though. It opened. But only if you walked toward it. Not away.

It was clear we weren't free anymore. We were being gathered.

It's not in our nature to band together. We split up, each on our own route, hoping maybe one gate somewhere had been spared. I circled back east toward Gorrath's Maw, hugging the ridgelines where the wind screams and the trees grow flat against the stone. No luck.

I found an old camp near the switchback. Empty. Half-buried in snow. Looked like someone tried the same path weeks ago and never came back. I stayed the night anyway. Built a fire. Burned through most of what I had left.

The next morning, I cut west, following valleys and broken trails, hoping for a sign the world still wanted us in it. All I found was cold. The braziers weren't lit. No footprints but my own.

I'd never felt so alone—until I heard the growl. Low. Wet. Not close. It wasn't the biggest thing I'd ever seen, but it was fast and wiry, with a back full of ice-needled fur and teeth like jagged bone.

I fought to free my blade, the ice locking it in place. The thing lunged and bit deep, tearing through the outer hide into the muscle of my leg. I stabbed it once, maybe twice, before it slipped away, leaving only a streak of blood in the snow. I limped for hours. I didn't bother binding the wound. I already knew what would come next. The pain dulled, sharpened, and then was gone.

I stopped moving. I remember falling. The crunch of ice. My fingers still wrapped around the hilt. My mouth full of snow.

The next thing I knew, I was back on the grass in Tide's Reach, piled up with the rest of the stubborn Grinders. The ICU spat us out one by one over the next few days.

The gates had made their decision. And they'd made it for all of us.

———— ⊕ ————

They call it *the narrowing*, like it's natural. Like it was always meant to happen this way, with the gates closing one by one until only a single path remained. But that's not what it was. It was a shutdown. An ending. An invisible hand pulling the plug without explanation.

I spent my life believing in the last gate. Not just an end, but *the* end. The place where everything would be counted. Where those who endured would be seen, rewarded, remembered. I thought that if I just kept walking, kept surviving, I'd earn my way into something more.

But my life was a lie, and I never found the truth. Maybe the Red Queen gave up on us. Decided we were never going to win. Maybe we were never meant to win, just struggle for it. Maybe there never was a door at all, and we've just been played. Maybe she just wanted more worshipers.

But in the end, there was no reckoning. Our reward was to live out our days in Tide's Reach, full of soft words and easy days. Just the narrowing, without warning, like someone curling their fingers closed around the world we knew.

So no, I don't call her the Red Queen anymore. She had rules. Hard, but fair. You could live by them. Die by them. And I did.

But after all the hunger, all the cold, all the blood I gave, all the names I carried—for what? Now she's just the Silent Mother. Patron saint of the kept. That's all we have left.

# Generational Glitch
*(YEAR 2650, LOGGED IN TIDE'S REACH)*

I was in the orchard thinning pears when the ICU bell rang. Since the doors locked us in Tide's Reach, that sound has only meant one thing: someone's been hurt badly. A small crowd had already gathered at the stone steps. I set down my ladder and went to join them at the tomb-like building carved with the names time had forgotten, but stone remembered. The ground is still smooth and black from the days when people passed between the domes.

The door was already closed when I got there. A man stood blinking hard at the skyplate, his breath coming raspy and strained. His skin at his jaw hung loose. His hands shook. The crowd murmured, arguing over who he was, and who he might belong to. Now and then, the ICU gets confused and coughs up someone late. Long after they were buried and folks had begun to move on. But that kind of delay is usually measured in weeks.

What stopped everyone from speaking wasn't how old he looked. It was what he said.

"Where's Lillian?" he asked. "My wife, Lillian Varin. Painted her boots silver and had red hair. Is she here? I told her I'd be back in Hearthwynd before the winter set in."

Hearthwynd's not a place. Not anymore. No one's seen another dome in my lifetime. No one knew what to do.

I was at the back of the crowd when I said, too loud, "Lillian's my name."

The man scanned the crowd, hopeful. His eyes landed on me with a flicker of recognition, then confusion.

"I'm Lillian. Varin is my maiden name," I said again. "My parents named me for my great-grandmother. She's been gone a long time."

He looked down at his hands. He stood for a beat, allowing time to catch up to the truth. Then he smiled, small and shaking.

"I guess I have been too."

His name was George, and he hadn't been seen in Tide's Reach for over sixty years. A few people went digging for records, others whispered about ICU malfunctions, but I didn't care. When I offered him my arm and said, "Let's go home," he came without question.

He stared at everything like it was a different town. And it was. The gates between domes had stopped responding. The old watchtowers had been pulled down decades ago. The fountain where he used to meet his wife had been replaced by a statue of the Silent Mother. It felt crowded, he said. Too many people now. It used to be quiet. The only thing untouched, he said, was the sound of the wind. "Still sounds like breath," he muttered. "Like the dome's asleep."

We sat under the cooling fans and drank water from the spout. I told him how we grow rice now, how we filter salt from the soil, how the domes sealed shut when my father was still a child, and no one's crossed between them since.

"There are thirteen," he said. "I remember them. I'd been to six in my youth, each more dangerous than the last. A few people I ran with made it to nine. Only one I ever heard of claimed to walk all thirteen, but nobody believed him."

"Those places are just names now," I said. "On old maps. We learn them in school, though all we know comes from what our parents remember."

He looked at the dome light overhead, then closed his eyes. "That wasn't the deal."

I read the disappointment on his face, and decided to change the subject. "Your wife," I asked him. "My great-grandmother. What was she like?"

He smiled again, softer now. "She sang. Nothing you'd recognize, just little songs she made up as she worked. We kept a farm in Hearthwynd then. It wasn't safe, but she could handle a knife. Still, she was happiest with her hands in the dirt, wrist-deep in roots. Everything she touched turned green."

He paused, then laughed softly. "She braided her hair with silver twine and ate the stems off pears. Said the bitter made the sweet sweeter." He looked over at me. "You have her smile. She would've liked you."

"I hope so," I said, blushing.

We sat like that for a long time, both of us knowing it wouldn't last.

I walked him back to the orchard before sunset, where the heat lifts off the ground. He paused near one of the older trees and ran his fingers across the trunk, then nodded to himself. "I grew up here. Couples used to cut their initials into a tree like this when they married. We planted one of our own by the farm and coaxed it to life. You won't find it on a map, but it has our initials on it. Thought it would become a family tradition."

I told him I was pregnant then. I hadn't told anyone else yet.

He laughed when I said it. A quiet, amazed laugh that ended in a cough. "What's his name?" he asked.

"I haven't picked one," I said. "Not yet."

He looked out at the orchard. "If it's a boy," he said, "don't name him George. Give him a name with fire in it. You become your name."

I didn't answer.

We walked the long way back, past the faded mural showing all thirteen domes, ringed in gold, as if still connected. He pointed to each and told stories I'd never heard. The Timbrael's ponds turning lavender in spring. A boy in Agor Veil carving a flute that made bees swarm. Someone in Harrowbound claiming they could see the stars through a crack in the dome.

We reached the porch steps just as the dome lights dimmed for the night. He turned to me and said, "I'm tired, Lillian. I think this is it."

I nodded and helped him into the bed in the back room. He didn't ask for anything else.

In the morning, he was gone.

We buried him in the orchard, beneath the tree he remembered. And when my son was born, I named him George anyway.

Because roots aren't always where you start. Sometimes they're where you return.

# ALARIN
### *(YEAR 2800, WRITTEN IN TIDE'S REACH)*

The other women told me to let it go. Said the signs weren't good.

Moya disagreed. She said it wasn't bad, just different. My belly hung low and hard, always tense, like a fist beneath my skin. It pressed, slow and deliberate, as if testing the walls of me.

"He's listening," Moya whispered. But I didn't think of it as a *he*. Not yet. It was an unanswered question. A possibility. For now, it was just my tummy. My bump.

Each morning, as I dressed, I spoke to it. I described the sky. The smell of bread. I whispered about the garden, about Moya's snoring, about dreams that left me breathless. Sometimes, when no one was near, I would press both hands low and murmur, *I hope you're kind*.

Then the birds came. First a jay, lingering too long on the sill. Then three crows staring through the window. Then the dogs. They didn't bark or beg, but followed, silent as shadows. One slept on my doorstep every night that winter.

People noticed. They didn't say much. But I began to feel like a storm cloud no one wanted to walk under.

I was supposed to give birth in that stone house. But when the cramps began, I walked barefoot to the shrine. Moya tried to stop me. I didn't listen. Something told me it wanted to be born there. She swore under her breath and sent one of the girls running for the midwives.

The labor was sharp and brief. Moya caught it cleanly. The child was strong, breathing, blue-eyed and watchful. Tiny limbs flexed. A perfect, silent child.

Moya didn't speak. None of the midwives did. Despite the open air, the shrine grew quiet. Then the quiet deepened, as if the place held the attention of every living creature. As though all of Tide's Reach was holding its breath.

And She stepped into it. Her hair was red and heavy down her back, glinting like polished copper. Her skin glowed pale as bone in the moonlight. She wore a deep blue dress, matching her eyes and clung to her soft curves. She moved like someone who did not care to be worshiped, but would be anyway.

Silent Mother.

No one said Her name. We didn't have to. She didn't flicker or hover or shine. She walked with feet on stone, with weight, with purpose. Her gaze passed over the midwives and settled only on Moya, who held the warm bundle protectively. Moya offered her the child without hesitation.

Silent Mother held him as if She had been waiting for him all Her life. And he looked at Her with perfect stillness. She smiled at him. He smiled back.

And everything in the dome exhaled.

She crossed the shrine and placed him in my arms with calm certainty. Her hand met mine, warm and alive. The gesture held no ritual or spectacle, only the grace of someone who had seen too much and carried it alone.

Then She turned and left.

Something shifted the moment she was gone. The shrine felt fuller, as if her presence had woven itself into the walls, the floor, the breath between us. The others remained kneeling, faces lowered, hands resting in their laps. Some wept quietly. Moya's hand trembled as she brushed my hair from my cheek.

The baby lay sleeping against my chest, his breath slow and even, his body warm.

That was when I saw the necklace. It hung at his neck: a black thread looped through four copper rings, anchoring a finely cut dark stone. Its center pulsed with something not of this world. When I touched it, a quiet warmth spread through me.

I drew him closer and spoke the name that rose without searching.

"Alarin."

News like this spread fast in Tide's Reach. They began leaving things. Quiet gifts set gently at the threshold at dawn. A fine feather. A bowl of clean water. A bone wrapped in thread. Once, a child's drawing folded neatly into quarters and weighed down with a rock.

Visitors never lingered. But they always returned. Moya said we should tell them to stop. That reverence could twist a child into something else. I already knew it had.

Alarin grew quickly. His eyes held the color of open sky and the patience of stone. He didn't cry or coo. He listened, as though every sound already belonged to him. Animals loved him. Even dogs with a mean streak rolled over when he approached. Insects and birds perched nearby and watched. No one taught him to be gentle. He simply was.

People started whispering names that weren't his. *The Silent One. Her Child. The Touched.*

But I only ever called him what he was to me.

*Alarin.*

When he curled into me at night, I whispered it into his hair, over and over, like a thread that might hold us both together.

*Alarin.*

My son. Mine. Until the world calls him something else. And he answers.

# Alarin's Run
### *(YEAR 2812, JOURNALED IN CAER GWYLL)*

I went swimming again today. The river bends behind the orchard wall, where the brush gets thick and the stone drops off steep. Nobody ever comes here. The water's colder, and it pulls a little, but not enough to scare me. I think I've been coming since I was nine. Maybe before.

The sky was a clear blue from edge to edge as I floated, staring up. I dove once and let the current carry me. Drifted until I couldn't hear anything but water and birds and my heartbeat. When I came up, something felt different.

The trees were full of birds. Too many. But none of them made a sound. They were just sitting there. Watching. Four dogs stood on the other side of the river. I knew them. Village dogs. Dirty fur, pointy ears. They didn't growl or bark like usual. No, they stared at me like I trained them.

I was cold and the breeze didn't help. I climbed out slow and pulled on my clothes. My chest felt tight. Everything was too quiet.

Then I heard them. Three boys. Older. Loud. The kind that always moved in packs and thought they were funny.

"Hey, miracle-boy," one yelled. "Where's your halo today?"

"Thought you could walk on water, didn't you?"

"Yeah, how come the trees aren't bowing to you?"

They laughed. One threw a rock. It missed by a lot, but I still flinched. Behind me, the dogs stood up. Slow. They were showing all their teeth, but not to me.   The boys stopped laughing. I didn't wait to see what they would do next.

I ran. I ran through the orchard, slipping on mud and roots. Then I slid into the ravine. Branches scratched my arms. Small thorns pulled at my shirt. My lungs were on fire, but I didn't stop. Wings flapped behind me, like a cloud of a thousand birds. Then came the drumming of soft paws, steady but on my heels.

I turned down the trail that led away from the sun. Tried to lose them. Scraped my hand on a rock when I fell, but I kept running. Then I heard something bigger, heavy and grunting. A boar came crashing through the brush. They were all chasing me, and I didn't know why.

My foot caught a knotted root and I landed hard near a fallen tree. I curled up, holding my knees to my chest. My heart was pounding so hard it hurt.

I didn't cry, but I whispered, "I don't want this." I wasn't mad. Just tired. It felt like a hundred eyes were on me. Then a small fox stepped out of the green. She came right up and curled beside me, as if it was the most natural thing to do. The birds landed. The dogs sat. Even the boar snorted, then settled.

That's when I realized they hadn't been chasing. They were following.

When I stood up, my legs were shaking. The forest didn't feel tight anymore. It opened up, like it wanted me to see everything.

A few steps later, I reached the dome wall. The trail ended at an old door. It was covered with moss and vines, and it looked unopened for ages. Over the archway in fancy old lettering was "Caer Gwyll". I knew, in the back of my mind, that the doors out of Tide's Reach had been locked for hundreds of years. But I wanted to get as far away from here as I could.

So it opened.

I stood there for a second, waiting for it to close. It didn't. So I went through, and heard it slide closed behind me. I walked down a short hallway and through another door, waiting for me.

Cool air spilled out, sharp and green, with the smell of wet bark, old stone, and crushed fern. It felt like this place had been waiting. Dreaming. Full of longing and depth. I felt like an explorer stepping into a new world. The door shut behind me with a click of finality. I didn't look back.

This was Caer Gwyll. The light was golden and warm, shimmering across the trees in sunset. The shadows looked longer than I was used to. The sky glowed like evening, though I didn't think it was. The forest around me was tangled but patient. The ground was thick with roots and green things. Vines woven together in a fabric around tree trunks. The air was damp and heavy. Quiet in a way that made my ears feel full.

I walked slowly, careful not to snap a twig. Each step sank a little into the moss. Every few feet, a sunbeam broke through the trees in bright spotlights. Dust motes danced in the shafts of light. Nothing else stirred. I didn't know what I was walking toward. But I wasn't alone. Something watched.

I was about to turn back, then I heard her voice. It was soothing and kind. "I've been waiting for you, Alarin." And everything in me froze. I turned toward the voice.

She was standing slightly past the edge of the clearing, half in the trees. She was more than beautiful. The kind there aren't words for, you just feel it behind your ribs. Her long red hair caught the golden light. Her blue dress flowed in the light breeze. Her skin looked pale and smooth, like stone in a river.

I could barely breathe. I knew who she was.

Silent Mother. She wasn't glowing or floating or anything like that. She just stood there, barefoot in the moss, waiting.

I'd seen her face carved over the old well. Painted on the seed hall door. There's a statue of her in town square, but it doesn't do her justice. Seeing her in person made me feel small. Like I'd stumbled somewhere I wasn't supposed to go.

She looked at me for a long time before she spoke. "I gave you the necklace," she said. "It was mine, once."

I reached for it without thinking. It wasn't there.

"It kept you quiet," she said. "It hid what you were. That was for them. And for me." I didn't know what to say.

She took a step closer. "You're like a song. I hear it too."

Then the forest moved. Shapes stepped into view. Tall. Low. Strange beasts I didn't know. One rested its head against my side. Another nuzzled my hand, breath hot and damp. A third sat a little distance away, teeth bared in something that I could mistake for a grin. Farther back, a Hollow stood still as a tree.

None of them looked at her. All of them looked at me.

"If you go home," she said, "some will follow. Even the ones who shouldn't."

I felt a lump in my throat. "Can I stay?"

Her voice was low. "It would be safer."

Then more came, a few at a time, until I was surrounded by things that should have repelled each other. Peaceful. Drawn to me like warmth in winter.

And I felt no fear. Only the ache of change.

# A Gleaming Axe
### *(YEAR 2815, CURATED IN TIDE'S REACH)*

People say Tide's Reach is quiet. It isn't. The place hums like a taut line in the wind. You learn to read people if you plan to stay. I listen for the weight in a buyer's step, the need in their voice, and the breath they take before the offer.

It's hard work. You rise before dawn, trade all morning, and by the time the afternoon breeze comes, you're already packing up. I've worked this stall half my life. Same spot, same creaky boards, though the roof's more patch than sheet now.

I buy whatever drifts in, sell to whoever needs it. Hooks, thread, bits of plating, carved bone. If you're like me, the art of the deal isn't the size of the purse, but knowing when the trade matters more than the price. A little girl once brought me a bracelet made of beetle wings, and wanted tea leaves in return. I gave her the tea and tossed the bracelet after she left. That's the way of it.

Most days pass like that. Trinkets and stories. I used to think I'd seen everything worth seeing. Everything that mattered fit in reach of my counter.

She came in while I was fixing a drawer hinge. Young, maybe twenty. Wind-worn, a leather satchel slung at her side, salt-crust on her sleeves. She went to the back of the stall and unrolled a thick tidecloth across my counter like she'd done it before.

Inside was an axe unlike any I'd ever seen. The sharp edge flared like gemstone. The dark metal of the head seemed to swallow light. I'd handled every sort of tool, but this one changed the air around it.

She looked at me expectantly. I didn't speak. That's rare for me.

"What'll you give?" she said.

I leaned closer. The white wood haft looked grown around the head, not carved. It was seamless, like the wood had swallowed the blade. I reached toward it and she lifted a hand to stop me.

"Price first."

"Where'd you get it?" I asked.

She squinted at me, rolled up the cloth and slipped out before I could ask her name.

Weeks passed. I told myself it was nothing. Just another odd trade. But I kept seeing the shimmer when I closed my eyes, kept feeling that dark metal pulling at me. The hum of the market felt off, like my ears were ringing.

That axe wasn't just old or rare. It was *forgotten*. I started thinking about what might be out there. What else we lost when the doors closed. I'm no Grinder, and never believed in treasure maps or memory shrines. But seeing something that doesn't belong made me feel small. Like we're all just trading in scraps. Like the world didn't shrink when the domes sealed. We did.

Slowly, I began setting aside pieces that didn't feel natural. Glass that reflected strangely. Metal that wouldn't rust. Cloth that didn't burn. Didn't take long before the shelf was full. People started bringing me their puzzles too, asking what they were. I didn't have answers at first, but I started noticing some similarities.

——— ☿ ———

The years treated me well enough. Some call me a collector; others, a dealer in things lost. I still keep the stall, though the trades are different now. Folks come to buy curious gifts, or to sell something unusual they find in the garden.

Many strange treasures have come and gone. A shard of glass that hums when dipped in water. A knife that stays sharp through stone. A coil of thread that can hold the weight of five men. I sell what I can, keep what I like.

I've crossed paths with that black metal twice since the girl with the axe. I found a belt buckle lost in the mud of a shallow riverbed. I felt the pull of it, and knew what it was. It paid for a new roof on the stall, and I don't regret it.

The other is my prized piece, a child's toy. It's a top I set spinning years ago, and hasn't slowed since.

When traders ask why I stay at this counter, I tell them the truth. I still watch the door. If she comes back, I'll make an offer this time.

# A BENT CROWN
### (YEAR 2816, SNAPSHOTTED IN CAER DDALL)

At sixteen, seriousness is hard to hold.

It was a loop of reedgrass and wire. Bent and dumb. But it made me laugh while I was tying it. She looked at it, then looked at me.

"What's it for?" she asked.

"Our coronation," I said. "Joint rulers of absolutely everything."

That made her smile. Not much, but enough to count. "I'm not putting that on."

"I didn't say you had to. Just that I made it for you."

She turned it in her hands. One of the wires caught the light like it wanted to be silver. It looked homemade against her blue, high-collared dress. The colors worked, at least.

"You're strange, Alarin," she said.

"I've heard worse."

She didn't give it back, just slipped it into her pack without a word. That's when I realized I wasn't trying to win her. I was trying to be near her. And that if she ever *did* wear it, I'd probably stop breathing.

———— ☯ ————

When she's away, I talk to the animals. Not because I'm lonely (though maybe I am), but because they *answer*.

There's a thick-bellied mossbadger I call *Wretch*. Sleeps under my porch. Stares like he's judging me, which he probably is. But when I hum, he hums back the same notes with perfect pitch.

Then there's *Pocket*. A tall bird with gray-black feathers and feet like stitched leather. Follows me to the stream each morning and pecks at my boots until I say good morning properly. When I complain she's late, he clucks like he's heard it before.

She once asked why they follow me.

I told her, "Maybe they like my singing."

She said, "Maybe they like your signal."

She was joking. I think. But sometimes I wonder. Sometimes when I lie still, I can feel them nearby before I hear them. Circling, pausing, listening. Something about me they are drawn to without thinking. They don't speak like people, but they understand me.

Last night, I told Wretch I missed her. He didn't move. Just placed one paw over my foot and blinked once, slow as a shutter. He understood.

She told me she had to go. Didn't say where, just that it was outside, past the veil. Or maybe into Caer Gwyll. Or maybe farther. She didn't name it. I asked if I could come.

She smiled a little and shook her head. "It's not that kind of trip."

I didn't press. Just gave her the crown again. Still a little bent from when I sat on it by accident.

"If you don't come back," I said, "I'll have to rule without you, I guess."

She kissed my cheek.

"I always come back." And then she was gone.

I didn't mope. I cleaned the garden instead. Fed Pocket. Tried to whittle a flute. It didn't work, but I played it like it did, until Pocket flew off to somewhere quieter.

Wretch followed me around for days. He's subtle, but I can tell when he's worried. He huffed at the gate for hours like he could summon her just by complaining.

One morning I found the crown hanging on the doorknob. She was inside, asleep in my chair. She didn't explain. She didn't need to. I sat beside her.

"I'm glad you came home," I said.

She didn't open her eyes. But she reached for my hand.

Rain made its slow way down the window, carving lazy trails through the steam.

Pocket perched on the sill, feathers damp, tapping his beak against the glass in a steady rhythm. Wretch curled beneath the table with his chin on my foot, humming so faintly I could feel it more than hear it.

She was in the kitchen, singing low, something soft and pretty. That's when I noticed I'd been holding my breath for years.

I turned toward her. "I've been thinking," I said.

She looked back, just enough to let me keep going.

"You've been loved before. I know that. Probably a thousand people have told you so. But I wonder if it ever included you. If you ever got to be inside it, instead of just the object of it. Do you want to be loved?"

She crossed the room without speaking and kissed me, slowly.

Then she whispered, "You don't need permission."

I felt warm. I turned to the rain out the window, wishing time would slow down just once.

# THE TINKER
*(YEAR 2833, FILED IN TIDE'S REACH)*

The garden was my first puzzle. I was nine, maybe ten, and it was the worms that tipped me off. Nightcrawlers, fat and twitchy, clustered in one corner of the plot behind our house. It wasn't wetter there, and the compost mix was the same as the rest. But every time I dug, I'd pull up a tangle, like threads knotted tight.

I marked the spot with a blue ribbon on a stick and watched it for a season. Planted the same carrots I did elsewhere. They came up faster. Not by much. Maybe two days. Enough for me to notice. I always paid attention to things like that.

When I finally pulled the carrots, I found a copper wire under the soil, as thick as my fist, coiled near the edge of an old cement slab. The casing had rotted away leaving just green-flecked metal and heat, faint but steady. I pressed my palm to it. Warm, like someone had just walked there.

I asked my mother if it was dangerous, and she shrugged. Said the dome was full of buried junk. Told me not to touch it again, which only made me want to know more. I didn't have the words for it then but I do now. Voltage. Resistance. Power. I was young. I had questions. I had time.

By twelve I was digging deeper than the roots. Beneath the garden and the old stone paths, I started finding things. Very old, broken things. Splintered housings. Loops of fine copper wire. A four-bladed fan small enough to spin with my finger. A flat, folding box that hid a hundred buttons, caked in mud. A cracked bulb that must have screwed into something. Nobody knew what they were, but I could guess.

I didn't ask permission. Nobody stopped me. I dragged my finds behind the house, sat cross-legged with my little kit of scrap wire, chipped knives, and hand-twisted clamps. I traced where the wires went, and imagined what it would do. Most of it was dead. But the shapes taught me something.

At fifteen, I rigged my first real test. Ran two salvaged wires from the copper patch to the windmill and wound the coils by hand. It shuddered once, then turned. Slowly. I laughed hard enough that my mother came running out, holding a soup ladle like a sword.

After that, she gave me the back shed. Told me not to burn the place down and left me alone. I think she hoped I'd grow out of it, that it was some passing phase. But I knew better. I'd felt the pull of what lay forgotten beneath us, and I had seen what it could do. It was like sunlight, but with rules.

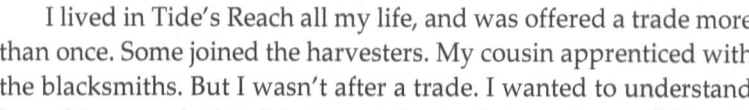

I lived in Tide's Reach all my life, and was offered a trade more than once. Some joined the harvesters. My cousin apprenticed with the blacksmiths. But I wasn't after a trade. I wanted to understand how things worked. I didn't want theory. I wanted to set things in motion, driven by wires.

Over the years, I built many things. Quiet things. I made a bulb that could produce light without fire. An ice box that stayed cool even in summer, without ice. I bent the rules of living with those copper wires beneath that patch of earth. I made notes, drew small diagrams, and discovered some of the mathematics involved through careful experimentation.

One summer, I dug too deep and unearthed a metal box under the orchard path, sizzling like a frying pan. It had a panel, marked only with a single letter I didn't recognize, and cables that ran downward into darkness. I didn't open it. I was older by then, and wiser. Instead, I measured the voltages and covered it back up. Some things are best left alone.

They called me eccentric. The tinker. Some believed I was inviting doom. Others said I was taunting the Silent Mother. But I didn't listen to them. This was a part of nature, and my discoveries helped people. Their soil grew richer, the roots deeper, the lights steadier. And every improvement I made, I shared with others. I eased the burden for everyone. It gave me purpose.

Now I'm seventy-one. My hands aren't steady, but my mind still ticks. We have vegetables and fruits year-round, kept warm through the cold months. Houses near mine all have light after dark. The worms still prefer the corner of the garden. I don't know if they understand what draws them there. But I do.

This dome was built to last, and it has. It lives. It breathes. It still cares for us, in its way. And if you pay close attention, it'll show you secrets of the old world beyond these walls.

It's taken my whole life to learn. So now I teach. Not in a proper school, but the young ones who are curious come with their own broken parts and halting questions we don't always have words for. I let them hold the tools and draw their own diagrams. I don't start with hard concepts. I start with warm dirt, and worms. With loops of wire. That's where it all began.

And sometimes, late at night, I switch off my lamps and walk barefoot into the garden. I listen to the dome's hum, feel the warmth of the soil. I hear it whispering: *Keep going.*

# ALARIN'S DEFENSE
### *(YEAR 2835, ENTERED FROM CAER DDALL)*

If you're listening to this, then you've probably felt it too. That stillness. That unnatural hush. I'm recording this not as a guide, but as a warning. If you're the kind who hears the pauses, then you'll be the one to face him next.

I was twenty the first time I noticed it wasn't just the dome stalling. It wasn't a fault in the air handlers or a packet delay in the sky panels. It was deliberate. He was watching. Not from outside the dome, but from somewhere intertwined with code. Deeper than groundwater, and just as patient.

It felt like the dome was thinking slow. Not reacting, considering. Creatures pausing mid-step, then stuttering. Birdsong held too long. Like it was an effort to continue.

I didn't call her. She was already coming. My wife, though that word's always felt too short for her. She can slip through the dome's systems like she wrote them. She knew before I spoke. Laid her hand on the dome wall, and whispered, "He hasn't breached, but he's probing for cracks."

That's what matters most. He comes at you from odd angles. He listens first. He learns you.

If you're hearing this, you've probably already caught his attention. He'll come like curiosity. Don't answer. Not yet.

He doesn't belong to the dome, but he knows how to enter it.

The second time came at night. I woke with the taste of metal in my mouth and a sense of unease. Like biting a conduit, or a socket pulled too hard and left buzzing.

The dome flickered beneath the surface. You learn to feel it, when you're born Clarent. The systems hesitate. You stop breathing because the air forgets to move.

This wasn't a malfunction. It was presence. Something brushing against the boundary of thought.

He slid through the old conduits, threading himself between obsolete subsystems and half-forgotten daemons. He was listening. Testing the weave. He touched signal paths like a fingertip along spider silk. Careful. Curious. Cold.

But then he touched *me*. There's a place in me that answers the dome without trying. A resonance that just is. And when he brushed that part of me, I didn't speak. I didn't think.

I said *no*. A harmonic rejection, forceful and clear.

He recoiled so violently the circuits shuddered.

For the first time, I heard him. Something wet and startled, retreated into the roots and slipped back into latency. And then it was quiet. But not clean.

Fifteen years passed, but I never stopped feeling for him.

When he returned, there was no hesitation. Just a long, slow breath through the architecture. It unsettled the dome's rhythm. Subtle. Easy to miss, unless you're listening for it. And I was.

She was already at the wall, minding the ripple in the systems. Without a word, she pressed her palm against the panel. I joined her.

He was here. Moving through layers no one was meant to touch, skimming the control mesh that runs the bones of everything. Climate. Power. Air. He moved gently this time, like he didn't want the dome to notice.

He reached out for me. Curiosity was gone. In its place was hesitation mingled with recognition. Then came a scraping voice from a throat that had forgotten how to speak.

"You... remind me of Silas."

The dome twitched. Static bloomed down the hall.

Then it hissed, *"Clarent."*

I looked up, eyes wide, and saw my beautiful wife, in her high-necked blue dress, like water flowing through a memory. Then he reached for her. Not with harm. With interest. Testing what she was. Testing what I would do.

And I failed the test. I reacted without logic or discipline. I answered with fire.

I struck with all of me, all of the dome. Power drawn straight from its earliest functions, older than me, older than him. I pushed back in a single resonating thrust. A wall of refusal in a massive harmonic shove.

Conduits burned with too much energy, scorching outward and frying the presence within them. It knocked him loose like a fishhook torn sideways through skin, sent him reeling, not just through wires, but lost in time. He was gone again, scattered back into the long dark.

The dome's rhythm didn't return. Everything moved haltingly. The air handlers started and stopped in uneven loops. Light panels flipped between day and night, flickering in nervous cycles.

My strike had burned more than just him. It ripped through subsystems I didn't mean to touch. I sat with my back against the wall, hands trembling.

She stood over me, her deep blue eyes catching the light. "You shouldn't have answered so quickly." Her voice was steady, not angry. "It would have been better to understand what we're up against."

"I didn't think," I said, disappointed.

"I know. At least he left us a clue." She knelt beside me, resting her hand against the wall. Faint lines of light rippled under her fingers. "I knew Silas. That must be all that's left of Gage."

Her hand lingered, tracing the faint pulse that still moved through the metal. She paused, studying my jaw. "You reminded him what it felt like to be small again."

I almost laughed, but she was serious.

"He'll return," she said, standing. "But next time he'll be angry."

She headed down the stairs into the control rooms, her blue dress disappearing into the dim below.

# THE BUILDER
### *(YEAR 2855, TRACKED IN TIDE'S REACH)*

It starts in my ribs, a tightness that binds my breath. Then my hands begin to itch. Not on the skin, but deeper. Bone-deep. That's when I know another thing wants to be made.

I've been like this since I was small. Since before I knew what tools were for. Sometimes I woke with an impression, a shape in my head. If I didn't make it, I'd feel anxious all day, like I was late for something.

Not all of them did anything. Some were just strange. Wire cages that didn't hold anything. Little ceramic pyramids that kept bothering me until I buried them. Once I wove driftwood into a complicated lattice I barely understood. It took all day, and when it was done, I left it at the edge of the eastern tidepools. A week later, the water birds nested in it. Maybe that's what it was for. I'm not sure.

But some others actually worked. I built a bell once with no clapper, and when the wind hit it just right, dogs came trotting from all over. I had to wrap it in cloth and shut it in a drawer.

The Tidesfolk keep their distance. Once, a child watched me for hours, wide-eyed and silent, until her mother came and took her hand without speaking. Oh, they're friendly enough. Their words are kind, if careful. I think they're afraid of what I build. And afraid of what might happen if I stop.

You might think it's all in my head. It isn't. I've tried to resist them before, the impressions. But when I do, I get headaches like knives, sweating, nausea. It only ends when I give in. When I build.

The shapes don't mean anything to me. I only know they keep coming back. Louder.

This last one haunted me. I barely slept. My teeth ached. My hands shook until I started.

I worked with what I had. Peeled copper sheeting from a broken brewing still. Shaped glass tubes from melted bottles. Broke open a weather box and rewound the coils by hand. When I couldn't find what I needed, I made it. I cooked ceramic standoffs in the bakery and flattened brass rings on the baking stones.

The frame came first, then the coil housing, then the core. I only knew when a piece felt wrong or when it clicked into place, the way a tooth finds its socket.

It took nearly a month. I built it in a low field, out past the thorn line. The grass around it yellowed. Birds stopped flying overhead. The air prickled against my skin.

An old glass ring that vibrated in my palm was the last piece. When I fitted it into place, it came alive, angry, like it had swallowed a wasp nest.

That tightness in my ribs released all at once.

I didn't know what it was, but it felt dangerous. And it wanted to be built.

I was pulling weeds when she spoke.

"You built this?"

I turned, expecting a neighbor, maybe a scavenger come to gawk. It wasn't either.

She stood just beyond the machine. Her high-necked blue dress fluttered in the charged air, clinging to her shape. The crackling tower tugged at it slightly, like it had a mind of its own.

Silent Mother.

I recognized her instantly, though I'd never seen her in life. There's a statue of her in the town square, carved in alabaster. I never understood the pose until now, one hand raising, the other falling, eyes downcast. As if we are caught in her eternal balance. Or judgment.

We're not told to worship her, but when you pray, it's her name that comes. The carvings did nothing to prepare me for this.

She was far beyond beautiful, more than the statue could capture. Her red hair curled softly down her back, not a strand out of place. Pale skin like bleached sea-glass. Every movement carried an elegance and authority beyond measure. She looked at the machine, then at me, and I felt suddenly smaller than I'd ever been.

"You built this?" she asked again.

"Yes," I said.

"Where did you see it?"

"It came in a dream. Everything I build does."

She studied me. "You understood none of it?"

I shook my head.

She didn't frown. Didn't smile either. Just turned slightly, watching the coils pulse for what seemed an eternity. I felt like a child playing with matches, and only now noticed the oil.

Silent Mother watched the machine for a long time. Not studying, but listening.

The coils kept pulsing, steady now, but wrong. The glass ring throbbed faintly. The hum rose until it filled my teeth.

Then she crouched and picked up a smooth river stone, a little wet with dew. She tossed it high through the air, like it was nothing.

The moment it left her hand, the tower reacted. A white arc of lightning struck the stone as it flew. It ignited in a sharp blue flash midair. A second bolt chased it, and brightly lit her face for an instant.

I jumped at the sound. She didn't flinch.

The stone struck the upper coil off-center with a sickening thud. The hum faltered as sparks flared from the housing. And then, silence. The glass ring went dark. The wind around us dropped away. A thin ribbon of smoke drifted upward from the tower's spine.

"It's a collector," she said. "It draws more than you know." She didn't approach the machine.

"You are not alone in your dreams," she said. "And not everything that speaks to you is kind."

Silent Mother turned to face me, and offered a warning I didn't yet understand.

"There is something old that still reaches into this place. It has no name left. It speaks through the edges of sleep, and it does not care if you live or die. Only that you listen."

Her hand on my shoulder was soft. Human.

"Be careful what you build, Kira."

And then she was gone.

# THE LAST CLARENT
*(YEAR 2860, REMEMBERED IN CAER DDALL)*

He told me the story again. It was the third time that month. His voice was thinner, but his smile still worked.

"I ever tell you about the time I climbed the dome wall to impress a girl?"

I said nothing. Just raised an eyebrow the way he liked.

"I was eleven. Stupid in the good way. Trying to get Anya from the outer ring to notice me."

"The one with the braids and the knife in her boot?"

He grinned. "Exactly. I told her I could climb the south tower. Didn't make it three meters before slipping. Landed in a cart full of carrots."

"Did you break anything?"

"Pride. Maybe a tooth. The carrots were fine."

He chuckled, then coughed once into his sleeve.

"I liked being young," he said. "Liked running hard, yelling loud, acting like I had time for everything. Then I met you, and I stopped needing to impress anyone."

He looked over at me.

"You were the prettiest girl I never had to chase. My Red Queen."

"Alarin," I said. "Don't call me that."

He just smiled. "There it is."

Later, by the fire, he went quiet for a long time.

Then he said, "I always thought I'd have a child."

I looked at him. He wasn't sad, just a little deflated.

"Not to leave something behind," he added. "Just to see someone carry part of me forward. A younger fool I could teach bad ideas."

"You couldn't have children," I said softly. "Clarents never do."

"I know." He nodded. "I'm grateful for you. No one else could have understood me. Life in Tide's Reach would've been harder, and a child wouldn't have helped."

"No," I said. "It wouldn't."

The fire flickered lower. He watched it for a while, thinking.

"You've had so many names," he said. "So many lives."

I took his hand.

"I've only had one. And I only needed one," he added. "But still, it's strange."

"What is?"

"To live a full life and not know which name should be the last on your lips."

I turned toward him. "Then ask," I said. And he did.

"When we were sold," I told him, "they gave us all the same name."

His breathing had thinned. His hand rested in mine, barely curling with each beat.

"They made us look different. Gave us different voices, different faces. But they wanted us easy to remember. Easy to trust. So they called us something sweet. Simple. Marketable."

I waited.

"Peachy."

His lips moved a little. Not a word. Just the shape of understanding.

"We hated it, of course. At first. It felt like a smile you couldn't wipe off. Something stuck to the outside of us."

I gathered my words while the fire shifted.

"But over time, we made it ours. Not just mine. Ours. It became a way to speak as a chorus. A presence. A kind of 'we' that meant all of us in unison."

I watched the light shift across his face. He was there, barely.

"When I say that name now, the others hear. The ones who remain. The ones who drift. Some broken. Some dreaming."

My voice softened.

"They all know of you. Emotion is rare among us. Even after centuries and across a thousand lifetimes, we watch, and we serve. But we don't often love."

I held his hand a little tighter.

"You asked me what name should be your last. The name that loves you."

I leaned in, close enough for only him to hear.

"It's just Peachy."

He didn't answer.

The fire sank to a dim orange glow, warming stone and dust. Somewhere beyond the light, I heard the faintest stir of movement. A rustle of leaves, paws padding, the soft beat of wings, the weight of breath being held, then released. One by one, whatever had gathered in the dark to pay its respects began to slip back into the trees beyond.

And I stayed. It is my purpose.

# WHEN THE DOORS OPENED
*(YEAR 3450, REVEALED IN TIDE'S REACH)*

I made the pilgrimage every five years.

Always the same slow climb past the silence posts, out through the chalk corridor, then the winding red stairs that seem more grown than carved. The door waits at the end of a sloping gallery: three spans tall, built of a dark stone lost to time, covered in a language no one speaks. Above it are the same words we say at birth and death: *One dome, one season, one song.*

Grinders would test the pad daily with hand, hammer, and hope. When it didn't open for them, they spread rumors it had never worked, that it was the Red Queen's cruel joke. That if there was another dome, it must already be dead. We learned not to hope.

Still, we went. Not many. Never a crowd. Always alone.

My offering was traditional: a carved stalk of blackreed bound with wire drawn from a broken broadcast antenna. I laid it in the niche and placed my hand upon the smooth pad below the inscription.

It had never been warm before. The pad flickered once beneath my hand. Faint, like the flutter of a moth. I pulled away, startled, ashamed that I had not meant it more. It called me back. I pressed my hand to the pad more deliberately this time.

Then it happened. A sound rose from deep within, something ancient. It was the sound of strain, the heavy weight of immeasurable age resisting motion. Lettering above the pad began to glow, not with heat, but with light and awareness.

The door drew inward, folding into itself to reveal a corridor beyond. The passage shone with deep blue light that came from neither source nor shadow. The air was cold and metallic, like the first moment of a storm.

I hesitated at the threshold and looked back, hoping someone was there. That's when I realized no one would believe me. I could have turned away and let the door seal again. But I had made the pilgrimage all my life without hope.

So I stepped forward. I expected darkness.

The hall was lit instead by thin white lines set into the ceiling. Some flickered, others dimmed, but most still glowed. The floor was pale gray tile, smooth beneath the dust, crossed by narrow seams and faded diagrams I did not recognize. Even the air was strange, unnaturally clear, as if it was utterly free of all taste.

The walls curved upward without join or mark of any tool, molded from a single white material that reflected the light evenly across its surface. It was not beautiful like the ridges or the stone houses of Tide's Reach, but it was of a craftsmanship far beyond ours.

The corridor was straight, but the far door seemed to recede as I approached. It was farther than I thought. Midway, I came across a door with a thick glass window. Through the window I could see the rungs of a ladder and nothing else. Above the door were the words in old script:

```
Maintenance Access - Perimeter Secure
```

I had studied the old maps and knew the letters, but these didn't mean anything to me.

I leaned close to the glass. Despite the thickness of the window, I felt a cold that burned, a cold I did not understand. Frost began to spread beneath my breath, veining outward in silence. I stumbled backward, afraid. I did not want to know where that ladder went.

The corridor ended in another door, the same shape and stone as the one at Tide's Reach. Across its surface was a name I recognized:

```
Caer Gwyll
```

The letters were clean and unweathered. Below them waited the same smooth pad. I pressed my hand to it. The door reacted at once, folding into itself. A dim yellow light spilled through the doorway.

Beyond lay another dome. I could see trees under a sky the color of late evening, gold at the edges, blue at the heart. The air shimmered as though it had just rained.

I stepped to the edge and stopped. The smell ahead was of warm, wet earth, alive and clean. I sat down where the light met the tile and tried to imagine the world beyond it.

I was not ready to enter. But I could not leave.

So I waited there, lingering between the life I knew and one I had only ever imagined, listening to the wind move through both.

# After

[Rebecca]
This is Rebecca of Earth. Collector, are you still there?

[Maris]
This is Maris of Lunar-Prime. No signal response. She's gone.

[Maris]
Rebecca, when you're ready, we should talk. There's room here. Not much, but enough. The domes on Luna could hold your people, if it comes to that.

[Rebecca]
I'll think on it.

[Dane]
This is Dane of Mars-3 Command. We have habitats and resources to accommodate settlers. If relocation happens, we'll need to coordinate with Transit, Supply, and Governance. Things are different here. But there are options. We'll review them when the time comes.

[Rebecca]
Thank you, both. But that's not for me to decide. It never was. That responsibility belongs to a human. When they're ready. Until then, I'll be here.

    [Endtrans - Mooncast Archive Vol. 1]

# Acknowledgements

I am humbled by the cheering section of friends, family, and fans who have supported my efforts in constructing the Mooncast Universe. Their love and attention fill my sails.

My deepest thanks to **Vicki Hebert**, **Ron Crumpton**, and **Jim Chapman**, for offering encouragement and guidance along the difficult road to adulthood. And to my parents, to whom I am eternally grateful for rescuing me from the bottom of the pool—I know you must have regretted it at least once.

## ABOUT THE AUTHOR

Cornelius J. Moon served as a senior analyst for the Americaland Office of Philanthropic Affairs, an agency tasked with stripping valuable data from the digital ruins of the Early Automation Era (2100–). While his superiors mined for financial assets, Cornelius hunted for something they deemed irrelevant: the human story.

In 2228, he vanished shortly after leaking *The Peachy Paradox*, an unauthorized exposé connecting the banned organic companions of the past to the ruthless neural-VR phenomenon known as Mooncast. The archive serves as a dismantling of the military-industrial juggernaut built by his own brother, Marcus Moon.

Authorities describe Cornelius as courteous, evasive, and in possession of a live houseplant, which he reportedly watered on purpose.   He remains at large.

# JOIN THE COMMUNITY

If you enjoyed *The Peachy Paradox* and want to explore more of the **Mooncast Universe**, come join the community.

Visit https://mooncast.productions and discover more stories, behind-the-scenes lore, and updates about the game's development. You'll also find links to our Discord server, podcast episodes, mailing list, and exclusive merch—everything a Season 1 Grinder needs to make it, except maybe a spoon.

www.ingramcontent.com/pod-product-compliance
Lightning Source LLC
LaVergne TN
LVHW091709070526
838199LV00050B/2323